DARK PURPOSE

A B Endacott

Cover designed by Marcus Moltzer
Cover illustration by Nicole Sizer
Map illustration by Ellen Liu

978-0-6481875-8-5

Books by the same author

The Second Country
Queendom of the Seven Lakes
King of the Seven Lakes

The Fourth Country
The Ruthless Land

The Third Country
Dark Intent

Coming Soon
Dark Heart
Untitled (First Country)

For Lucas,
Who I would follow into rebellion,
For the strength of his consideration
And unwavering loyalty to those he loves.

Now could I drink hot blood
And do such bitter business as the day
would quake to look on

Shakespeare, *Hamlet*

The City of Oranis

ONE

"Again, Freya," Astrom said, stepping back.

"I'm tired," Freya protested, rubbing the spot on her arm where Astrom's staff had smacked her.

"Do you think that the Kade will stop in battle to allow you to rest?" the other woman demanded, her voice impatient but not unkind.

"I'm a healer, not a fighter," Freya argued, tired of the endless practice she had been forced to undergo that day and on all the other days that had come before.

"The only thing that not knowing how to fight will do is get you killed," Makkyd said from her seat near the edge of the room.

Freya looked resentfully at Astrom's physique. The muscles in the woman's arms were as hard as the stone she worked. In comparison to her, Freya was uncomfortably conscious of her frailty. Healing work required a different kind of strength, but Makkyd was correct: if it came to any kind of physical confrontation, Freya's lack of training would see her dead. Taking a deep breath, she picked up the wooden staff she had dropped and settled back into a fighter's crouch, readying herself for the next beating that she was certain she would sustain at her teacher's hands. There was something almost insulting about the easy strength and speed Astrom possessed. Especially when compared to Freya's efforts. Astrom leaned back for a moment and then almost lazily stepped forward, her staff a blur as it moved through the air. The endless hours of practice drilled into her over the past cycles had

Freya stepping to the side and bringing her own staff up to block Astrom's attack before her mind had even registered what was happening. Her body curved to one side and she stepped behind Astrom, whipping her staff up and around to lie against Astrom's neck.

The watching room erupted into cheers and whoops as Astrom stepped aside, bowing slightly to Freya. "You always hold back until you're tired," she noted, making the bow into a stretch to her toes. The long braid into which her brown hair was customarily pulled swung down across her shoulder.

Freya shrugged, stretching out her arms and groaning as she felt the bruises from the session make themselves known.

She didn't like fighting, but it had become a mandatory part of her life in the Resistance. Cycles of training and practice had given her a rudimentary understanding of how to handle a few weapons, although she had settled into fighting with the staff, despite Astrom's chuckled mantra that with a staff there was no keen edge on which she could injure herself. Her healer's teachings meant she did not feel truly comfortable with any weapon in her hands. Using them to inflict the sort of damage she had spent her life learning to fix was anathema to everything she believed.

"You've come a long way." Makkyd, the leader of the Resistance, clapped her on the back. Her hand landed directly on one of the places that Astrom's staff had hit her particularly hard. Freya winced but Makkyd did not seem to notice. Astrom did, and shot Freya a look of amusement and sympathy.

"I've been training hard enough," Freya said lightly, closing her eyes and letting her mind focus on the dissonant notes the bruises sounded in her mind, soothing them back into the harmony.

Aware of what she was doing, Astrom stepped forward and extended her arms in a subtle request. Freya obliged, placing a hand on Astrom's wrist and stretching out her mind toward her friend's body to hear the vibrant hum of her body. She found the injuries and righted the discord that their presence caused. She didn't even feel the fatigue which used to sap her capacity to focus for anything when she first started using her ability for anything but the smallest healing work.

"That was so fast," Astrom marvelled quietly, careful not to be overheard by the onlookers. Very few in the Resistance were aware of the powers that true and deep piety could bestow. Only the most trusted members – those whose faith had remained un-challenged even during the years of Kade rule – had discovered their abilities. Freya had only been aware of her ability for a few cycles but she had become quickly accustomed to the way the knowledge of her power sat within her, the way someone's body would sing to her as soon as her fingers brushed their skin. She now couldn't imagine life without the explicit knowledge of that ability.

She smiled in acknowledgement of the comment. "By the way, you'd pulled a muscle, probably from something you did in your workshop," she whispered to Astrom.

Astrom's laugh drew a grin to Freya's face. "No wonder you won that last one!"

Freya shook her head, running her fingers through her dark crop of hair. "Don't be a sore loser," she teased. The easy repartee between them had sprung up over the cycles in which Astrom had taken Freya under her wing and mercilessly trained her – a special project, of sorts – even giving her one-on-one sessions when pos-sible. While Freya struggled against the impulse to be offended that her ineptitude was deemed so severe she required special at-tention, her teacher had been endlessly patient and encouraging, and she couldn't find it within herself to resent Astrom for the endless bruises she had inflicted upon Freya. Indeed, they had be-come close, friends – Freya's first in a long, long time.

They moved to the room's edge and two others stepped for-ward into the makeshift ring, taking the staffs from Freya and As-trom and settling into fighting stances. Freya sat on the sidelines and watched as they moved backward and forward, exchanging blows, but neither gaining the advantage. She quickly grew bored and her gaze began to rove around the room. The number of people within the Resistance had swelled over the past few fivedays as the Kade crackdowns had become increasingly severe. Despite the fact that it had been several cycles since the brutal attacks of the Followers of the Dark Gods, the justifications for the increasingly severe edicts the Kade had put into effect over the recent fivedays were that they were taking no chances with the safety of Oranis's citizens. This translated into the Healing Centre that she administered seeing more and more individuals who bore signs of the Kade's brutality, sustained because they were deemed to be in breach of some Kade order. It was little wonder that the people were starting to seek out the Resistance. These sessions in which the Resistance trained their fighters were becoming more populated and more frequent. Freya wondered how long it would take before the Resistance was discovered. She wasn't the only one. In the leadership meetings, more than once the wisdom of holding such sessions had been raised, but each time Makkyd's reply was the same: it was more important that their own followers see they were presenting a viable threat to the Kade and that, when it did come to fighting, their people were actually competent.

Freya realised with a start that Ashtyn was sequestered in a corner of the workshop-turned-sparring space, almost out of sight. He must have seen her fighting. She was glad she had been unaware of his presence before she had stepped into the space with Astrom. Almost certainly, she wouldn't have managed to get that final victory had she known his eyes were on her every movement. As though he could feel her gaze on him, his eyes found hers. She quickly looked away, feeling heat travel across her face. It had been cycles since she had burst in on the Resistance meeting, frantic to recommit herself to them despite her prior defiant departure from the group. She could not stand to be any kind of part of the Kade's stranglehold on the Third Country for a moment longer, was desperate to be part of something that actively worked against it. At that meeting, he had looked at he with an undisguised mixture of apprehension, uncertainty, and longing written across his face. She had turned her head so she didn't have to look at him. Her feelings had been too complicated, too difficult, for her to face him, and they hadn't changed much in the intervening time. The way he looked at her hadn't changed, either. It made her uncomfortable, uncertain, around him. She had not forgiven him for the way in which he had seduced her – turning her into an adulterer in the process – so he could then introduce her to the Resistance. It had been far easier for her to forgive Makkyd and the Resistance as a whole for targeting her for recruitment, instructing Ashtyn to deceive her so as to bring her to them, than it had been for her to forgive him. Perhaps it was his claim that he had fallen in love with her that meant she couldn't move beyond the lingering betrayal that the discovery had brought; she didn't know if he was telling her the truth or simply telling her another lie to try to ease his conscience. But really, even if he was telling the truth, she wasn't certain she could forget that the relationship that had blossomed between them had been formed while he was trying to manipulate her. She pushed aside the memory of his lips on her skin and forced her attention back to the middle of the room. Some things were better left unthought and this was one of them. Her life was already difficult enough juggling the pretence of loyal Kade collaborator against her secret life within the Resistance without reintroducing the added complication of her romantic sentiments.

Eventually, the practice finished. People left Astrom's workshop in small groups. Freya watched them as they departed, noting the fatigue and exhilaration. She no longer received looks of surprise – this group of people, the more senior, trusted members of the Resistance, were now accustomed to her presence here, although every so often she still caught them regarding her with curiosity. She couldn't blame them. She had developed a reputation within Oranis for being favoured by the Kade for her obedience to them. To suddenly see her placed among the leadership of the Resistance might well be cause for confusion, even concern. But she was finished allowing the Kade to hurt innocent people so that she could live comfortably and safely. Hopefully, she had proved that with her presence over the past cycles and the dedication she had demonstrated when she and Astrom had sparred in front of them. Makkyd's comment was that the more Freya was seen by the people within the Resistance who could be trusted with the knowledge of Freya's membership, the more she would cease to be the collaborator and instead be a symbol of defiance against the Kade. Freya wasn't certain she liked the idea of being a symbol, but she definitely disliked being viewed as someone who betrayed her own people for a life of comfort.

"You know, there's an air of anticipation in the city that I haven't seen before," she commented as she helped Astrom push the benches back into their usual places.

"That's true. You can only rule with the kind of force the Kade's employed for so long before people begin to start seriously contemplating an alternative," Makkyd replied, bringing over a tray of tools and placing it on a table.

"You sound almost thrilled that the Kade is being so vile," Freya said, struggling to pull a worktable over.

Ashtyn came over to help her, easily moving it by himself. She refused to meet his eyes and turned away from him as soon as the table was in place.

"I hardly enjoy the ongoing violence brought against our own people, Freya," Makkyd replied acerbically. "But I can appreciate the opportunity it presents."

Freya brought over two stools. Ashtyn took one from her, his hands brushing against her own as he did. Her skin tingled where their hands had touched and she told her body to stop reacting to him like this – not that it would obey her.

"I suppose that's why you're our glorious leader," she retorted dryly, realising too late that she had echoed Ashtyn's description of Makkyd the first time he had brought her to the Resistance. Now her eyes did flick over to him, and she saw him looking at her, knowing it, too. She blushed again.

"I suppose that must be it," Makkyd said, seemingly oblivious to Freya and Ashtyn's shared look or indeed the awkward moment that had bloomed from it.

They finished replacing the furniture and the small number of people who remained, the leadership of the Resistance, gathered around a table. With practiced efficiency they shared news and speculated on how what they had just divulged might affect what was taking place across the city. The regular, more structured meetings of the Resistance leadership had recently been replaced by these informal updates. It meant that Makkyd could be told what they learned from their various positions scattered across the city, and often. Freya had quickly realised that Makkyd was more than just the person who made the final decision: she was the mastermind of the Resistance. She designed the strategies they pursued and ensured that the many elements of the subversive organisation seamlessly worked to undermine the authority of the Kade and remain a hidden phantom that the Kade simply couldn't pin down, despite their best efforts. Freya was always amazed that Makkyd hardly ever wrote down anything, citing security precautions, yet she remembered the tiniest, most inconsequential details with ease.

Over the past few fivedays, the possibility of an uprising was looking ever more likely as discontent grew within the city, requiring plans to constantly be amended and immediate responses to issues as they arose; hence, the less formal meetings. Makkyd's brilliant mind held all those plans, immediately adjusting them and giving necessary instructions. Freya had never seen her fazed by anything: not reports of a beating, or of permits being inexplicably revoked, or of the announcement of more severe curfews.

Makkyd's mouth would simply tighten for a moment, then she would announce what they would do in reply.

"Bardan, are our supplies safe?" Makkyd asked, looking at the portly man.

The merchant, who had been the first person in the Resistance Freya had met, clasped his hands together and propped his elbows on the table. "As safe as they'll be anywhere in Oranis. Raids and impromptu inspections are occurring on a daily basis. I've placed our more...controversial supplies in the secret areas Ashtyn has built, and the rest is documented as legitimate, thanks to Lyssa's talents."

Freya felt a stab of bitterness at the fact that Lyssa's discovery that she could alter ink even after it had dried on paper was thanks to Freya's own inquisitiveness. Had she not asked whether it was possible, she suspected Lyssa would never have thought to experiment with it. Yet here was Lyssa getting all the credit for Freya's idea. Her jealousy wasn't helped by the fact that Lyssa had, from the very first time she had met Freya, taken an instant and vehement dislike to her. Their relationship had not improved. Lyssa made snide remarks at Freya's expense whenever the opportunity arose, criticising Freya's fighting technique, the amount of medical supplies she diverted into Resistance warehouses, Freya's progress in honing her ability to heal with only her mind. More than once Freya had fought her exasperation with Makkyd for not stepping in and chiding Lyssa for her pettiness. Although she hated to admit it, Lyssa's goading had made her train harder and improve faster. She wondered if Makkyd realised that. Knowing Makkyd, she probably had, which was exactly why she did nothing to silence the beautiful artist. As much as she was sometimes ruthless, that was fair; her position was not to care for her people, but to get a job done. And, if rebellion came to pass, that job could become quite messy.

Makkyd's question cut through Freya's thoughts. "Freya, our sources indicate that there's a large shipment of barat coming in. How much do you think you'd be able to get for us?"

Startled, Freya looked at her. "You seem to know more than me. I wasn't even aware that a shipment was arriving." Freya's discovery that the lethal barat flower could be used as a topical remedy for vile rashes that covered the whole body, a symptom of the sweating sickness that had recently run through the city, had led to a significant increase in demand for the dangerous plant.

"Keep an eye out for it then. Having some of it in our stocks could be very useful," Makkyd told her.

"What would we use it for?" Freya asked, suspicion unfurling within her. Even though she had made her decision to join the Resistance knowing she would be helping to hurt, even kill people, she still didn't like the prospect that something as unpleasant as barat poison may be unleashed by them.

Makkyd shrugged with a nonchalance that Freya couldn't quite believe. "It's a useful thing to have," she replied. She immediately directed a question about weapons to Ashtyn, the group's armourer, which forestalled other questions Freya wanted to ask regarding her plans for the dangerous substance.

Years of keeping her thoughts and opinions carefully away from her features meant that Freya's suspicion about Makkyd's plans remained far away from her features. Inwardly, she heaved a sigh. She had discarded any naivety that the Resistance would eschew morally questionable actions in pursuit of liberating the Third Country from the Kade's grasp. She knew that the Kade and the Resistance both did bad things, but she had chosen to join the Resistance because she believed the Resistance was fighting for a better world while the Kade sought to maintain their power and abuse the Pious population purely for the fact that they had been born into worshipping the wrong god. It was a choice she had made knowing what that entailed. But that didn't ease the weight which pulled at her conscience.

The meeting concluded not long after and the rest of the Resistance members dispersed back into Oranis to resume their places within the Kade's world. Freya took the white over-robe that signified her healer's profession off a peg on the wall. She slipped it over the light shift and trews she had stripped down to for training. As was often the case, her eyes slid down to the green band sewn into one sleeve. It denoted her status as a Pious, her undesirability. And yet she had been promoted by the Kade into the highest position of any Pious within the city. Her skill and displays of dedication to the Kade in the years since it had seized control of the Third Country had led it to overlook her birth to promote her far above her peers. The fact that the bottom hem of her robes was edged with the red, purple and blue colours of the Kade only served to highlight her unique position within Kade society. She sometimes wondered if it was another technique of control, to try to elicit disunity amongst the Pious by evoking jealousy toward one of their own. But the Chief Healer had always emphasised Freya's invaluable contributions to the Kade governance, at times even speaking to Freya with warmth and candour – or what constituted warmth and candour for her.

Freya shook her head. She didn't know what was causing this pensiveness, but it wasn't helping anything.

As she straightened her robe, she felt Ashtyn come up behind her. Her whole body tensed.

"It's been nearly a year since we first met."

She thought she detected a note of uncertainty in his voice. At least his comment gave a likely explanation to why she was suddenly so introspective – the upcoming anniversary of when her whole life had been inverted.

"Am I supposed to celebrate?" She tried to keep her voice neutral but a sting of bitterness crept in.

"I just thought..."

"Yes?" She turned around to look up at him. She was still as attracted to him as she had been when she had first met him. Being that close to him still made her breath catch, made her stupidly conscious of how she held herself, of where his body was in relation to hers.

He seemed to recover himself slightly. "I just thought you may like to know."

"I didn't realise it had been that long," she replied quietly, looking away from him so that she didn't have to meet his eyes.

Before he could say anything else, she darted around him and left the room. Despite herself, she glanced back at him and their eyes met. He looked as though he was about to say something across the distance between them, but seemed to think the better of it. She wasn't sure if that left her relieved or disappointed.

TWO

On her way home, she passed a Kade official's transport cart. It was deemed unfitting for the more senior members of the Kade to be seen walking through the streets. Safety was also a concern, but it wouldn't do for the Kade to admit they felt any weakness, and Freya had been involved with the Kade governance for long enough to know that one of their foremost concerns was appearance. So to present a reminder of their importance, senior Kade officials were transported in small carts that housed at most two people. Freya had travelled in one twice since taking up her position as chief healer of the Centre, and both times she had found the experience stuffy and uncomfortable. It seemed a ridiculous thing to impose upon oneself to be apart from the rest of the world for the sake of seeming important.

The carts were pulled by hearat – beasts of burden preferred for their manoeuvrability inside cities when compared to the larger manaxas merchants used for their plodding endurance to transport goods across the Third Country. The transport cart Freya passed was sitting motionless in the middle of the street, its Kade owner standing beside it, looking with red-faced ire at the driver's legs which stuck out from underneath the cart. The hearat that drew it stood placidly, its long ears twitching as it waited. It seemed to be the only one unperturbed by the unfolding scene. Freya smiled to herself as she strode past. A great many of the Kade carts had been mysteriously encountering difficulties of late. It had led to a significant number of very inelegant scenes on the part of frustrated Kade officials. Freya's favourite story had been that of a Kade official who had been so angry that during a rant which was replete with wrathful gesticulations, she had slapped the hearat. The animal had flicked its long, thick tail in response, catching the Kade official off-balance and sending her straight down onto her backside. Apparently it had been quite a comical scene. Incidents like this alone wouldn't bring down the Kade but it niggled at their pretence of complete control. It was a start.

As she walked in the front door, Symon emerged from his workroom and called out to her. "How was your day?"

She wondered if he really cared or if he was simply performing his role dutifully, as always.

"It was fine," she replied, putting her things down and going to the kitchen. Symon had left a plate of food out for her. It was cold by now, but she knew that it would be delicious, regardless. Symon was an excellent cook.

"You've eaten?" she asked as she picked up the plate. He nodded and she began to eat, surprised by the sharp claws of hunger that seized her as the scent of food filled her nose. It took her three bites before she realised that he'd cooked the meat in a sauce that was particularly enjoyable.

"Really, Freya, surely you can sit down," Symon objected.

Freya shrugged but went to the table, shovelling food into her mouth as she walked.

He sat down next to her, playing with some imagined dirt on the tabletop.

"Is everything all right?" Freya asked. It was unusual for Symon to fidget or seem nervous. Or indeed to sit with her while she ate after coming home late.

He was silent for a moment, seeming to collect his thoughts and choose his words.

"Symon?" she prompted.

He fixed his dark eyes on her. "I think that it's time for us to seriously consider having children."

Freya dropped her spoon with a clatter. "What? Now?"

He nodded, almost shyly, his gaze trickling away from hers to rest on the table between them.

Freya looked down at her meal to avoid looking at him. He didn't know that she had been taking mandras root to prevent children for years now. It wouldn't have mattered anyway. Freya couldn't remember the last time she had been in any danger of falling pregnant with Symon's child. She knew that their relationship was a transactional one, born from the mutual recognition of the need to survive following the Kade's brutal takeover eight years earlier. Together they had become the perfect couple, excellent at their respective jobs and utterly loyal to the regime. They had succeeded in Kade society where many of their faith had failed. To the outward observer, they had completely discarded their Pious origins and their previous worship of the Goddess and taken to the mandated worship of the Kade gods with vigour. Until a year ago when the cracks in Freya's obedience had been pried open.

"What's brought this on?" She was filled with a small but insistent flutter of panic. It was fuelled equally by the prospect of having a child, even if it was theoretical, and by what creating a child would entail.

"The Kade like families. They reward families," he said. It was true. Children could be taught to unquestioningly worship the Kade gods. There was no need to employ coercive measures such as those levelled at the Pious. It was brilliant, really. Within a generation, the resentment against the Kade for their prohibition of worshipping the Goddess would be all but eliminated.

"But...I've not been in this position at the Healing Centre for even half a year," Freya protested. "Surely we can't afford to compromise our dedication to work?"

"Freya, you're practically the best healer in the city and I'm all but the best tailor. The only way we can progress higher into Kade society is if we show that we're dedicated enough to produce children."

"I'm still the one who has to carry it," she pointed out. "You know I sometimes work so late that it's past curfew when I'm done and I have to sleep at the Centre." She wasn't only referring to the question of how such hours and habits may be affected by carrying a child. Without so many words, she was trying to point out that her routine may impede their ability to actually engage in the act required to conceive a child. Although, intimacy between them was currently all but non-existent, so her routine wasn't going to much affect things in that area, anyway.

"I didn't say that we should start trying right away," he replied, and she relaxed a little.

"But I do think it's within our interests to start planning. Besides, we certainly can easily support a child."

He was correct. Freya was chief of a Healing Centre and Symon was one of the most highly sought tailors in Oranis. They each earned more than two or three regular people. Their wealth reflected their success as members of Kade society. Not even two cycles ago, they had moved out of the Pious district and into the city's Kade living district. The waivers allowing them to live outside the confines of the Pious district had been signed by the Chief Healer herself. It made them the first Pious to have been allowed to leave the Pious district. This testament to their success and position of favour was underlined by the fact that their home was richly furnished.

Freya forced herself to look at him and smile. Regardless of what she felt, it was of the utmost importance that he not suspect she no longer remained loyal to the Kade. "You're right. It's the natural next step."

Satisfied, he stood up and took a step toward the door. He paused and hovered by her for a moment. Then in a quick and clumsy movement, he stooped down and kissed her cheek before returning to his workroom. Freya couldn't remember the last time he had done that.

She sat and finished eating, alone with her thoughts. What she mulled over the most was her abject panic at the prospect of having to feign trying to conceive a child with Symon. She was satisfied with the complete lack of physicality in their relationship.

It meant that the pretence of life with him was far easier to sustain. But the more she pondered, the more she realised that it wasn't the thought of having to be intimate with Symon that unsettled her the most. It was the fact that he was willing to have a child not because he wanted children, but because he believed that a child would further his standing with the Kade. To view your own flesh and blood as something that could simply benefit you seemed unbearably callous. She was reminded of an exchange with Zarech, captured leader of the anarchic Followers of the Dark Gods. She had been assigned to tend him following his capture and then through the repeated beatings he sustained over the course of many interrogations. He had defied her expectation that he would be a raving lunatic and she had formed a wary attachment to him over the cycles in which she had tended his wounds. He had asked her why she had not had children and she had replied that she didn't want to bring children into a world which was dominated by repression and fear. It had been as true then as it was now. Any children she bore she wanted to keep safe from the harms of the world. To allow any child of hers to be raised in a society where everybody was forced to worship the Kade gods and lived in fear of the terrible and brutal consequences of breaking the impossibly strict rules was criminal.

She shook her head. Zarech was dead. She suspected he had used his own abilities to blow up the Central Healing Centre where he had been kept, plunging the city into chaos and provoking an even fiercer repression by the Kade. Freya often wondered whether he had made sure she was out of the Centre before destroying it. She couldn't quite shake the sense that he had spared her on a whim of tenderness. It ran contrary to the beliefs of his faith whose gods demanded chaos at any price, but then again, Zarech had been more complicated than that. He had been a Pious man whose family was killed during the Kade takeover. Following this, he had converted to worship of the Dark Gods and committed himself to fulfilling their destructive vision. As much as she could never believe she would ally with a cause that demanded such a terrible price of other people, she could understand why Zarech had.

Freya regretted his death, almost resented it. He had forced her to look at herself during their time together, made her question why she was so desperate to live as a subjugated citizen in the pursuit of illusory safety. She almost wished now that she could talk about Symon's proposition with him. It was preposterous of course. Zarech was a mass murderer. He wanted to destroy any semblance of society and leave in its place complete chaos. But even though she had known this, she had never felt like that was the case when she had talked with him. She felt like he had understood her, even cared about her. He had been the first to do so since her own parents and sister had been killed by the Kade for her sister's defiance. She wondered what Zarech would say about Symon's suggestion. More than simply ponder what he may have said, she actively wished she could speak with him, to unburden her complex mix of feelings to him.

But such thoughts were unproductive. Regret over things that were beyond her control was not going to help her survive now. She cleaned her plate and went into her own workroom.

It seemed there were always reports to read and write. But she was more often than not grateful for the mass of work that her position required of her. It kept her away from Symon and gave her a moment's reprieve from the intensity of rebellion. This was what she knew – even if it wasn't dealing with the body and how it worked, it was still the business of healing. She had surprised herself with her ability to look at a report from one of the wards and find within the words what needed to be done to be more efficient in tending to patients. She picked up an inventory and explanation of the Healing Centre's stockrooms, intending to determine how they could be better organised. However, thoughts of stockrooms led her right back to thoughts of the Resistance: Freya's careful reorganisation and management of the stockrooms masked the medicines that she surreptitiously siphoned off to the Resistance. And just today, Makkyd had tasked her with stealing one of the city's most controlled substances – barat flower – without getting discovered.

She sighed, a heavy sound that had her shoulders sagging. She wasn't going to get any work done. That much was swiftly becoming obvious. It wasn't that she minded juggling the two lives – she had made that decision and it felt right to be a part of the Resistance. It was simply that sometimes she wanted a reprieve from the intrigue. She wanted to simply be, to not worry about keeping her façade carefully maintained to ensure that she wasn't followed or discovered. Just a moment where she could truly relax would be wonderful. That being said, life under Kade rule was a constant façade of carefully constructed model citizenship. It was just a different sort of pretence.

Running her fingers through her hair, Freya pushed the papers to one side and stood up. It was too early to go to sleep but too late to leave without facing the risk of running into Guardian patrols and having to answer difficult questions.

A feeling of restlessness awoke inside her. She prowled through the house with its lovely furnishings, not really doing anything beyond moving from room to room. Symon came out of his workroom after the fifth time she passed his door, exasperation written into the hands propped on his hips.

"What on earth are you doing?" he demanded.

"I don't know," she admitted. "I don't feel like doing work and it's too late to go out."

He looked at her for a moment, bemusement across his face. Symon didn't understand the concept of not wanting to work. He lived for his work, often to the exclusion of everything else, including her. Normally Freya did, too.

"Well, if you don't have anything you want to do, I suppose we could always...practise."

With a sense of mild horror, Freya realised what he was pro-posing. "Uh..." She wasn't sure what she could say to extricate herself from the proposition.

Symon covered the distance between them and put his hand heavily on her waist. There was a grim sense of determination and purpose to the gesture that made Freya's eyes widen.

"Are you sure?" She tried to hide how nervous she felt but was now certain she was entirely unsuccessful.

"Freya, we're joined." He sounded pained. She couldn't blame him. He put his free hand on the other side of her waist and slowly brought his eyes up to meet hers. She saw his own uncer-tainty and discomfort alongside the ever-present undercurrent of determination to survive. "This is what's supposed to happen."

He was correct. It just felt so...wrong, somehow. They hadn't been so close in a very long time. His hands upon her brought no excitement. But she didn't want to give him any cause to feel that she wasn't as committed to being a loyal Kade citizen as he was. Forcing herself to smile, she lifted her arms and draped them around his shoulders. "You're right. I suppose we could practise," she said.

Symon was as meticulous as ever, leading her into their bed-room and folding each item of clothing he took off her. In different circumstances, Freya would have found it comical. Instead, she just waited patiently for him to finish removing the last piece of clothing. Finally, they were both completely naked. She felt the strength of her muscles and the way they gave her body a new shape, formed from the intense practice of the recent cycles, and saw his scrawniness by comparison. She wondered if he saw the muscles on her. Worry that he may question her about it clouded her mind, but it seemed that he was too intent upon his purpose. When he pulled her to him and kissed her, it was clumsy, as though he were following instructions rather than the dictates and desires of his body. Freya couldn't remember when he had last kissed her. She fought back her instinct to draw back from him and instead ran her fingers along his back as though she were enjoying it.

As they did every morning, the morning bells for prayer woke her. Freya rolled over to prod Symon awake as she normally did – until the previous night, that had been the extent of their intimacy for several cycles – and found him looking at her, a small smile on his face.

"Good morning." His words were still slurred with whatever dreams had lingered into wakefulness, but his eyes were alert and fixed on her.

"Mmm," she responded, aggrieved that he was so awake while drowsiness still clung to her. She was surprised, too. Normally, she had to coax him several times before he arose.

"How did you sleep?"

Not yet awake enough to properly speak, Freya rolled out of bed and went to find clothes before she replied. "Fine. You?" She picked up the robe that Symon had neatly folded the previous evening – convenient, if nothing else – and pulled it on.

"Very well, actually. Are you all right?" His question was so unexpected that it drew a look of surprise from her. "You seemed tense last night," he said in answer to her question as he pulled on his own clothes.

"I guess it had just been a long time since we'd done that," she replied cautiously.

An expression flashed across his face, too fast for her to discern, and Symon stepped forward as though to embrace her.

"We'd better get to the square," Freya said hurriedly. He stopped himself and nodded, leading the way through the house and out into the predawn streets.

Freya followed him quietly. It hadn't been so bad, the lovemaking. She shuddered a little as she thought the word. Symon had always been a very dutiful lover. But she couldn't help but compare him now to Ashtyn. During the short time that they had been lovers she had been consumed by the overwhelming need to be with him, to feel him against her. She had never felt like that about Symon, and for all his judiciousness, the previous evening had left her feeling entirely unsatisfied. Truth be told, she still thought about Ashtyn's touch with an acute longing, and that morning she struggled to keep that desire at bay. But that was only her body's desires, not that of her mind or even her heart. She wrested her mind away from those thoughts and focused instead on the prayers ahead of her.

The prayers to the Kade gods every morning were a test of the devotion of Oranis's people. While it wasn't as rigorously expected of Kade citizens as it was of Pious, as the Kade leadership had intensified the restrictions on the people, Freya had noted a distinct increase in the number of people in the Kade district's worship square. It seemed that being born Kade no longer guaranteed complete protection from their rulers' draconian brutality.

The Ordained began the chanting and prayers that typified every worship. The resentment Freya had always felt at being forced to participate in the worship of gods not her own simmered as it always did. As she always did, she kept that sentiment safely inside her and her face carefully attentive. The two Ordained began to walk through the square, waving smouldering arax root back and forth. The plant's fumes sent the gathered people into a trance-like state that cleared the mind. The use of the plant was intended to channel the worshipper's mind so that they could focus on the gods to whom they were praying. Freya inhaled deeply, letting the drug do its work on her. Symon had once asked her if the drug was being used to condition citizens into obedience. He had been wrong about that, but by mandating the worship only of Kade gods, the Kade had sapped the lifeblood of the other gods and given it only to theirs. Freya's blood boiled with indignation and fury whenever she thought about it. She had once asked Makkyd why they didn't simply tell the citizens of the Third Country the truth about the existence of the gods and what the Kade had done to the Goddess. Surely, she argued, if people found out that the Kade leadership was complicit in the attempt to kill a god, their outrage would be a powerful ally to the Resistance. Makkyd had outlined the mayhem the revelation may cause and the fact the Resistance may not be able to properly harness such mayhem to their advantage. Additionally, Makkyd had noted, as far as they could gather from the surviving Pious religious texts, the abilities of the faithful existed because the strength of their faith enabled them to reach out and touch the gods. How that could be explained to all the citizens of Oranis in a way that they could even begin to understand was itself a near-impossible task, let alone in a way that the Resistance could twist to their cause. The delicate balance within the Third Country meant that something so monumental could not be carelessly revealed; the consequences could not all be foreseen and as such, it was too dangerous. Freya had been forced to concede that Makkyd had a point.

She breathed in and out, listening with one ear to the chant of the Ordained, and in her mind reciting a prayer to the Goddess. She had once thought that the Ordained and Guardians who watched the worshippers were able to see if someone wasn't truly praying to the Kade gods but she had long since discarded that fear. There were worse things to fear in the world.

THREE

She couldn't help but think of the Healing Centre as hers. It was a curious thing that amid the world of intrigue and the secret life it required of her, Freya was very much content with her work and what she had achieved there. It was her world, arranged in accordance with her design. Everybody obeyed her commands without question.

Her days were invariably filled with an assortment of issues requiring her attention: wards to reorder, training programs to oversee, lax workers to discipline. Her workload was added to by secret trips to the storerooms and the careful forgery of records to hide her theft of supplies for the Resistance. She never ceased to be surprised by how easy it was to steal from right under the Kade's nose. When she was certain she was able to remove the medicines or ingredients without them being missed, Freya would leave the crates in a particular location and merchants who delivered supplies to the Centre would in turn collect what she left for them. It was a perfect way for her to remain anonymous; she had established from her first day that she liked to go through the storerooms regularly – as she liked to go through every part of her Centre, even the morgue – and because the supplies were simply left for collection, the merchants who were allied to the Resistance had no way of knowing who was procuring the supplies. Probably, they assumed it was someone in the storerooms, not the overseer of the Centre herself.

Intrigue aside, Freya loved her work and the fact that she was in a position of authority. She had wanted to walk the path of a healer for as long as she could remember, and even though her position meant she did not do much healing now, she still found a great deal of enjoyment in what she did. She knew her decisions and instructions made a difference to the lives of the people of Oranis. Even if she could personally perform a healer's task better than anybody else, it did not stack up against the number of lives saved by the instructions she gave the many healers at the Centre, improving the quality of the treatment and care given to the patients. Makkyd had told her that in a world in which the Resistance came to power, she was to take the role of Chief Healer. A part of her was terrified at the prospect of assuming such a position of importance. Another part was thrilled at the idea that she would be able to co-ordinate the healers of the city so completely. A world of possibilities was opened up by Makkyd's plan for her. As a result, she always considered in the back of her mind how what she saw in her own Centre could be applied or changed across the city. Occasionally, she frightened herself with her ambition and single-minded purpose. She was preparing to assume a role that would only become available through bloodshed.

Freya swept through the wards on her daily inspection, looking with a critical eye for anything out of place or that could be done better. Were the more infirm patients being properly washed and turned? Were the patients being fed meals best suited to their maladies? Were injuries being tended efficiently and frequently? Most days, everything ran well. It pleased her that she had created a world that was so well ordered. Today, the elation running through her was particularly buoyant. She had managed to secret away some of the barat flowers that Makkyd had requested, thanks to a flash of inspiration to alter the labels on some boxes. Even as she moved between the wards, the marked crate was being picked up and the Resistance's latest prize was being delivered to their warehouses. That was something for her to consider if she ever did take the position of Chief Healer, though: how to ensure nobody could siphon off ingredients from the Healing Centre supplies. At least she had the head start, knowing the various tricks she had employed.

She paused by the ward that held newly arrived patients, drawn by the sound of their injuries and maladies. As her ability had developed, she had begun to hear the ailments of people around her. She was even able to faintly hear sickness or injury from a different room if there were a large enough number of patients clustered together. The maladies rang in her head as a dissonance to the usual background hum of everyday life. She had begun to call the sound of every individual's body the lifesong, as the dissonance or harmony told her everything she needed to know about the health of the person. She had intended to pass by the arrivals ward today, but the sound of so many people in pain drew her in.

Often, as the weakened, fading lifesong of someone whose body was giving out reached her, she needed to fight the impulse to put her hands on them and right it with a simple effort of will. So far, she had never given in. The only opportunity she had to use her healing ability was on the few Resistance members who knew about the abilities of the faithful. It was too dangerous to try healing anybody outside that small group for the questions such an ability may prompt. Freya accepted that the Third Country wasn't ready for that kind of truth about the world yet. After all, rumours about the fantastical abilities of the monks in the Fourth Country and wild tales of what went on in the nearly inaccessible First Country speculated about such things, but that was very different to being certain that magic, for want of a better term, existed and could be possessed by anybody. If her ability were discovered by the Kade, it could lead to the genocide of the Pious for fear that there were more like her, and that they may pose a serious threat to the Kade. Yet despite her agreement with the need for secrecy,

Freya often had to strengthen her resolve and allow people to go on dying so that her secret was safe. She hated herself for it.

She walked a few paces into the ward, drawn to one of the beds. It was occupied by a heavily bandaged woman. Her eyes were fixed upon the ceiling; her lips moved without sound. The injuries that ravaged the woman's body were a harsh, angry noise which assaulted Freya's senses.

Her mind flashed back to her tumultuous re-entrance into the world of the Resistance so many cycles earlier.

After her parents and sister had been killed before her very eyes, she had thought the only thing defiance did was assure your own death, and Ashtyn's betrayal had only seemed to reconfirm that rebellion brought heartbreak and nothing else. And then she had been ordered to allow a Pious girl to die simply in order to attend to an injured member of the Kade. With that order, Freya's loyalty to the Kade had snapped; being loyal to the Kade may have ensured her safety, but it guaranteed the death of innocent people for no reason. If personal safety required her to sacrifice lives according to some arbitrary designation, she couldn't live with herself. She knew the Resistance may ask her to do difficult things, even allow people to die when she could save them, but at least it was in the service of bettering the world rather than saving herself. She knew the Resistance would probably use her, perhaps at times callously. But the Kade definitely used her. This way, she was at least making a choice about how and why she was somebody's instrument.

After she had burst into the Resistance meeting, full of choler and disgust at herself for allowing a child to die, Makkyd had requested she remain behind.

"What caused you to change your mind?" Makkyd asked the question only once the room had cleared.

"I was made to sacrifice a life that didn't need to be sacrificed."

Makkyd considered the answer with a grave expression in eyes a shade of brown that looked as though the red of her hair had bled down into them. "I'll need more than that," she said.

So Freya had told her. About her sister and parents, about her quest for safety, about the girl the Chief Healer had forced her to let die. After she finished, Makkyd sat, the only indication that she was thinking a slight line across her forehead.

"What if I asked you to do the same thing?" Makkyd eventually asked.

Freya's surprise and unease must have shown on her face.

"Make no mistake; we will rise up in this lifetime. But it must happen when the time is right. Rebellion is a delicate thing, Freya. And the Kade is very powerful. The only way we can ensure that we take power and remain there is to be careful and patient, to sometimes do awful things. I need to know that if you are in a position similar to today's, you will be able to make the right decision, to not use your ability to heal someone when it could save them. It will be difficult, but I need to know that you can do it."

In response to that, Freya had bitten her lip hard enough that she had tasted the sweet-salty tang of her own blood until she willed the cut closed. She was a healer. The training she had received had emphasised that hers was the business of healing, not of taking lives or allowing lives to go to waste.

Makkyd continued. "I never said that the business of rebellion was easy. This will not be easy. But this way, at least each life that you might be forced to sacrifice helps you go undetected while you help us to create a better world. I won't blame you if you walk away now. This is at times a dark path and it isn't for everybody. But if you stay, at least the next time you must allow one of your own people to die, their death won't be meaningless."

Freya knew she was being manipulated but that didn't make what Makkyd was saying any less true. She struggled with the callous logic behind the claim and the way it butted up against the awful prospect of allowing a life to slip away.

"Doesn't what you've asked me to do make us just like the Kade?"

Makkyd sighed. The sound contained the weight of all the lives she carried. "I've thought long and hard about that," she admitted. "It makes us different from them because we didn't set the terms of this situation. We have to manage with the circumstances we have, not what we'd like to have. In an ideal world, we would never have to do something that we find repulsive, like allow someone to die. But this isn't an ideal world. I suppose really, the difference is that we struggle to live with ourselves afterward."

"Does saying that ever make you feel better?" Freya asked.

Makkyd's chuckle was a bitter sound. "Sometimes for a moment."

Now here Freya was, again facing the awful task of having to sacrifice someone for a greater cause. The dissonance of the woman's lifesong spread through Freya's mind as she laid a hand on an exposed patch of undamaged skin. Every time she stood in front of someone who she could save, she thought of that exchange with Makkyd. How much longer, she wondered, would they have to go through with this ghastly task; would she even be able to use her ability to save those she could once the Resistance threw off the Kade rule, or would there be yet another supposedly compelling reason to force her to let people die? Yet she held fast to the belief that her position gave more to the Resistance than her saving one person's life.

"What happened to her?" she asked the initiate who was shadowing her as she walked through the ward. One of her first instructions had been to ensure that all initiates or first-ranked healers were able to provide the full details of the patients assigned to them to any healer who might come into the ward. She had seen the cost of ignorance far too many times.

"She was in a warehouse when it caught fire," the initiate replied instantly.

Freya nodded in approval at the speed of the response. "Caught fire?"

"Yes. Nobody has any idea how it started."

"What was in the warehouse?" Freya slipped through the lifesong of the woman in further investigation as she listened to the initiate, privately reeling at the extent of the injuries hidden behind the neat bandages.

"I don't know. It was a Kade warehouse. Surely you heard about it?"

"Of course." Freya remembered reading a report about a Kade warehouse burning almost to the ground a few days ago. The report hadn't mentioned whether or not people had been inside, nor had she even considered it. She had only been grimly pleased that the Kade was being forced to deal with yet another problem.

"Does she have any children?"

The reply came back immediately. "Two."

"How old?"

"Ah, I don't know," the initiate said, obviously abashed.

"We should probably start noting that," Freya murmured. It wasn't relevant to the condition of the woman in front of her, but she had been taught to distance herself from the body in front of her while also remembering that she was treating a person who had an entire life of their own. Holding those almost paradoxical states of thinking in one's mind made for the best healer; compassionate, but not overwhelmed. The knowledge of the age of the woman's children was a small thing, but it was important to Freya that her healers remembered that they were dealing with people, not simply bodies, and in so doing, did the best they could by every patient. Knowing something as seemingly trivial as the age of a patient's children was a way to instil that. She made a note on the wax tablet she carried to ensure she instructed all healers to record the age of patients' children. Judging by the apparent age of the woman, she couldn't imagine her children were particularly old.

"Those poor children," she murmured. She lingered a moment longer, and then she moved on.

FOUR

It seemed that all she ever did when she had time to spare from her duties at the Healing Centre was attend training sessions for the senior members of the Resistance. Sometimes, it would just be her and Astrom – if she was lucky, they would occasionally have a snack or drink afterward and spend a sliver of time together talking, relaxing. She enjoyed those times and the odd sense of normalcy that accompanied them; as strange as it was to feel normal after practising the use of weapons, it had been far too many years since she had freely laughed and chatted with a friend. Today there wasn't a group practice scheduled across the time when Astrom's workshop was available, but a few people had made their way to there, seeking to speak with Astrom or to use the practice space her workshop offered. Freya was disappointed. She had hoped for she could quickly relieve some of her pent up frustration.

Symon had made clumsy advances three of the past four nights, all of which culminated in lovemaking that she had to endure. The only reason it hadn't been all four nights was that she had locked herself away in her workroom one evening under the false claim that she needed to finish writing a report. She had reorganised all of her papers, re-written some of her notes to include new observations, and then finally, when she heard him still moving in the next room, idly drawn a sharp knife across her arm again and again to see if she could seal her skin before blood seeped out. Gory, but to her it had been better than the prospect of withstanding Symon's clumsy ardour.

She had told Flen, one of her assistants, that she was going to the spice market to compare the quality of what was delivered to the Centre against what could be bought in the marketplace. Freya's frequent inspections of the storerooms ensured that any substandard quality was quickly detected and the merchants were spoken to, leaving them in no doubt that she would not tolerate poor ingredients – especially when they were to help people get better. Flen hadn't looked at all surprised at her announcement – Freya's reputation was that of ensuring the very best, after all. She had slipped out of the Centre and made her way across the mid-day-hot streets to Astrom's workshop only to find she had to wait to spend time with her friend.

With only a few cycles of training, Freya still was far from being a skilled fighter. But she had found herself approaching the task with the same kind of stubborn determination that she had tackled the requirements for botany during her first years as an apprentice. She would not be proved inept simply because of an initial lack of knowledge. Besides, she reasoned that the more she trained, the more likely it would be that she might actually survive if she ever ended up in a fight.

She patiently took a seat at the edge of the room and watched three different bouts. The first was with knives. There was a certain artistry in the way they stayed constantly dancing away from each other until one broke and lunged in, then quickly darted back again. Freya hated training with knives most of all; the jumping backwards and forwards, needing to be light on her toes, had made her feel like she was going to be sick. The second bout was with a half pike and a short sword. It was fortuitous she was present, as one of the participants was injured by the pike despite the dulled practice edge. Freya tended to the wound as the third bout began; unarmed combat.

When she finally got to spar with Astrom, she was pushed to her very limit. Astrom didn't pull even one of the many blows which landed on Freya. Freya didn't mind, though. The discomfort took her way from the petty frustrations which were writhing within her. Quickly, she lost herself in the rhythm of the movements, her body twisting and moving automatically as Astrom bore down on her. The pace was truly ferocious. Had she the time to spare a thought, Freya would have lamented the fact that she was so markedly inferior to Astrom. It was all she could to do keep up, and finally she faltered. That was all Astrom needed. She swept Freya's foot out from under her so that she landed on her back, winded.

Freya grimaced as she took Astrom's proffered hand to help her stand. "I'll never be as good as you." She winced as she finally felt the effect of several bruises and one nasty cut.

"You're getting better," she was told with a patronising encouragement she knew too well.

"But what if I ever have to fight someone who's better than me for real?"

The sound of others sparring in the huge space meant that nobody else could hear the conversation. She was glad. It occurred to her only after she had spoken that such comments weren't good for morale. No leader should so openly worry about the possibility of being killed.

"Then you stick to the basics. Be disciplined. Don't do anything stupid. Even the best make mistakes," Astrom advised.

Freya wasn't reassured. "Surely there's something else I can do?"

From her side, Ashtyn spoke. She hadn't even been aware that he had come into the room. "What about your ability?"

She jumped. "What do you mean?" she asked him tersely. *So long, and I still can't behave normally around him*, she thought to herself as she shifted slightly away from him. If he noticed her shuffle, he said nothing.

"I've been wondering about how we could expand our capabilities, ever since you asked Lyssa about the ink," he said, keeping his voice low so nobody could overhear.

"Yes?" She was intrigued despite herself.

"You only really consider healing. But what if you could do the opposite?"

She stared at him, not certain that she understood what he was saying.

Astrom, however, was looking thoughtful. "You're right, you know. We've always assumed that we know the limits of what we could do. But Lyssa taught us otherwise."

"Are you saying that I should harm people with my ability?" Freya asked.

Ashtyn's look was all she needed to set her off.

"That's a disgusting idea. I'm a healer. I save lives, I don't take them."

"What are you learning to do here, then?" Astrom said, with infuriating calm.

"I'm learning to defend myself," she snapped.

"Go on, Freya, just try it," Ashtyn suggested. "You can experiment on me."

"Are you crazy?" she said under her breath, realising that people were starting to stare at them. "I have no idea what would happen. I could kill you. But I think you're missing the more important point. I. Am. A. Healer."

"I thought you were worried about being beaten by someone better than you." He raised his hands as though in self defence.

"I am. And?" She gripped her hands around the practice staff she was still holding, trying to calm her outrage.

"This may be a way to give you an advantage if such a situation were ever to arise."

"You really are out of your mind." It was all too much for her to bear. With little regard to what the others in the room may think, she threw down her staff and stormed out the room.

Freya found herself in the central courtyard of Astrom's building; like all larger buildings in Oranis, the workshop was built around a garden. The rooms that walled the garden housed Astrom's apprentices, her workshops, storerooms, and storefront, but despite the number of people who might have been in the space, the area was mercifully unoccupied. Freya ignored the seats scattered around the garden and slumped to a spot in the sun on the pebbled ground, trying to allow the heat of the warm rays to soak into her, to soothe her.

Just as her breathing was beginning to slow, she heard the crunch of footsteps from the direction she had come. She tensed, knowing without having to look that it was Ashtyn. She refused to say anything, to be the one to break the silence. He was the one who had sought her out. If he wanted to speak with her, he had to say something. She didn't even open her eyes when he sat down in front of her.

"You know I'm here," he said. In different circumstances, it would have been a playful game between the two of them. It was a tiny stab to her heart to realise that.

"What do you want?" She fought to keep the hurt and anger out of her voice. She hated the way the emotions welled up so uncontrollably within her whenever he was around.

He was quiet for so long that she opened her eyes. He was staring into her face. "Ashtyn?" she prompted.

"Are you growing your hair?"

"Huh?" Her hand involuntarily went to the bun into which her dark hair was drawn up. She was growing it out of the short, sharp style that Kade women typically preferred. But she didn't want to give him even this and stayed quiet.

"It looks longer."

"Why do you want to know?" She wondered why she had been able to forgive Makkyd and everybody else in the Resistance leadership who had known that she had been targeted and recruited, but not Ashtyn. Even though he had been the one who had shadowed her, made contact with her, and eventually introduced her to the organisation, she surely should still have been able to forgive him for his deception. He had only been following orders, and in service to a cause to which she had ultimately pledged herself. But she couldn't forgive him. She couldn't forgive herself for not realising he had come to her with an agenda. The space within her that had been filled with how passionately she had felt about him was still too hollow for her to be able to move beyond that hurt.

"So that I can write it in my ledger of facts about you." He was finally exasperated enough to resort to sarcasm. The absurdity of his reply had her lips curving into a small smile, despite her best efforts.

"Ah, she smiles. I'll have to note that as well."

She couldn't help it, his words surprised a little laugh from her.

They sat together in the sun for a moment, the brittle tension between them lessened by her laughter. This time, Freya was the one to break the silence.

"I'm sorry I reacted that way to your suggestion. You were only trying to help."

"Do you still want to try it?"

"What?" The earnestness with which he offered amazed her. He had no idea what the outcome would be, yet he was genuinely offering to let her experiment on him with little apparent worry.

"I have faith you won't rip me apart," he replied. "Besides, if you do kill me, at least we'll know it works." He chuckled, seemingly unconcerned by the prospect.

Fighting mild horror at his macabre sense of humour, Freya beckoned for him to extend his arm. "It's easier to concentrate if I'm touching you."

She took his arm in her hands, her fingers settling against the warmth of his skin. The flutter which she had come to anticipate when their skin brushed was pushed aside by preoccupation with what she was about to do. She concentrated on the hum from his lifesong. Her focus on it complete, she picked at the sound with her mind, forcing it to become discordant. She tugged at that note, gently but firmly, and before her eyes, the skin on Ashtyn's arm peeled apart. She then took that wrong note and realigned it, watching as the gash sealed itself.

"Did it hurt?"

He shook his head. "It tickled a little, but that was about it." He shook his arm, and peered at the unblemished skin.

Freya sat silent for a moment, considering the enormity of what she had just done, and of his readiness to throw himself into the unknown. She would never allow anyone to experiment on her like that, and couldn't fathom why anybody would be willing to do so. Yet he had without even a moment's hesitation. "I still don't know why you trusted me to do that. I wouldn't let anybody experiment on me." She leaned back, tilting her face upward to enjoy the feel of the sun on it. The warmth was an anchor, burning away the extremities of her amazement.

"I'd trust you to the end of the earth." He didn't say it with any gravitas, but that made it all the more profound. His statement rendered Freya silent, no response adequate or appropriate.

"Do you think that the Goddess is getting stronger?" she asked, seizing upon the first thought that would take them away from the dangerous territory of sentiment.

"When you pray to Her does it feel any different?" He didn't seem to notice or mind that she hadn't responded to his comment.

This was the first conversation they had shared since she had screamed at him to leave her alone following her discovery that he had been sent to recruit her. It wasn't easy, it didn't flow, but certainly it was a conversation. And she'd endured worse exchanges.

"Praying does feel a little different," she admitted. Her hand reflexively went to her wrist where the green band was normally sewn into her sleeve, but she was wearing sleeveless underclothes for training so instead her fingers rubbed along bare skin. "But it may simply be that I haven't properly prayed to Her in such a long time that I'm only now truly remembering what it is to pray." She was silent for a moment longer. "I'd hate to think that we're doing all of this, putting ourselves through all this danger and it makes no difference to Her," she added.

"Are you doing this for Her or for you?" Ashtyn asked. Something in his voice made her open her eyes to look at him.

"Both," she replied after a moment. When he didn't say anything she realised that he was waiting for her to elaborate. "I'm a part of this because I want to be able to pray to Her without worrying that I'll be found out. Is that a good enough reason?"

He shrugged. "So long as it's good enough for you, what business is it of mine?"

Something in the way he spoke chafed against the still-tender rawness of his deception. "You're right. You only care whether or not I serve your cause." She threw the accusation at him, then bit her lip, regret at the outburst of bitterness coursing through her. She hadn't expected the anger to overtake her so powerfully that she would speak without thinking. She didn't want to be childish like this. But being around him seemed to drive all emotional control from her. That only served to leave her more uncertain and more tense when she found herself near him.

He fixed her with a level green-eyed stare. "You really don't know me, do you, Freya?"

She felt heat that had nothing to do with the sun rushing to her face. "Of course I do."

Again, he simply stared at her. It wasn't a stare that challenged her, it was a level, evaluating gaze. It was far worse than had he just responded with anger of his own.

"I'm sorry to have disturbed you," he said eventually. "I'm glad that you have an extra way to defend yourself." He walked away, the crunching pebbles beneath his feet fading into silence.

Freya sat alone, shame pricking at her. He was right. She didn't know him, not really. She hadn't known that he had been assigned to shadow and recruit her. She hadn't known whether he had genuinely cared for her or if seducing her had simply been the easiest way for him to bring her into the Resistance. She still didn't know, and she didn't trust herself to even guess. She had allowed her judgement to be fooled once before and it had made her wary.

She stayed in the sun, letting the warmth soak through her, trying to forget the expression on his face as he had walked away.

A few minutes later the crunch of footsteps sounded again. This time, she couldn't tell who it was. She opened her eyes to see Makkyd approaching her. She came to sit in front of Freya in almost the exact same place that Ashtyn had been only a few minutes before.

Being alone with Makkyd made Freya nervous. When the short woman regarded her, Freya felt as though her very self was being scrutinised. It was disconcerting to think that someone could see down to her very core. Yet it was also one of the things that made Makkyd the ideal person to orchestrate the Resistance movement. She knew how to discern who would be an ideal recruit and – more importantly – who would be loyal. But it also made casual conversation next to impossible.

"Is everything all right?" Freya asked.

"You tell me," Makkyd replied, her evenness of tone reminding Freya of Ashtyn's calm demeanour.

When Freya didn't reply, Makkyd continued. "I heard that you and Ashtyn had a disagreement in the training room."

"What concern is it of yours?" Freya regarded Makkyd warily. Makkyd was not the type to engage in personal discussion.

The redheaded woman shrugged, evidently willing to wait for Freya to respond.

Freya sighed. "Yes, I became angry with him."

"How long will you remain angry with him?"

Freya knew without requiring elaboration that Makkyd wasn't referring to the disagreement of that day.

She sighed again. "I don't want to be angry with him anymore," she admitted.

"So don't be."

"I try. And then suddenly I can't stand being around him." Freya realised that she had involuntarily clenched her hands. She took deep breaths, forcing herself to relax. With deliberate motions, she uncurled her fingers so that her hands lay flat upon her thighs.

"It sounds like you aren't trying very hard." Makkyd's tone was neutral but Freya knew she was being reproached.

"I am trying. It's just that he looks at me with this expression on his face, and I don't know what he wants from me, and all I can remember is that he seduced me and lied to me..." Freya pulled herself up, uncomfortable at sharing so much with Makkyd who was a woman with her own forest of secrets.

"Have you ever spoken with him about it?" Makkyd asked.

Freya shook her head.

"You and he may one day have to work closely together. Have you considered that?"

Again, Freya shook her head.

"Your lives may depend on each other. The lives of others may depend on you two not bickering and actually working together."

"So what should I do?" Freya asked. The helplessness and frustration she felt at being unable to trust herself, or Ashtyn, pushed her to turn to Makkyd for advice.

"Deal with it. Move on. There aren't enough of us at this level to enable you to avoid him." It was closer to an order than a suggestion.

"And how many of us are there, exactly?" Freya asked, seizing on that question to leave behind the embarrassment that Makkyd's curt instruction had brought forth. Makkyd had hinted at the far-reaching nature of the Resistance and its assorted supporters and sympathisers, but was tight lipped about exact numbers. For security, she always said.

Makkyd's smile was almost lazy. "Enough."

Clearly she wasn't going to find out any more than that. Despite her abashment, she returned to the subject of Ashtyn, almost against her will, as curiosity to know what insight she could gain overleapt all else, especially after his comment that she didn't know him. It had found its mark and nettled her from somewhere underneath her skin. After all, Makkyd had known him far longer than Freya. "Do you know what Ashtyn wants from me?"

Makkyd shrugged, shifting slightly. "That isn't the sort of conversation I have with my people."

Freya looked down, shamed that her problems with Ashtyn had required Makkyd to come and speak with her. She would have given any of the healers under her authority a thorough dressing down for allowing their personal problems getting in the way of their work yet she couldn't ask the same of herself.

"But," Makkyd continued, "if I had to speculate, I think that he would die for you without a moment's hesitation."

Freya looked down, laughing softly. "He'd die for a lot of things, though. He'd die for the Resistance. I'd rather he'd live for me."

"You either accept who he is, or you don't. But you need to be able to be around him without any outbursts." Makkyd shrugged again, her tone uncompromising.

"Makkyd..." Freya hesitated, not wanting to pry.

"Yes?"

"Are you bound?" She unthinkingly using the Pious term for a union between two people.

"I was. Before the takeover."

"What happened?"

"He was killed." There was no sadness in Makkyd's voice. She stated a fact, brusquely.

"Oh. I'm so sorry." Freya looked at the lines of the other woman's face, trying to discern any display of grief or anger. She saw nothing other than absolute composure.

"We all lost people in the takeover. It affected all of us differently. Remember that." The finality to her tone indicated she was unwilling to discuss the subject any further.

After a moment, Freya spoke again. "I'm sorry. I'll try to manage with Ashtyn."

"I'm not asking you to try. I'm asking you to do it." Makkyd didn't say it unkindly, but it was nevertheless a reminder to Freya who was in charge.

Chastened, Freya looked down at her hands.

"I actually ran into Ashtyn before I came to see you. He said that you had discovered a new capability."

Freya nodded and told her about what she had done with Ashtyn. Before she had driven him away.

"That could be very useful." Makkyd's voice held speculation with the finest sliver of excitement.

"I'm not sure it's something I want to use," Freya said. Makkyd looked at her for further explanation. "I'm a healer. My obligation is to heal and my ability comes from that. I don't know that it's right for me to use that knowledge, that power, to hurt someone."

"Freya, this is a tool. Do you think that people like Ashtyn and Astrom don't use tools in their workshops because they're sharp?"

"Yes, but—"

Makkyd interrupted her. "You are no longer simply a healer. You are a member of the Resistance. And a part of that means you may have to kill people."

"There's a difference between killing someone in the middle of a fight with say a knife, and killing them with just the touch of my hand and a thought." Freya pointed out. Silently, she also thought that there was an enormous difference between taking action to allow someone to die, and actively killing a person. But she didn't voice the thought aloud, not wanting to push Makkyd too much.

"Is there? Either way, they're dead. In combat though, there's a chance that you'll die."

"But it still doesn't feel right," she protested.

"Maybe that's what keeps us different from the Kade," Makkyd suggested. Echoes of their conversation after Freya's return to the Resistance sounded through her mind. She wondered for how much longer she would keep having this conversation, would keep being asked to do things which went against her very identity.

"I'm sure there are Kade members who also don't want to kill anyone," Freya argued.

"Freya, if things were ideal, I'd still have my Talesh, we could worship the Goddess freely, and you wouldn't have to allow the lives of Pious people to go to waste to protect your own life. But they aren't. So you either fight for that or you don't. But I thought we didn't need to have this conversation." Makkyd's voice held the slightest note of warning.

"You're right." Freya had known all along that Makkyd was correct. She just hadn't liked that she was.

"If it makes you feel any better, I don't particularly like the idea myself. But I remember what I'm fighting for," Makkyd added.

Freya nodded. "I just don't know that I could bring myself to do it if it came to that."

Makkyd stood up, stretching her stocky form with a slight groan. She put her hand on Freya's shoulder and gave it a small squeeze. "When the time comes, I know you'll be able to do what's necessary."

"Maybe that's what I'm afraid of," Freya whispered to the retreating back of her leader.

FIVE

The rap on the door startled her. Not because she was unaccustomed to people knocking, but because the type of knock was unusual. It conveyed the expectation of doors being immediately opened upon being heard. The single sound conveyed none of the deference Freya had become accustomed to as chief of the Healing Centre.

Freya smoothed her perfectly ordered uniform as she called for the visitor to come in.

The Chief Healer strode in, filling the room with her presence. As the older woman closed the door behind her, Freya glimpsed her guards taking up positions on either side of the door. Freya rose to greet her, coming out from behind her desk. She offered the Kade salute, clenching her fist across her heart and drawing her hand down her torso. "My lady, you honour me with your visit – how can I help you?"

The Chief Healer was a striking woman in both presence and looks. Her aura of authority had everybody in any room she entered instinctively turning to look at her. Her high cheekbones and silver hair gave her a slightly severe aesthetic, but one of impeccable elegance and self-assurance, too.

"Do not worry yourself, Freya. I'm not here on any particularly urgent business." The corners of her mouth softened for half a second. Rumour had it that she had a soft spot for Freya. Freya knew, however, that being favoured by somebody like the Chief Healer was about as much a guarantee of her safety as being close to a wild animal. It may come to accept you, but at its heart, it could – and would – still kill you. As one of the most powerful members of the Kade governing elite, the Chief Healer had the power to reduce Freya's fortunes to nothing more substantial than ashes on a whim.

Freya was acutely conscious of the green band on the sleeve of her healer's robe. While both women's white robes were edged with the blue, purple and crimson colours of the Kade to denote them as members of the Kade governance, the green band on Freya's wrist served served as a reminder of her birthright. It took all of her self-control to keep from running her fingers along the band on her sleeve.

The Chief Healer sat down and looked at Freya with the efficient thoroughness that was a product of their shared profession. "You've changed your hair."

This time Freya's self-control did fail her, and she put a nervous hand to the pinned knot at the back of her head. "Yes, it kept getting in the way."

It was partly true. During the hours of leaning over papers, she lost count of the number of times her hair had escaped from behind her ears and fallen across her eyes. The way the strands scooped underneath her chin meant they were too short to tie them back, too. Of course, that annoyance wasn't nearly as compelling as her desire to shake off the hairstyle favoured by Kade women and display the long locks worn by the Pious women of her childhood, elaborately pinning their hair up to keep it out of the way. Freya could still remember watching her mother's black tresses tumbling down as she unpinned her hair. It was a memory suffused with warmth and comfort.

"It's certainly a departure from the style currently in fashion," the Chief Healer commented. Her own silver hair was cut in the Kade style; short and sharp to hug her jawline. It made her look efficient, clinical. The kind of person whose orders should be followed, and quickly.

"Fashion became impractical," Freya said with a bold lightness that she didn't quite feel.

The Chief Healer surveyed her for a moment, then the ghost of a smile flitted across her face. "You've changed. Leadership does that to a person."

Freya resisted the urge to shrug. It felt too informal, too disrespectful. But she couldn't deny that the Chief Healer had a point.

"Are you well, Freya?"

"Yes, thank you for asking." Small talk wasn't exactly something the Chief Healer seemed to enjoy. Freya wasn't certain where this line of conversation was headed but she knew better than to question it.

"How are you finding your position?"

"It's very different from being in the wards all the time," Freya said cautiously.

"Do you like your work?"

"It's certainly different."

"Maybe we should make you a diplomat," the Chief Healer said dryly.

Freya elaborated on her initial response, the initial behest in the Chief Healer's expression prompting her. "I see a different side to healing. Even if I don't really do much anymore."

"It's all right, I miss it, too." She had admitted as much to Freya previously. It had been an odd thing to realise that the Chief Healer may not have wanted to be in the position she currently held.

"I never said that I missed it." She chose her words carefully, fearful of sounding ungrateful.

"You didn't have to. You're too much like me."

Freya shifted, uncertain whether she was comfortable being compared to this woman. On the one hand, the Chief Healer had pioneered more medical techniques than anyone before her in addition to totally changing the manner in which the network of healers was organised across Oranis and the Third Country. On the other hand, she was a high-ranking member of the Kade who would reduce her to nothing without a second thought if Freya failed to do exactly what the leadership wanted. Moreover, this woman was part of the people who effectively wanted to kill her Goddess by denying her the worship of the Pious.

"I've said it to you before." The Chief Healer shifted in her chair to make herself more comfortable. "If you're too good at what you do, you'll be asked to serve rather than do what you love."

"I do enjoy what I do now," Freya protested weakly.

"But you don't love it," the Chief Healer said.

Freya looked down. There was nothing else to say, really.

"Do you regret taking promotions?" Freya asked after a pause, hoping she had read the feel of the space between them correctly and that she did indeed have the latitude to ask such a question.

"I wasn't really given a choice," the Chief Healer replied. Another parallel between them. Freya wished she could simply hate this woman. The idea that one day she may need to lock her away or even see her killed was not one that sat comfortably with her.

The older woman folded her hands in her lap as she fixed Freya with a level gaze. "But to answer your question, no, I don't regret taking those promotions. I did a lot of good. I would never have been able to do that had I not all but stopped doing actual healing work. Sometimes you have to give up what you love in order to do the right thing. I made my peace with that eight years ago."

Freya wanted to ask her what she thought of the Kade takeover, whether or not she had agreed with it, if she had been involved or simply conscripted in the aftermath. Surely as a healer, this woman couldn't have condoned the violence that the Kade practised to secure their authority. Not for the first time, Freya wondered if she knew of the abilities true faith unlocked. But the voice of caution in her head whispered to her that she could trust nobody, to not even ask a question that hinted at such things, to give nothing away. So she remained silent.

"I do enjoy talking with you, Freya." The older woman's tone stopped just shy of warm – for her, a great degree of emotional expression. "You understand. Not many people do."

Freya was again rendered speechless.

"But this chatter has taken me far from the reason for my visit. I wanted to advise you that we may have an even more senior role for you. You've not only proved yourself, but you surpassed almost everybody's expectations." At this, she did smile. It stayed on her face a full second.

"Almost?"

"*I* always knew you would excel."

"You humble me, my lady," Freya stammered.

"Soon we will be giving you a new assignment. All we need to do is find a replacement for you here. They won't do as good a job as you, so it will fall to you to make sure that they deviate from your methods as little as possible." She stood, smoothing her al-ready-immaculate robes. She moved toward the door, then paused. "Oh, there's another matter." She almost sounded casual, as though this other matter had almost slipped her mind. Freya knew better than to believe that.

"Yes?"

"We do need one thing of you."

"Of course." Freya worked to maintain her own semblance of casualness as she waited for what she was certain had been the real reason for the Chief Healer's visit.

"I realise that you have moved from the Pious district, but if you would be able to reconnect with some of your acquaintances from there it could be quite beneficial to us. We believe there is a rebellion fermenting. You may have heard reports of warehouses being damaged, of cargo being contaminated, of various acts of petty vandalism all across Oranis. Between you and I, documents have been misplaced within our bureaucracy, some of them important enough to cause a degree of consternation. There is a worry amongst some of us that these events are not simply random incidents but co-ordinated in some way. If you were to indicate discontent with the Kade to your Pious friends, some of the malcontents may reach out to you. Given the position you hold, you would be an ideal recruit for a resistance movement. Once you've been contacted by these people, if you could let us know their identities, it would be most appreciated."

Freya fought to keep her face straight. "What makes you think that these people would reach out to me?"

"They've done it to others in similar positions to you before," the Chief Healer replied casually. "This won't be a problem for you, will it?" she asked, turning to face Freya fully, scrutiny sharpening her eyes.

Freya felt that a flush was creeping up her neck, that her fingers were obviously trembling, that her breathing had gone ragged. Fighting to hide her reaction, she smiled. "Anything to help you, and the Kade, my lady."

"Good. I knew you would be willing to do this. Someone will come to you here for a report." The Chief Healer nodded once, seemingly satisfied, and left the room.

Freya waited several minutes after she had left, half expecting her to burst back into the room to see if Freya had fallen apart in a sign of her guilt. Only when Freya was certain that the Chief Healer would not return did the breath leave her body in one great exhalation as she sank to the floor, bypassing the chair and her desk entirely. She had done a great deal in her servitude to the Kade: she had forsaken her birthright, she had forsaken her Goddess, she had unquestioningly healed someone again and again so the Kade could torture him, she had even allowed a young girl to die in order to treat a member of the Kade. But she had never informed. Informants sought to ingratiate themselves with the Kade by doing nothing other than turning in their own people, often on the flimsiest of grounds. Informants had only been particularly prevalent in the first year or so after the Kade's rise to power, scurrying to officials and whispering in their ears that they had seen neighbours not praying during prayers, that they had glimpsed a shrine to the Goddess through the window of another person's house. Most informants had been rewarded with the promise of safety and a comfortable job. They were easy to spot. It was something about their eyes, a scrutinising appraisal of everybody with whom they spoke, that gave them away. But they had earned a certain immunity, so only the bravest of souls dared go after them. As the Kade's grasp across the Third Country had strengthened, informants and the awful outcomes that they bred became less and less commonplace. But the filthy stain of mistrust they had engendered lingered across the Third Country. Then in the ensuing chaos and panic that followed last year's set explosions in the marketplace and the Main Healing Centre, the Kade had begun to encourage people to turn on each other once more.

Freya had always taken a certain measure of comfort in the fact that she had attained her place in Kade society through her dedication to her job. She worked hard, she didn't say anything that would have caused trouble, and she certainly didn't look at the people who surrounded her to see if they weren't living in exact accordance with the severe expectations of the Kade.

That being said, her success had isolated her almost as effectively. She was still a collaborator. It had been lonely, but she had accepted it was the price she had to pay for security and comfort. Until the day she had met Ashtyn amid the fire and chaos of the destruction of the marketplace. She had never thought there was something worth dying for until she met him.

The thick weave of the carpet beneath her fingers brought her back from her state of anxious reflection. She stood and smoothed her already perfect hair in a gesture of comforting habit. She needed to decide how she was going to deal with this. Makkyd had promised that outright rebellion was within their grasp but never given any specific idea about when they would act. That uncertainty left Freya in a very unpleasant position: she couldn't defer in the hope that the Resistance would make their move, and if she didn't report on people, questions would be asked of her loyalty. That could not happen. Such questions might lead to a closer scrutiny of her and might in turn lead the Kade governance straight to the Resistance. She had to have a plan on how she would approach this. Obviously, she couldn't turn in a member of the Resistance. But equally, she couldn't report on an innocent Pious. It was a conundrum that she didn't want to deal with alone. The memory of Zarech's calm face tantalised her. Whatever games he had played with her, she had always found that her discussions with him ultimately led her to view choices before her with greater clarity, even if she hadn't enjoyed the way he forced her to see what lay in front of her.

As she calmed down, Freya arrived at the conclusion that she must speak with Makkyd or Astrom the first opportunity she had. Makkyd would definitely know what to do, and Astrom would have some useful suggestions of her own, while also being able to offer her brusque compassion. Freya found herself wanting the understanding and sympathy that the stoneworker's stormy grey eyes could offer. In truth, she wanted the reassurance of somebody helping her decide how to proceed.

She finished her work early, the need to be outside in the fresh air urging her to quickly complete the remaining tasks. Dusk had just fallen as she left her Healing Centre. The Guardians outside the main door greeted her. "Early night, my lady," one of them said. It never failed to make Freya a little uneasy, the way in which some of the people who worked in or around the Centre would address her with the term of respect reserved for Kade officials.

"Yes, things are running smoothly, Sord." She smiled at the young man who often took the dusk until dark shift. She exchanged pleasantries with him on her way out on the evenings when he had a shift. He was a very polite young man. She found it difficult to reconcile his friendly nature with the violence that his uniform represented. Then again, she was being trained to perpetrate violence and her uniform represented a promise to only heal.

"That's good. You certainly do stay late most nights, my lady." He smiled at her, his face open and cheerful.

"Running a Centre takes a lot of work," she replied.

"Still, surely tailor Tuk must miss you."

Thinking of Symon's clumsy attempts to romance her, she gave a little uncomfortable laugh. "Well, I suppose you've got a point. Anyway, I'm going home nowhere near the beginning of curfew tonight so you can be pleased about that."

"The city's a bit restless this time of day, one of us should escort you home." A small frown creased his forehead.

"That's very sweet of you, Sord, but I'm sure I'll be fine," she said.

"But my lady, last night an official disappeared on his way home, cart and all. Foul play is suspected. If a Kade official can disappear, who knows what may happen to you. And if anything were to happen to you, it would be my fault," he protested.

"Sord, I'm hardly important enough to be attacked. If I can walk home alone close to the darkest hour of the evening, then I'm sure I can walk home alone when the streets are still light and filled with people." She tried to be stern, but she only succeeded in smiling at him again. He couldn't have been more than a few years younger than her, but she felt as though they were an eternity apart in age. The weight that fell upon those who had suffered during the takeover simply didn't seem to be upon him.

Clearly unhappy with her refusal, he shifted from foot to foot.

"I promise I will see you tomorrow evening," she told him, giving him a little wave as she set off.

Despite her assurances to Sord, as she walked through the streets of Oranis, she had to admit he was correct. There was a restlessness to the city. As people poured through the streets, having just finished their working day, mingling and talking, there was a sense of discomfort, even of anger. Any discontent was kept in check by the heavy presence of Guardians and the severity – and publicity – of punishments for those who broke the Kade laws. But Freya did wonder how long it would take before even that was not enough to suppress the sentiment, especially with the prevalence of mysterious fires and disappearances nipping at the façade of Kade authority.

The walk home was a relatively short one, but Freya savoured each moment of it. Despite the hushed fear which tempered the actions of every person, she loved Oranis most when it was filled with people. It was far lovelier than the empty streets down which she normally walked, long after the sun had set. The dusk hours brought a particular luminescence to the pink stone of the buildings. Every so often, older buildings made from the off-white aegat stone, streaked with bronze-coloured veins, would appear; buildings that had survived the turmoil and stood proud as markers of their endurance. Freya took her time, enjoying the sense of life that flowed through the sunset-illuminated streets. The atmosphere of concern did much to separate the Oranis in which she lived now from the Oranis of her child's memory, but underneath it all, it was the same city, the same people. And she loved it so much that it was a fierce ache in her chest.

As she opened the door to her house, the thought occurred to her that if she really needed to inform on someone, she could always report that Symon had been behaving unusually. That may remove the problem of his unwanted ardour. Inwardly chiding herself for her callousness, she stepped inside.

SIX

The way Symon's presence filled the house announced that he was home almost more effectively than the greeting he called out from his workroom. Freya couldn't help but wonder if he ever actually went to the tailor's anymore or if he had started doing all of his sewing in his workroom at home. She wished she could be in the house without being pursued by the knowledge that he could hear her every move. It made her feel as though she were on some version of the battleground of which Astrom spoke during their training, where the slightest mistake would lead to the most fatal of punishments. Often, she was left unbearably tired from the constant strain of having to hide the reality of her life and maintain the appearance of a devoted Kade supporter. Even in sleep she was careful, dreams of secrecy and incriminating evidence prowling through her mind more often than they didn't. It made sleeping at the Centre on nights she worked late enough to be past curfew or too close to it for her to feel she could leave the Centre without risking trouble, appealing. She suppressed a near-hysterical laugh as she contemplated her idea of informing on Symon to simply acquire a moment for herself in her own home. She shook her head at the dark callousness which had taken root inside her. A year ago, she would never have thought something like that, let alone found any humour in it.

"You're here early." Symon emerged from his workshop to greet her with an embrace and kiss on the cheek. This was a new addition to their routine. Freya endured the gesture of affection and even reciprocated. Anything to keep up the façade of a perfect Kade life.

"I did all I needed to do today." There was more defensiveness than she wanted in her voice. She blamed it on the request made of her to inform and the insidious doubt that it called forth.

His single chuckle was an unusual sound from him. Symon wasn't really a chuckler. "Freya, there's always something you find to do. You're terrible like that."

Hating that he knew her so well, she shrugged. "I wanted to take a moment for myself. I've been feeling a little tired recently." It wasn't even untrue, although she steeled herself for him to ask her further questions. But he surprised her.

"You may be interested to see what I've been working on." Gently, he took her hand and led her into his workshop.

She was intrigued. Symon never asked her to look at his work. He had no need to show off his skill; the quality of his craftsmanship spoke for itself. More often than not, he responded with grumpiness when she came in to look at the masterpiece of fabric he was assembling; her questions took him away from doing his work. She had come to believe that his designs held the tenderness that his demeanour seemed to lack, perhaps taking it from him in tithe for creating such breathtaking garments.

He steered her toward the bench and released her so he could use both hands to carefully pick up a small scrap of cloth. It was a baby's birth garment. As with everything that Symon made, it was exquisite. The cloth was the best quality, the embroidery along the hems was unbelievably fine, the stitching without flaw.

"It's beautiful. Did sometime commission it?" She ran the tips of her fingers gently across it. The material was as soft as it looked. Beneath the fabric she could feel the warmth of his hands. It was the most intimate she'd felt with him in a long, long time.

"I commissioned it. It's for our child," he said.

"But it's in the Kade style." The words left her mouth before she had properly considered them. Immediately, she bit her tongue, cursing her stupidity.

"Of course it is."

"Yes, of course, I don't know what I was thinking," she murmured, turning her attention back to the material under her fingers, trying to shake off her comment and the fear of what implications Symon may draw from it.

"I know it's a big adjustment, and that things haven't always been comfortable between us, particularly romantically." Symon looked at the cloth as he spoke. "But I want to have a family with you. I think we can be happy, especially thanks to our position."

Freya couldn't reply. This was an unusual, if not unprecedented, honesty and openness from Symon. Showing vulnerability had never been something he considered acceptable. Yet here he was, doing just that. It rendered her completely lost for words.

"If we have a girl, I thought we could call her Rohana." There was an uncertainty in his voice when he offered.

Freya stared at him. "But..." His suggestion that they name their child after her younger sister who had been killed for her unwillingness to subjugate herself before the Kade authorities was a singular show of defiance for Symon. She couldn't believe he would be so bold as to propose such a thing.

"I know how much you cared for her. We've proved our loyalty enough in myriad ways. Wouldn't it make you happy?" His dark eyes searched hers, for once his expression naked enough for her to read his earnestness.

"It...would." She spoke slowly to give herself time to order her thoughts; Symon had completely taken her by surprise. "It's a lovely thing for you to think of." She took the beautiful tiny garment from his hands and put it down so she could embrace him. Her arms wrapped around him, her body softened into his, and their heads gently nestled together. His gesture – both of them –

had surprised and touched her in ways she hadn't thought he could.

It had never occurred to Freya that Symon may actually want children for any reason other than the social benefit they may bring. His own life had been mostly devoid of family as he had spent his first few years in a Pious orphanage. When his aptitude for sewing was discovered at an early age, he had been taken in by one of the finest Pious tailors. The woman had no children of her own and it was commonly known that she treated Symon like her own son. Shortly after the Kade took power, she disappeared. Whispers had always held that someone had turned her in for continuing to worship the Goddess, but nobody had ever offered proof of those claims. Symon had been relocated to a different tailor where he swiftly finished his apprenticeship and gained a reputation as one of the best young tailors in the city. He had barely spoken to Freya of the woman who had been mother and mentor to him for so many years and as a result she had assumed the prospect of a family wasn't something that particularly appealed to him, especially considering his seeming lack of interest in the subject. But it seemed she had been wrong.

She looked at him properly, then. Normally, she regarded him in glances, letting her eyes slide quickly away from his features. The habit maintained the distance between them, ensured that they shared little true intimacy. Freya didn't like the idea that if she allowed her eyes to lock with his he might be able to see the deep dark part of herself that she had kept hidden from even herself for a very long time. Shadows from the gas lights flickered over his face, making it difficult to see the nuances of his expression. Not that more illumination necessarily would have helped. Symon was a master of keeping his thoughts concealed. Whatever secrets he may have were his alone. A chill claimed her as suspicion eased its way across her mind with characteristic insidiousness as she considered the rumour Symon's mentor had been turned in by an informant. Perhaps that informant had been someone close to her, someone who had been like a son to her. Symon had never suggested with any word or gesture that he had been an informant, but that meant nothing. He had often relayed to her the careless pieces of gossip or information – some of which were quite sensitive – that had been shared between the people he was measuring and fitting. He certainly had access to information from which he could profit, and he also possessed the desire to succeed in the Kade's world which might push someone into doing the unconscionable. She wondered to what extent his promotions to the better-paying Kade tailors were the result of his skill or of another type of favour he had somehow curried with the Kade. Perhaps that was why he had never spoken to her of his teacher – some form of guilt? Maybe what she had interpreted as a disinterest in family had simply been him trying to forget what he had done to attain his position within Kade society.

"I didn't know that you wanted children this badly," she ventured, trying to push the suspicions from her head. Now was not the time to mull over them.

"I wanted our lives to be safe and stable so that we could have a good place for children." He sounded surprised, as though he had assumed she knew he felt this way. "Everything I've done has been to get us to that position."

Freya wondered if he was obliquely referring to being an informant or if she was simply seeing shadows where there were none. The problem was that now the idea had taken root in her mind, it refused to be contained and it coloured every other thought.

"I'm hungry, have you eaten?" She changed the subject, uncomfortable with so much of what lay before her. It was an inelegant way to shift the focus, but some distant relative of panic had begun to claw its way up the back of her throat, forcing her to deferr to the imperative to move away from questions of family and betrayal.

"No. I can start making dinner for us if you'd like," he offered, seemingly unbothered by the abruptness of her question.

In truth, she had forgotten who he had been when they first met. It had been an age ago when both of them had been so much younger and almost everybody believed that the world would be safe forever. Her first impression of Symon was of an innocuous young man. They met when her mother had taken her to get a set of robes made. He had taken her measurements, a thin boy with light blond hair and dark, dark eyes, blushing as he wrapped the measuring cord around her waist and breasts. He hadn't been the first boy who had shown an interest in her, but something about his fierce bashfulness had intrigued her.

It had been ten years since then, but she could still clearly remember the ambition she had discovered burning so forcefully within him. On that day they first met, she asked him how long he had left of his apprenticeship. "One more year. But I'm going to be the finest tailor in Oranis." It hadn't been a boast but a simple statement of conviction. She had giggled, looking over her shoulder to see if his mentor, conversing with her mother, had overheard. True to the word of his youthful self though, she doubted that there were many tailors finer than Symon in the city, or indeed the entirety of the Third Country.

The memory of his ambition unsettled her. He had always spoken of the comfort they would attain once they finished their apprenticeships. At the time, she had been taken aback by his certainty that they would be bound, let alone that they would both be successful enough to live luxuriously. Now with darker thoughts and still-darker doubts weighing down the edges of her mind, she wondered what the fourteen-year-old boy who had blushed when he touched her had been willing to do to acquire the status and wealth that his identity as a Pious orphan had denied him.

"You know, Freya, we're lucky," he called back as he led the way into the kitchen.

"Oh?" She moved cautiously to join him, adjusting the gas valve in the wall as she came in so that the flame burned more fiercely, throwing more light into the area.

"Well, I never knew my family and yours are all gone. We don't have any pressure to feel as though we should raise our children in a way other than our choosing. It makes it easier," he explained, raising his voice a little so that he could still be heard over the rhythmic beat of the knife as he started chopping vegetables.

"I suppose I've never thought about it that way." She chose to ignore the fact that he glossed over the Kade's brutal murder of her parents. It was a jarring discord to the earlier understanding he had shown about how devastated she had been by their deaths. But that was Symon, enigmatic to the point that Freya had decided it was utterly impossible to understand how his mind actually worked. She also chose to ignore the fleeting stab of grief which pierced her as his remark reminded her that when it did come time for her to have children, she would do so without her mother or father's guidance.

"Raising children without the influence of our parents means we can teach them the Kade ways without feeling the stare of our families' disapproval," he continued.

Freya wondered if Symon knew that teaching children the Kade way of life meant to deny the Goddess the strength of worshippers while empowering the Kade gods, or that some Kade followers knew of the abilities they could receive in return for their devotion. It seemed unlikely. After all, she hadn't known as such until Zarech had revealed that truth to her. He had been one of the Goddess' Children – the clergy for the Pious. She wondered what he would say to Symon's comments. She could even picture Zarech's level stare, asking how wordlessly she truly felt about Symon's proposal – about even the prospect of bringing children into a world where she couldn't keep them safe or raise them in the way she truly believed.

"Yes, we'd just receive the disapproval of our community for raising our children as Kade," she replied.

He put down the knife and turned to face her. "We live in a Kade district. The people who are our neighbours are our community now aren't Pious." There was a level of admonishment in his tone.

She sighed. This was a dangerous conversation. One better left alone. "You're right. Sometimes I forget," she said.

They ate together in their customary silence. The excitement, even tenderness, that Symon had seemed to exhibit when he had shown her the birthing robe had receded and he resorted to his usual inscrutably calm demeanour. Not for the first time, Freya realised that the man to whom she was joined was a stranger and always had been.

When he first courted her he had ardently begged her to become bound to him. But she had demurred. She couldn't say why she had been so reluctant to accept his request, but she certainly had been just shy of unsettled by this intense boy's infatuation with her, and it gave her pause.

And then everything changed. The Kade had risen up, overthrown the Dual Accord that shared power between the Kade and Pious, and in so doing destroyed the old way of life and the old certainties that she had held close. Symon had come to her again. The memory of the tree under which they sat when he had implored her to join with him was vivid because she had stared intently up at the interplaying shapes of the sharp green leaves rather than looking at him as he spoke. He had shocked her with how easily he cast aside the Pious notion of being bound to a person and instead spoke of being joined in the Kade way

"But everything is so uncertain," she had protested, privately vowing never to be joined. The Pious binding of two souls to share a life together was far more intimate than the simple joining of assets and households in the Kade custom. Her younger self believed such matters were entirely to do with love rather than pragmatism and she had revolted against anything that tarnished her belief that love should and could be the most important factor in decisions about how to share and live one's life

"We have an opportunity to show the Kade that we are worthy of their favour if we become joined now. It's a statement of our fealty. This could give us chances we never dreamed of," he had replied, eagerness and excitement in his voice.

Again, she had equivocated. She didn't know if she wished to become bound or joined to him, and with all the chaos and violence that stalked Oranis, it simply didn't feel right to answer questions of love and commitment. But when her family was killed by Kade officials only a few fivedays later, she had seen the wisdom to his argument. There was no purpose in fighting the Kade. That sort of behaviour only got everybody killed. So instead she showed her commitment to adopting the Kade ways wholeheartedly and joined with Symon as soon as the burial rites – Kade ones, of course – had been performed for her family.

"You look troubled." Symon's comment interrupted her musing.

"I'm just thinking about when we first courted," she replied. It wasn't untrue; like so much of her life now, it just wasn't the whole truth.

"The first time I saw you, I thought that you were the most beautiful thing I had ever seen." He spoke like he was stating a fact rather than allowing the force of the memory to engulf him.

"And now?" She was curious despite herself. Call it vanity.

"You're even more beautiful. I knew that with you by my side, I could be anything. *We* could be anything." He spoke in his characteristically understated way, but that didn't detract from the depth of emotion in his words.

"And were you proved correct?"

The corners of his mouth crept upwards. "We've done quite well so far, don't you think?"

"I suppose."

Whatever he was going to say next was cut off by an insistent rapping on the front door.

"I'll go," Freya said, glad for the interruption. Even though her own recollections had led them down this route, tangled guilt for her infidelity had begun to nip at her. It left her ready to move on to less emotionally tumultuous matters.

The rapping continued until she opened the door, ready to yell at whoever it was for their insolence. The angry shout died on her lips when she saw Ashtyn, the part subject of her guilt, before her, as though she had summoned him with her thoughts. Unlike Symon, whose face betrayed nearly nothing, she had no trouble reading that Ashtyn was deeply shaken.

Before she could say anything, Ashtyn shook his head, the tight motion warning her to remain silent. "My lady, here are the instruments that you ordered. I thought given the urgency of your order, you may want them at once," he said.

Wordlessly, Freya stepped forward to take the proffered package. The look he gave her was lingering; worry and something far more complex in the way his features were arrayed pulled forth an answering ache in her chest. With obvious effort he nodded once, then left.

She retreated inside and shut the door, her fingers probing the package. The urgency to open it made them tremble.

"Who was so desperate to see you?" Symon called out.

"Oh, just a gildsman. I ordered some instruments to be made in order to try a new treatment I've been working on and he thought to deliver them the second they were finished. I should examine them to make sure of the quality."

"See? You always find some work you need to do," he replied, faint amusement lightening his words. For him, it was akin to up-roarious laughter.

Freya went into her workroom and made sure the door was locked before she turned her attention to the package. Whatever message it contained had to be urgent for Ashtyn to be the messenger, and at this time of night, too. It was tightly wrapped in thin material and she undid it carefully, not knowing what she would find inside. The Resistance communicated across several ways: verbal, coded messages, symbols. The method they used was chosen at random to ensure there was no clear pattern for the Kade to track. The package contained a set of medical tools. Freya inspected them and concluded quickly that there was nothing special about them. That left the cloth. She held it up and found the message, written in a Resistance code. Shock shuddered through her as she deciphered it. She read it twice more to ensure she hadn't decoded it incorrectly, but there was no doubt about the words: 'Makkyd taken by the Kade. Meet at Bardan's warehouse first chance possible.'

SEVEN

Freya waited a few minutes even though the delay left her over-
taken by the sensation that insects were crawling under her skin.
Before she decided how she would excuse herself to Symon, before
she flung herself out of the house and ran blindly through the
streets to get to Bardan's warehouse, she forced herself to stop.
She breathed deeply, drawing upon techniques taught to her at the
very beginning of her healer's training. It had been a long time
since she had stood in front of a patient overcome by panic and
needed to fall back upon the breathing to calm her, but the familiar
count as she breathed in and out now helped settle her heart back
into the well-worn rut of its usual rhythm. After she felt her body
yield to calm, she took ten long breaths to force her mind to still
itself. She took a further moment to examine the many thoughts
which all sought precedence in her mind. First, there was fear that
Makkyd's capture could endanger her. Shadowing that was shame
that her first and loudest thought was one of self-interest. Beyond
fear for her own safety was the worry about what Makkyd's capture might do for the Resistance. Makkyd was the only one who
knew every single part of the movement. Keeping knowledge in
one person's mind was a strength and a weakness – given her
capture, it definitely seemed a weakness. That in turn gave rise to
a sense of frustration at Makkyd's secrecy, but as she considered
it a little longer, Freya didn't know what she would propose as an
alternative way to safeguard the Resistance against traitors or the

carelessness or capture of a different member, so her frustration ebbed.

Freya took a breath and as she expelled it, she visualised all of those thoughts being blown out along with her spent air. Taking even a minute or two of extra time to give those thoughts space and then acknowledge she could only act on them once she had learned more about what had happened left her with the calm sense that she could get through at least the most immediate issue: getting to Bardan's warehouse.

She exited her workroom and went back into the dining area. "I think I have to run back to the Healing Centre," she told Symon who had just finished his meal and stood to see her to the door.

"Really?" He sounded more amused than upset.

"Really. I left a report there that I need," she lied.

"Will you be all right walking through the streets?" He was asking what she thought about it, not simply expressing concern in her ability to look after herself. She appreciated that about Symon.

"You know that you're the second person to ask me that today?"

"Is there someone else after your heart?" He made a valiant effort at teasing her, but Symon wasn't exactly adept at humour. Had the circumstances been different, she would have indulged in guilt given her affair with Ashtyn. As it was, her thoughts were too fixed upon maintaining the calm she had fought to settle around herself.

"Hardly. It was just a Guardian at the Centre who asked." She brushed aside the gentle hand he placed on her, turning and going into the entranceway where she picked a dark over-robe off a peg on the wall and slipped it on.

"Is everything all right, Freya? You said you wanted some time away from work yet you're running back now." She could feel Symon looking at her as she walked to the door.

"Yes, of course. I'm just frustrated." The lie slipped easily off her tongue, the light tone a counter to the knots which sought to gather in her stomach.

"All right then. Hurry home." He strode to catch up with her and put his arms around her, drawing her to him and brushing his lips against her cheek.

Darkness had fallen completely over Oranis. The streets were almost devoid of people. The few that remained moved swiftly, fear of encountering a patrol of Guardians giving their strides extra length. Even in the Kade district where Freya and Symon lived, people were clearly uncomfortable being outside after dark. Brutality was the new norm. It was common knowledge that Guardians frequently interrogated anybody they encountered after dark, even Kade citizens, and their interrogations were rough more often than not. Uncertainty had become the overriding characteristic of the city. The consequent silence in which the streets were bundled gave the night air an eerie quality.

Freya's position as the chief of a Healing Centre meant she could get away with being occasionally out after the curfew on the grounds of her work; provided she offered a convincing lie about being out on business, she should be allowed to pass. But that immunity wasn't something she had ever wanted to test. It was one of the reasons she stayed at the Centre on nights she worked late; given her role within the Resistance, she wanted to avoid any questions about her movements. But despite her position, she was all too aware that running into a patrol of Guardians would be a risk. The green strip on the sleeve of her over-robe and the Guardians' propensity toward violence were both more than enough to see her as a patient in her own Centre if she was unlucky. Her lie would get her only so far. The warehouse district was out of her way. But she had lived for too long in fear of the Kade's reprisals. She had come to understand that her life was less important than fighting for a better world. So she ventured through the streets of

Oranis, painted dark shades of blue and grey by the evening, with fear that was securely leashed.

Luck, or the Goddess, or a combination of both, was on her side and she made it to Bardan's warehouse without encountering any patrols.

She knocked on the door, feeling unbearably vulnerable as she waited for it to be opened. Surely if a patrol rounded the corner and saw her, she would be pulled up. Her self-control slipped in the moments while she waited for the door to be opened. Something about the near-silence of the dark streets made each second stretch out into a realm of possible danger and her fear took her imagination hostage, conjuring the most gruesome of scenarios, most of which ended with her dead. Her knees nearly gave in with relief when Bardan answered the door, his normally jovial face a grave mask. Freya let him pull her into one of his trademark smothering hugs. Despite his bulk, she could feel the slight tremble in his frame. It was comforting to know that she was not alone in feeling afraid.

"Is anybody else here?" she asked once he released her.

"You're one of the first. Ashtyn's still delivering the messages, I think. You may as well stay out here and keep me company." He gestured to a chair against the wall.

Freya sat, grateful to give her trembling knees a respite. "What happened?"

"We're not sure. We think perhaps an informant reported on suspicious behaviour. But we can't be sure."

"What does this mean for the Resistance? Will they be coming for us?" As she had done in her work room, she fought down the wave of fear that sought to rise within her.

"We don't know yet. We know very little, actually. Try to stay calm." Despite the darkness, Bardan must have seen the expression on her face. "The only reason we know she was taken is because one of our people happened to be delivering a report to her at the exact moment she was dragged out by the Guardians. Lyssa is contacting our people within the Kade administration to find out more. It's important not to panic until we have more information." Bardan ran a hand across his face, his own worry clearly evident.

"Why am I here?" Freya asked. "I don't know that many of our people, I can't deliver messages, I've not really been involved in any significant planning..." She raised her hands helplessly.

"Freya, you *are* important." His voice was gentle. "You're a part of the leadership, you're our healer. Besides, you know more than you think you do. We need every senior person to try and piece together the whole of Makkyd's plan. She's the only one who knows how far we extend, who our members are, and what various schemes are being conducted across the city. It's worse because we don't keep any paper records in case they're discovered. Together, we may be able to assemble a picture of all our operations. Everybody who's been party to any discussions is going to be needed in case they remember something." The size of the task ahead seemed to overwhelm Bardan who again ran a hand across his face again.

"It's so much for one person to know," Freya whispered, the tickle of her voice almost lost in the huge warehouse.

"Honestly, I think Makkyd would rather even she knew nothing, but she's so Goddess-cursed clever that most of what we do is dreamed up in that devious red head of hers, so she knows it because she came up with it," Bardan said.

They sat together in silence as more people trickled through the door and passed through to the meeting room concealed within the heart of the warehouse. Freya didn't go with them, preferring to stay in silence with Bardan rather than make stilted conversation with everybody else.

"How long has the Resistance existed?" she asked him after the fifth person had arrived. She had never thought to ask before. It hadn't seemed as important as the fact that it did exist.

"Since the very beginning. I joined two years after the take-over, but there are a few who have been here since the day the Kade claimed control. They built a foothold in warehouses, and learned everything about the Kade, waiting for the right time to strike. Actually, there were several different groups who wanted to find ways to resist the Kade. But over the years, Makkyd and Astrom found them and convinced them to unite into what we're part of now."

"Why did you join?" she asked.

"It was my neighbour. He didn't pray enough in the squares, despite many suggestions from the Kade that he should. One evening his home caught fire. I'm sure you've heard the stories."

She nodded, leaning her head back against the cool wall of the building.

"He had a daughter who was the same age as my own. Sometimes they would play together. She died in the fire."

"Oh." It hadn't occurred to Freya that any members of the Resistance had families. She simply assumed if they did have families, it was in another life, one destroyed when their loved ones had been snatched away from them by the Kade. "How old is your daughter?"

"Eight, nearly nine. She doesn't even remember a time when the Kade weren't in power. She's a perfect little Kade child. She doesn't even have to wear green."

"But you—"

He cut her off. "I am not allowed to speak of the Goddess to her. Why would she be marked out for something she knows nothing about? The Kade want to remove the Goddess from our society, not entrench instability by keeping a group of people oppressed forever."

"Surely you could teach her about the Goddess in secret," she suggested.

"I dare not. She's young. If she were to let slip, I would be dead and she may come to harm...I certainly would never see her again."

Her fingers found the green band on her sleeve and traced along it as she spoke. "So, if your daughter knows nothing of the Goddess, what will life be like for her if we succeed?"

"Then I will give her what the Kade will never give her: a choice," Bardan answered softly. The darkness made it hard to see his face, so she had no hint to how he would feel if his daughter chose to worship the Kade gods in the end.

"Bardan?" she ventured.

"Yes, Freya?"

"Aren't you worried about your daughter if fighting breaks out?"

"I'm going to send her and her mother away. I have an aunt who lives on a farm. My aunt's a tough old thing. She should be able to keep them safe."

"Does your woman know that you're part of the Resistance?"

"Of course. We were bound before we were joined," he said simply.

They lapsed into silence which neither sought to break. After a time, Ashtyn arrived.

"Freya's here," Bardan told him, gesturing toward her. Uncertainly, Freya got to her feet to greet him.

"Are you all right?" Ashtyn walked over to her. It seemed as though he wanted to reach out to her but he restrained himself. She wasn't sure if she was glad of it or disappointed.

"Of course. Are you? You didn't run into any Guardians?" She hated the palpability of her concern for him, the way seeing him unhurt in front of her went further to chasing away the gnawing worry at the bottom of her stomach than any of Bardan's reassurances.

"It was fine. I've snuck around outside a lot before." He tried to affect his usual grin, the one that spoke of mischief and fun, but it wasn't convincing. "How many have arrived?" He addressed the question to Bardan as the grin slipped away.

"Seven, including Freya and myself. Enough to start?"

"Wait a little longer. Lyssa shouldn't be far behind me." Ashtyn turned to Freya. "Come on, let's go in."

The expectation that she would follow him roused her anger. "I'd rather stay here," she said, her tone sharper than she intended.

A spasm of hurt flashed across his face. "All right then." He turned and moved noiselessly across the warehouse.

"Ouch." Bardan whistled softly to punctuate his observation. The noise echoed off the walls.

"It's not him. I don't want to be in that room not doing anything but sitting, looking at each other...waiting," Freya said, regret for snapping at Ashtyn replacing the anger.

"He has nothing to do with it?" Bardan asked, his voice pointed.

"It doesn't help. Especially because he all but told me what to do," Freya admitted. "Why does everybody keep commenting on him and me anyway? It's none of their business!" she exclaimed in sudden ire.

"Because you two are so in love with each other that it's preposterous to witness," he answered.

Her mouth swung open and as she searched for the words to reply, he continued. "But it's a question of safety, actually. If you two are bickering, as you often are these days, how would that play out in a situation of combat or danger? If you disagree with him, that would take time. It could cost your life and the lives of everybody around you. Disunity like that is dangerous."

Freya began to disagree, then she stopped herself. He was correct – as Makkyd had been when she had made a nearly identical point in Astrom's workshop. "Even if I am in love with him, and even if I could get past everything that's happened, I'm still joined to Symon."

He chuckled, clearly not missing that she had evaded his point. "And what if there wasn't Symon?"

"Then..." In her darkest heart she had thought about how Symon might be removed from her life. She didn't like what those thoughts suggested about herself. In truth, though, she genuinely did not know what would happen if Symon were no longer an obstacle. That possibility existed in a completely different world.

"How many before me went to his bed?" she asked finally, seizing on the final betrayal which remained unchallenged; the prospect that seducing her had been something he'd done with countless other prospective recruits as part of a tried and tested way to win them to the Resistance.

"I really wouldn't know. But does it matter? Whatever he did before he met you, I can tell you, as someone who's known him for years that he's never even glanced at anyone in the way he looks at you."

She bit her lip at his words but it didn't stop her from asking, "how does he look at me?"

"Like he worships you."

More than anything, the plainness of the way he spoke robbed the breath from her lungs. Silence filled the cavernous space of the warehouse as she struggled and failed to find something to say in reply.

Bardan kindly stepped in to fill the quiet. "If you ever need to talk, I'm here."

"Thank you," Freya whispered, her eyes burning with unshed tears at the gentleness in his voice. "It's nice to know I have a friend. If your daughter ever needs anything..."

"I'll come straight to you." She could hear the smile in his voice.

It wasn't long before Lyssa arrived, her face shrouded by a long scarf wound around her neck. She threw a withering glance at Freya, saying nothing before stalking toward the secret door.

Seething at the artist's ability to direct malevolence at her despite the severity of the situation, Freya followed her with Bardan bringing up the rear. The three moved without speaking through the short tunnel and entered the hidden meeting room. As Freya had expected, the room was totally silent. At their entrance, Astrom stepped into the centre of the room.

"Thank you all for coming. I know for some of you it was particularly difficult to get here. I think the first thing for us is to get a clear idea of what we know and try to figure out what we need to do. Bardan?"

He stood. "From what we know, we suspect that someone informed on her. But we can't rule out the possibility that someone within our ranks is a traitor. They'd have to be fairly senior as we've worked to keep Makkyd's position as secret as possible, for her, and our, safety."

Freya looked around the room, wondering if any of the people there was a traitor. She was almost certain that Bardan and Ashtyn weren't, but she had to uncomfortably admit that she barely knew any of the others. She hadn't really gone to a lot of effort to get to know them, instead focusing on what Makkyd asked of her. She was regretting that now.

"How imperative is it that we recover her?" Lyssa asked.

"This is the woman who built us up from nothing. We shouldn't even ask such questions," Ashtyn snapped.

Freya couldn't help but feel a glowing ember of satisfaction at Lyssa being reprimanded.

"Yes, and I'm not saying that we shouldn't get her back. But it may not be possible to do it straight away. It's an option we should at least consider," the artist replied, a hint of temper and obstinance in her voice.

"She's right, we have to at least entertain the idea of what might happen if we don't get Makkyd back," Bardan said tiredly. "However, Makkyd is the only one of us who knows everything crucial. Over the years that the Kade has ruled Oranis, she found all other malcontents, all the different groups, and she, with Astrom's help, convinced them to join with us, follow her lead. Not only does her being a captive jeopardise everything, but without her, we're a headless beast with limbs that answer only to her. We need to get her back for both of those reasons."

The room fell silent as the implications of Makkyd's absence yet again hit everybody. "Once we get her back, we're going to have to have a serious talk with her about her record keeping," Astrom said dryly. "I'm supposed to be second in command and I know basically nothing."

"You see how we must live though, not trusting anyone," someone else said.

"Which is exactly why we have to get her back, because of what we're fighting for," Astrom said firmly. "Now, we're still getting information, but we need to plan so that we're ready to move at a moment's notice. If everything falls correctly, we'll act tomorrow. We need to retrieve her before they start to interrogate her."

Freya shuddered, remembering the injuries inflicted on Zarech that she had been forced to heal. He had never seemed to be concerned or upset, but she could tell from the extent of the wounds how brutally he had been questioned. The prospect of similar things being done to Makkyd was awful. Makkyd was a tough woman and she wouldn't break easily. But relying on her stubbornness was a terrible plan.

"All right. Who do we need?" Bardan asked, his tone business-like.

"We need Ashtyn to go – he'll be able to break locks. Probably Freya, also," Astrom said.

"Wait, what?" Freya looked up, alarmed.

"You're a healer," Lyssa sneered as though it were perfectly obvious. "If Makkyd is injured, we need you to heal her so that we can move her."

"But I wouldn't be any use in combat," Freya objected.

"Don't be so sure. You've improved a great deal since you started," Astrom said. "Besides, that's why you'll be with three others who are amongst our best. They'll look after you, don't worry about that."

"And I'm not useless either," Ashtyn interjected.

Freya swallowed, remembering Bardan's comments in the warehouse. The thought of going on something so dangerous with Ashtyn made her uncomfortable. She didn't want to contradict him, but she found herself disagreeing with him so often and so powerfully that she found herself unable to restrain her words of protest.

"Is there a problem with you going that I don't know about?" Astrom asked.

Freya looked at Bardan, who gave her an encouraging smile. "No. If Makkyd's been interrogated then Lyssa's right, you'll probably need me. I can do this."

EIGHT

Every second of the next day was filled with agony as Freya waited for word from the Resistance on when they were going to make their move. She went in to the Healing Centre, knowing her absence would arouse too much suspicion and that she needed to at least try to keep herself occupied. However, despite her resolve to try to distract herself with work, she accomplished nothing. She listlessly ordered and re-ordered the stacks of reports on her desk, but none of the words she read found purchase in her mind. She undertook her usual round of the wards, but couldn't focus on anything. She knew it was impossible that the Centre was operating perfectly, but despite her best effort to discern details that needed to be fixed, she found nothing to critique or compliment. Her thoughts were too filled with the task ahead of her, terror of having to work with Ashtyn, and the gnawing fear that she would let everybody down.

After the lunch hour time itself seemed to stop its usual march forward to focus instead on tormenting her. Freya was ready to scream with frustration. Part of healing required patience to see whether a treatment was taking effect, but that was her least favourite part. She was in her rooms when a runner arrived with a message. She looked at the slim girl of maybe fourteen, noting the green band sewn into her clothing. It wasn't unusual; a great many of the city's runners were Pious adolescents who weren't able to gain access to the professions. When they began to slow down, unable to speed through the city's streets to carry messages that required deft feet to ensure swift delivery, they were put in minor administrative positions. It was one of the Kade's initiatives offered to the city's poor. It would have been a very good system were the runners not mostly Pious; Kade citizens were given preference when it came to who was selected to enter training and apprenticeships. Even the Kade's charity was a reminder of its unfairness.

It meant that there were a great many Pious runners in the city and a great many Pious administrators working in the Kade halls of governance. Freya wondered how many of them were truly loyal to the Kade. After all, almost all of them were there because a Kade citizen got an apprenticeship or training instead. Even though the Kade provided them with a job, it was a sizeable difference in earnings and prestige from an actual profession. It was a powerful motive for resentment and fertile ground from which to recruit. Freya wondered if the Kade governance even realised how many people who had cause to resent them had been placed across every part of the city by the Kade themselves and with access to nearly every strata, or if those people were simply invisible to them: young Pious people whose birthright and status were so lowly that they couldn't possibly be viewed as capable of posing a threat. But those unseen, unnoticed people had access to so many pieces of information that, when put together, it gave away far more than the Kade governance would ever be happy to realise.

She took the message from the girl, rolling the scroll in her fingers. "Do you need a reply?"

The girl shook her head. "It should all be clear in there," she said, regarding Freya with eyes the colour of a stormy sky. Eyes that were too serious for a young girl, Freya reflected. She wondered what this girl had been through that had left her looking like that.

The scroll contained a coded message to return to Bardan's warehouse that evening. Relief that soon she would be taking action hammered through her. That was swiftly pursued by anticipation. Night would take far too long to fall tonight.

The rest of the day was a total waste, at once too long and also entirely unforgettable. Freya was preoccupied with the restlessness building within her. It clawed at her, hungering for action rather than this passive waiting. With every second that passed, Makkyd was likely suffering at the hands of people skilled in the art of pain and the way it undid a person's resolve to remain silent. With every second that passed came the chance that Makkyd may let something – even the most seemingly inconsequential detail – slip. And that might be enough for the Kade to begin to unravel the careful and complex secrecy of the Resistance. Her anticipation was broken only by intermittent fears that somebody would come bursting into her rooms to arrest her on the basis of information which had been coerced out of Makkyd about Freya's involvement with the Resistance. She found herself not overly concerned with her own safety but instead consumed by the thought that if she were discovered now, she couldn't do any more to usurp the Kade. She wasn't prepared to be stopped just yet.

Finally the warm light outside began to be replaced by the gentle blue tones of twilight. The view of the garden below, perfectly tended into a visual feast of colour and geometric design, faded into shadows and suggestions. Freya summoned a runner and asked him to take a message which told Symon that she would be home late, if at all. She slept in the pallet in her rooms because she had worked past the curfew often enough that it wasn't an unusual or suspicious thing for her to do, although her earlier wonderings about Symon left her with a certain sense of paranoia, especially given the extra attention he had been paying to her of late. There was a time when he hadn't even seemed to notice the empty space on her side of their shared bed. Even as she hadn't missed him, her pride had stung at his apparent indifference. Now that she would have preferred he not pay attention to her absence, he was. Her frustration at the inconvenience stuck out in her mind as callous, especially as it overweighed her worry that Symon might find her behaviour suspicious and potentially inform on her, but she dismissed her introspection. This was not the time to contemplate who she was becoming now that she had slipped the restrictive yoke of the fear she had placed around her own heart.

Once the city was completely cloaked by night, she slipped from the Healing Centre. As had been the case the previous evening, the streets were almost devoid of people. The scale of blues coating the buildings and streets, interspersed with islands of colour made violent by the illumination of sporadic street lamps, gave the empty streets a melancholic air rather than the gleefully mischievous sense that dominated the night-time streets of Freya's childhood. Arched recesses of doorways became shadows that seemed to shy away from the street, as though what was transpiring in Oranis had even the buildings trying to step backward; away from it. Her whole body hummed with nervous energy rather than the fear and anxiety that had all but overwhelmed her the night before. The need to get Makkyd back gave each step a little extra determination. The need to return the city to what it should be – a place of light and warmth and freedom –permeated every decision she made and every action she took.

"How are you feeling?" Bardan asked as he greeted her with a hug.

"Ready."

"That's our girl." He smiled, pulling her into another rough embrace.

Instead of sitting with him as she had the previous evening, she went straight through to the hidden room. Ashytn was there by himself, dressed all in black and sharpening a knife. He looked at her as she came in, the light from the gas flames making his green eyes glitter.

"Are you all right?" he asked.

"I think so," she replied.

He stared at her for a moment longer, then handed black clothes to her. Mutely, she stripped off her white healer's over-robe and the loose tan-coloured clothes underneath, down to her underwear. She paused for the briefest of moments, surprised that this seemed as normal to her as any task in the Healing Centre. She glanced up to see Ashtyn looking at her near-naked body. Modesty hadn't even entered her mind but now she felt a flush creeping along her neck and face. Realising that she was aware of his gaze, he too blushed.

"Sorry," he mumbled, averting his eyes.

Freya quickly pulled on the form-fitting dark trousers and tunic, chasing away the memory of the heat that Ashtyn's lingering eyes had evoked. This was hardly the time for such thoughts. She experimentally stretched out her arms and nodded, satisfied that she had enough freedom of movement.

As she was adjusting the tunic so that it sat a little more snugly, two more people joined them. They too were from within the very upper echelon of the Resistance leadership, the weaver twins Sek and Ellan. Despite their peaceful profession, Freya had seen them in the practice rooms at Astrom's workshop. She wasn't certain what their abilities were, but she half expected it to be something that gave them astoundingly quick movement. If she had thought Astrom was skilled, these two left her friend to shame. They most often fought each other as nobody else was really fast enough to keep up with either of them. Freya was glad that they would be with her.

The twins quickly and wordlessly donned their dark clothes, then the four of them sat and waited in silence. Freya was grateful for it and the way it offered space for her to collect herself for what was to come. She stared at the way the skin on her hands looked so pale as she rested them against the black cloth of her trousers.

Astrom and Bardan entered the room. Astrom began speaking with little ceremony. "We know Makkyd is in the city prison. That's on the border of the governance and market districts. You are to go in and find her, then bring her back here. We need to get her out tonight before they decide she's more value to them dead than alive."

"They may kill her?" Ashtyn asked. He sounded afraid.

"If they realise exactly how valuable she is to the Resistance, it's possible that they may choose to eliminate her and all the knowledge she has," Astrom replied. She didn't sound at all scared by the prospect. She was simply laying the truth before them.

Ashytn swore. "All right, so let's go." He stood up.

"We need to move through the city inconspicuously," Freya pointed out, although she privately echoed his desire for action. Her fingers went to her wrist to trace the green band sewn into her sleeve but found only smooth cloth.

"Do you really think we hadn't thought of that?" Astrom strode across the room to open a hidden door that Freya hadn't known existed. A short man stepped in. Thick shaggy brown hair covered every inch of exposed skin, giving him the appearance of a ball of fur.

"About time." His voice was coarse, his words formed with the roughness with which many traders spoke. "Me arse was getting' so numb I thought it would fall off."

"Thank you, Olek." Astrom's lips were pressed into a thin line.

Ashtyn hid a smile behind his hand.

"Speaking of arses, for a resistance you certainly do sit around on yours more than you act," Olek continued, either blithely unaware of Astrom's wince at his liberal use of the word 'arse' or completely indifferent to the jarring effect of his coarseness. He caught sight of Freya. "Who's this? Certainly a fine piece for you all to admire." He looked her over appreciatively.

Freya gaped, unsure what to say. Men and women were considered equal under both Kade and Pious worldviews, and given that she had often outranked men, she had always been treated with total respect, even deference. She had never been reduced to such objectification.

"This is our resident healer. You'll have to forgive her shock. She's unaccustomed to bawdiness," Ashtyn said, his eyes glinting with amusement despite the urgency of the moment.

"I feel no need to resort to crudities if that's what you mean," Freya replied, her voice formal as her healer's mask of composure slipped into place.

"There's no shame in being our delicate flower," Ashtyn teased.

Freya expected anger to flow through her at Ashtyn's comment, but her lips instead struggled to suppress hysterical laughter. The seriousness of the moment eased away for a breath and she revelled in the reprieve. It made the prospect of what was to come farther away and as such, somehow easier to face.

"Hang on," Olek interjected, his eyes flicking between Freya and Ashtyn. "Are you two going at it?"

"That's none of your business," Freya told him stiffly, all her amusement having taken flight.

"People bicker like you two means they're havin' it on or they want to." Olek shrugged. "I just wanted to know so I could make sure you two were separate. It's mighty close quarters in that wagon and I wouldn't want there to be any stains to clean up." He was so sincere in his comment that Ashtyn burst out laughing. Freya turned bright red and glared across the room at the hairy man.

"I'm sure I'll be able to contain myself," she muttered, remembering Ashtyn's eyes on her as she changed. She banished the thoughts, amazed that they sought passage through her mind when the situation was so serious.

"Maybe you're just in need of a good tumble. Loosen you up some." The little man grinned, showing a mouth full of yellowed teeth with a regular sprinkling of gaps. "I'd be more than happy to oblige." Then again, it seemed perhaps situations of this kind brought the libido to the fore.

Before Freya could decline his kind offer, Astrom stepped in. "Olek, court Freya later. We need to move."

His eyes widened. "Wait. Healer. Freya. You're not Freyanna Kusch?"

Uneasy, Freya nodded.

"But you're a bloody collaborator," he exclaimed.

Freya took a breath to calm herself. She knew her name was often followed by the descriptor of collaborator, but it was unnerving to hear her reputation thrown back at her. "Clearly not, given I'm here."

He ignored Freya's comment, turning to address Astrom. "Are you sure you can trust her? She's been given riches for her service to our lords and masters. Can you be sure that she's so happy to give that all up?" He threw a glance at Ashtyn. "Sleeping with the enemy there, friend."

At this, Freya felt a hot anger rise within her. "I see no green band upon your sleeve. Why should *I* trust *you*?"

"This one's got beady little eyes." He turned back to face her. "Aye, I'm Kade. But seven years of their rule and what has that gotten me? Half my wares are taken with no word of thanks, and then I have to pay tax for that joy. If I'm being screwed by someone, I at least like to get off. Why would *you* bite the hand that pleasures you?"

Freya smiled faintly. "Fashion and wealth aren't always compelling reasons to do something."

Olek's snort contained an entire treatise's worth of derision. "You talk like them, too. As though someone's rammed a rod right up your arse."

"All the better to, how would you say, screw them when they least suspect it," she retorted.

He looked at her for a moment, consideration written into the narrowing of his eyes, then he nodded. "A fine pair we make. A collaborator and a blood traitor. Think of how fine a pair we'd make naked." He grinned, again showing that spectacular dental display.

Freya repressed a shudder at the prospect of him naked. She consoled herself with the thought that his hair probably was as good as a second set of clothes.

"Now that we all trust and love each other, shall we get on with the business at hand?" Astrom snapped.

"Certainly. Once you're all ready, my wagon and I will be waiting outside the cargo entrance." He left the room, taking all the levity that had so briefly entered it with him.

Silently, they finished getting ready. They donned black shoes made from a leather so soft that it would create only the smallest noise as they walked. Their black tunics were hooded, secured with a string that tied under the chin. With the hoods up, it was almost impossible to see anybody's face. The clothing gave the group the illusory appearance of being moving shadows.

As they were arming themselves with a myriad of weapons; blades, combat knives, and throwing knives, Freya found her way to Ashtyn's side. He secured two knives into sheaths on his forearms and double checked that no glint of metal was visible through the opening of his sleeve. She rested her hand on his shoulder with the most light and uncertain of touches. He raised his eyebrows in question.

"I just wanted to say...I'm sorry for being difficult," she stuttered, feeling the blush again rise along her neck. She was glad the hood hid most of her face.

The way he tilted his head meant that most of his face was thrown into shadow by his own hood and she couldn't see his expression. "I appreciate you saying."

"I just don't want our differences to cause any trouble getting Makkyd out," she stammered.

He was silent for a moment before he answered, his voice stilted. "I wasn't planning on letting them." In complete defiance to how easy she usually found it to read him, she couldn't tell if he was angry, hurt, or something else. She turned away, wondering if she'd somehow made things between them worse.

"Freya?"

She turned back to him.

"I'm glad you said something. I—"

Astrom's voice rang through the room, cutting off what he was going to say next.

"All right, let's get you away. I wanted to come with you, but Bardan pointed out to me that it would be irresponsible of me to put the rest of our knowledge of the Resistance on the line." Astrom made no effort to hide her obvious unhappiness at the decision for her to stay behind. And although the reasoning was more than fair, Freya shared her friend's sentiment. She would have found comfort in her friend's presence tonight.

Freya gave Ashtyn a tiny smile, nerves pushing her to seek the reassurance she received in the smile he returned to her.

NINE

Olek and his wagon were waiting in the street. The night was dark and the sparse gas streetlamps across the warehouse district gave the shadows which wrapped around the streets a bottomless quality.

They climbed onto the wagon bed. Olek had spoken truthfully, it was a tight fit, especially lying down. They were squeezed together, shoulders digging into each other.

"Mind you don't prick yourselves with your weapons," Olek cautioned as he placed half-filled sacks over their legs and lower bodies. Freya fought to hold away the instinctive panic that wanted her to be able to move her limbs freely rather than be all but buried in the dark restriction of the wagon. Olek pulled an oiled cloth over them. The stiff, greasy material settled just a breath from Freya's nose. In the dark, her legs weighed down, hemmed in by one of the twins on her left and Ashtyn on her right, Freya's resolve to action, to do whatever was required to end the Kade, wavered and the impulse to struggle and yell until she was let out stole the evenness of breath from her.

Olek's footsteps beat in from outside, then silence fell for a moment. Freya's panicked mind wondered if he was going to betray them by bellowing out to a squadron of waiting Guardians. But then the wagon rocked as he climbed aboard and they began to move. The motion of the carriage reminded her of her powerlessness, and the thin measure of self-control began to fray, forcing her breath out in uneven pants. Long, warm fingers found hers, squeezing in reassurance. Freya's fear receded and she was grateful that Ashtyn knew what was needed to comfort her.

The ride was bumpy and long. Perhaps her perception of the journey's duration was simply elongated by the discomfort of the cramped, wholly black world, but Freya felt they must have travelled half the night. Finally the wagon stopped. Freya's suspicion had her tense as she waited for the feel of knives sliding into her from the Guardians to whom Olek had sold them. Instead, the heavy cloth was thrown back and replaced with the looming face of the hairy man.

"Quickly, out," he whispered, the whites of his eyes almost luminescent in the dark as he glanced around nervously. The four eased cramped limbs and climbed out. "I'll be waiting here," Olek rasped.

Even though he had brought them here safely, Freya could not let go of her suspicion. For all his comments, he was a Kade citizen and he would be richly rewarded for delivering key members of the Resistance. But she knew they had no choice but to trust Olek. Seeming to sense her unease, the round man grabbed her by the arm. "Don't worry, I will be here," he promised, the sincerity of his tone at odds with his earlier bawdy demeanour.

He released her arm and knelt by the side of the wagon, deftly pulling apart one of the wheels. Freya watched for a moment before Ashtyn lightly touched her arm. She pulled herself back to the task at hand and the four slipped away.

Olek had deposited them two streets away from the prison building. Staying deep in the shadows and listening for the sound of Guardians' footsteps, the four moved as swiftly as possible toward the building where Makkyd was being held.

Thunder rumbled overhead, but that was all that the sky seemed to offer as they reached the prison. They paused in the shadowed doorway of a building across the road while they surveyed the building and street before them. Then, at a signal from one of the twins – in what they were wearing, it was almost impossible to tell Ashtyn apart from either of the twins let alone one from the other – they dashed across the street. The prison had been a school before the Kade takeover. In the days of the Dual Accord, there had been a place outside the city walls where criminals had been kept away from society. But the Kade's justice was a harsh one. If someone was guilty of a serious crime, they disappeared, were put to hard labour, or executed. The prison was used only to hold people who were either awaiting sentence or being interrogated by the Kade, so it was more convenient for them to be kept close. As a result, the school had been commandeered and converted.

Freya wondered how many people were being tortured or awaiting a brutal sentence. It seemed wrong to rescue one person when so many were also in the building – a great many of them innocent. But the truth was that Makkyd's knowledge would help more than even the number of people imprisoned, so Freya clung to that cold logic even though it offered little consolation.

Freya followed the lead of the other three, every nerve tingling. Tonight, the Kade's unmerciful approach to justice worked in their favour; the building had not been designed as a prison with only one entrance and exit. The now-superfluous doors had been sealed with ugly, thick iron bars. For the jailbreakers though, that wasn't a problem.

Ashtyn stopped before one of the barred doors and gestured for the other three to step back. He placed his hand on the bars, his focus locked entirely on the metal in his hands. The iron began to glow and Ashtyn pulled the bars effortlessly aside, creating enough space for a person to slip through. He released the bars then put his hands on the mechanism of the door. Freya tried to see what he was doing, but the lock was almost entirely covered by Ashtyn's hands. Within a few moments, the door swung open. All four winced at the shrieking protest of the disused hinges and looked around to see if the sound had reached the ears of anybody nearby. When the sound of footsteps or the appearance of an investigatory silhouette didn't eventuate, one of the twins stepped through, pausing for a moment, then gesturing for the others to follow

The inside of the prison held a heaviness. Pain – past, present, and promised – wended its way around them, as though it the sentiment oozed out of the stone walls. They had entered at the end of a long corridor with a high ceiling. Only every fifth gas flame in the walls was lit, making it almost impossible to see clearly. The murky light offered enough illumination, though, to see that the walls had gone uncleaned in the years of Kade rule. The building was grimy and barren.

"Do we know where Makkyd is?" Freya whispered, and flinched as the susurration of her voice echoed off the bare stone walls.

"We know she's on the second floor," one of the twins replied, cupping his hand around his mouth to try to minimise the sound. Ashtyn and the twins drew weapons. Belatedly, Freya drew her own knife, wondering what she was doing in the group. She had been given a knife for that evening instead of the staff with which she was most adept. It was an unstated but unmissable reminder that combat was not her forte. Ashtyn and the twins seemed so sure of what they were doing. She simply felt as though she was going to hold them up. Shadows and knives were not ways with which she was familiar. The nervous energy that had burned within her flickered and went out in the face of where she was and what she was doing. If they got caught by the Kade, they were going to die.

The four padded along the empty corridor and turned left at the end. A guard paced aimlessly in a pool of light cast by a gas flame at the base of a set of stairs. Freya didn't have time to look further before she saw a blade flying silently through the air. It landed solidly in the guard's back as she pivoted away from them.

One of the twins was already running toward her, his feet thudding softly on the floor. He reached the Guardian as she fell. The tiny whimpers she was making carried along the corridor. The twin twisted her neck violently. The crack was the loudest thing about the entire episode.

Freya stared in shock at the sight of the man kneeling by the body of the Guardian, looking furtively about in case anybody had heard anything. It had all happened so quickly. Ashtyn touched her arm. She flinched, gasping. Her surprised breath was not nearly as loud as the crack of the woman's neck had been.

"Are you all right?" He leaned close so that his voice wouldn't carry beyond her ear.

She took a deep breath. She had seen death before, had seen bodies before. She took another breath. Then nodded. It was only then that she realised everybody was waiting for her.

They moved up the stairs, one of the twins a little farther ahead. Distant thunder growled outside.

A second Guardian sat on a chair at the entrance of the corridor on the second floor. Freya wondered if he was supposed to be sitting or if he, like the woman downstairs, had been overcome by boredom. One of the twins ran at him. The honed edge of his knife flashed brightly in the dim light. Freya looked away but she couldn't stop from hearing. A moment later, the sound of approaching footsteps signalled another Guardian who had presumably come to investigate the sick gurgling sound. In a single fluid motion, the second twin drew a knife and threw it at the approaching Guardian, not even stopping to see where it had hit as he followed the knife's path. Whereas she hadn't been able to look across the grimy, dark space at the way the man on the chair had been dispatched, Freya found she couldn't look away as the twin reached the Guardian only a moment after his knife. Another knife was pushed quickly up and into the Guardian's chest. She thought she could feel the Guardian's lifesong suddenly extinguished, even though she was on the other side of the room. Almost gently, the Guardian's body was lowered to the floor.

Both twins looked around the area, waiting for more to come. When none did, they walked over to Freya and Ashtyn.

"We need to be methodical about this," one of the twins whispered, glancing around the landing as he spoke, knife held ready in his hand. There was blood on the blade.

"Should we split up?" the other twin asked his brother.

Neither Ashtyn nor Freya objected, both deferring to the skill of the weavers.

The first twin thought for a moment, then shook his head. "Better if we stick together. There are four corridors. We go down each one together as fast as possible. I'll lead, you take rear."

The four went down the first corridor. Of the ten rooms, three held prisoners. A quick glance through the slits in the heavy doors, which had obviously been retrofitted into the far more slender stonework of the door frames, confirmed that none of the prisoners was Makkyd. A Guardian patrolling the second corridor was quickly dispatched by the twins, but still no Makkyd. They found her in the third corridor. Her distinctive coppery hair marked her out even through the tiny gap in the door. Ashtyn made short work of the door and they went inside. Makkyd glanced up, her face smeared with dirt as though it had been pushed into the filthy floor – forcefully. Her face slackened in relief when she recognised them. The room was unexpectedly spacious. It had probably been a classroom. But the only suggestion of its former life was a large board of slate on one wall. The room in which they stood surpassed the worst nightmare version of a schoolroom. The windows had been bricked up in an obviously hasty fashion, and as such allowed in only the tiniest slices of light – a torturous reminder of what prisoners would likely never see again. The stone walls had been gouged as though someone – or several someones – had tried in desperation to chip away at them in some futile attempt at escape. Even in the shadowy darkness of the room, Freya could see that the wooden floors were stained in places with what she could only assume was blood. She didn't pause to investigate. A foul smell sat in the room, emanating from a bucket in one corner, presumably for Makkyd to relieve herself. The cell was truly a haven for misery and the death of hope.

Before she had even reached Makkyd's side, Freya knew it was good she had been assigned to go. Makkyd's injuries weren't going to kill her immediately, but she was in bad shape. Her leg had been broken, she was suffering damage to her internal organs, and she had a slight concussion. The wrongness was written through Makkyd's lifesong, speaking to how the injuries had been sustained; there was something about inflicted injuries that sounded particularly awful. There was an almost sweet quality to the way natural ailments or injuries pulled a lifesong out of harmony. But there was nothing pleasant about the sound of deliberate wounds, and that made it hard for her to focus on healing them.

She tried to let her mind settle on Makkyd's injuries rather than the crashing, discordant horror of them, and she breathed deeply as she pulled Makkyd's lifesong back into alignment. Thoughts of the dead Guardians and the brutal skills of the twins prowled in the back of her mind, trying to draw away her concentration, but she denied them her focus. It took her several minutes, but when she stepped back, she was satisfied that she had done the job.

"Thank you, Freya. You really are quite something," Makkyd said, her voice even but weak.

Ashtyn held out a hand to help Makkyd stand.

Once Makkyd was on her feet, she tested her weight on the leg that had been broken, finding it bore her weight.

"You're still going to feel weak," Freya cautioned.

"I'll manage," Makkyd said, her shoulder squaring as she released Ashtyn's arm and walked toward the end of the cell.

It only took a few steps for her to stumble. Ashtyn caught her, one arm going around her waist to support her. Freya was reminded of the first time she had met Ashtyn, immediately after the explosions in the marketplace. He had been ready to catch her then, too, when she had been unsteady on her feet.

"I thought you healed her," he said to Freya, no recrimination in his voice, only tight worry.

"I did. But that doesn't stop her from being exhausted or her body still having to deal with whatever they've given her. I can only do so much in the time that we have."

"Oh, I take my praise back then," Makkyd with dry humour, slinging an arm around Ashtyn to keep herself steady. The humour felt so forced in the awful room.

"Well, at least we know you're going to be all right," Ashtyn told her, walking with her toward the door.

The path back through the corridor to the landing of the second floor was slow. The growl of thunder sounded again, ever so briefly masking the slight groans their footfalls drew from the wooden floorboards of the second floor. As they passed the bodies of the Guardians, Freya tried not to look at them.

The twins led the way back to the stairs and held up hands to stop them. The sound of footsteps echoed from down below. They all knew what was to come; a body lay at the foot of those stairs.

The footsteps slowed. "Nisha?" someone called at the same time that one of the twins whispered to his brother, "go."

Not waiting for a response, he hurtled down the stairs, trying to get to the Guardian before the alarm was raised. A shout was cut off, but it was a shout nevertheless.

Ashtyn wordlessly passed Makkyd to Freya and grimly drew his weapons. Freya staggered a little as she took the brunt of Makkyd's weight. She wrapped her arm around her leader's waist, her fingers digging into hard muscles on Makkyd's side. Flanked by Ashtyn and the other twin, they made their way as swiftly down the stairs as possible. A sheen of sweat covered Makkyd's forehead as she tried to move as quickly as she could.

Pounding footsteps were dull thuds on the stone floor of the ground floor. Freya's heart began to beat a jerky rhythm. Her legs started shaking as she prepared to run, dragging Makkyd along if necessary.

"Back to where we came in," Ashtyn directed. He led the way as the twins stayed behind them, ready to intercept the person whose footfalls approached.

They reached the door. Ashtyn pulled it open and held it wide for Freya to help Makkyd get out onto the street. Despite the dark, it was far easier to see, and the rips and bloodstains on Makkyd's clothes came into better relief. Freya stared for a moment, wondering what exactly her leader had sustained in the two days she had been captive. Another violent rumble of thunder prompted her to move, and she helped Makkyd through the doorway.

The others piled out and Ashtyn hurriedly closed the door, his hands already heating the metal. "Can't let them see what I did," he muttered, pulling the red-hot bars back into place. The twins urged Freya on, not letting her wait for him to finish. She heard voices from within the building as they navigated through the streets to where they left Olek. Thunder sounded again, loud and low across the city. Her arm began to ache with the leaden weight of Makkyd and she wondered what would happen if Olek had left. There was no way they would be able to get Makkyd to safety without being sighted. Their clandestine demeanour, Makkyd's obvious state of injury, and the dirt and blood smeared all over her marked them as doing something very illegal. The sound of running footsteps behind them nearly made her buckle, but it was only Ashtyn. He slipped an arm underneath the other side of Makkyd, taking most of her weight from Freya. It made walking the final stretch of the deserted streets far easier.

Olek was waiting by the wagon. Guilt stabbed Freya for her doubt. Olek wordlessly handed Makkyd a billowing tunic which she pulled over the filthy clothes, then helped her up onto the driver's seat with surprising gentleness. "You too," he said to Freya. Shouting from a few streets away cut through the air. Freya obeyed, knowing with awful certainty that she needed to trust the competence of the others to keep her alive. She was so far out of her depth that it felt almost as though she had slipped into a dream but for the ache in her arm from supporting Makkyd and the fear that made her heart beat so fast and her bladder tremble.

Olek heaved himself up next to Makkyd, wedging her between himself and Freya so that she was sitting upright. The wagon started to move.

"Wait, what about Ashtyn and the twins?" Freya asked.

He shook his head. "Can't risk it."

"Ashtyn!" Freya twisted so she could look at him still standing on the street. Panic swirled within her at the idea of him being left behind to deal with the Guardians.

"I'll be fine," he called, the promise just loud enough for her to hear over another roll of thunder as the wagon left them behind.

They made it three streets until two Guardians appeared, calling for them to halt. Olek did so. Fear became a physical presence sitting beside her, whispering into her ear every awful way in which she could die or be beaten.

"Just me, my woman, and my sister coming back from a late deal," Olek called. Freya didn't understand how he could sound so cheerful.

"Your woman has unusually red hair," one of the Guardians called suspiciously.

"Not a crime, is it?"

The Guardians approached, one on either side of the wagon. "No, but—" The Guardian closest to Olek started to say. He was cut off by the plump man, moving with surprising speed, drawing a knife and plunging it into his neck.

The Guardian next to Freya went to draw her own weapon. Time seemed to slow down as thunder seemed to make the very buildings of Oranis shake. She reacted without thinking, swooping forward to grasp the woman's wrist. Her lifesong surged into Freya's perception, a strong vibrant symphony. Forcing it to stop was like putting a dampener on a drum; it needed effort, but Freya had plenty of incentive. It was over in one second, maybe two. The woman's body crumpled to the ground without so much as a mark on her.

TEN

Freya spent the ride through Oranis in a daze. The focus on getting safely back to Bardan's warehouse made it impossible to tell whether Makkyd or Olek had seen how easily she had stopped the heart of the Guardian. That woman had gone in a second from being *some*body to *a* body, and Freya had caused it with nothing but the force of her own will.

The clatter of the wagon's wheels on the smooth paving stones seemed impossibly loud – louder even than the thunder which continued to intermittently rumble overhead despite the absence of rain it heralded. Freya was sure that the rattle of the wagon would surely rouse anyone they passed to investigate what fool would break the curfew. In Freya's mind, the noise put into sound the enormity of what she had done – could do.

The warehouse district seemed so much larger than Freya knew it to be, but finally, they arrived at Bardan's warehouse. Freya would have missed it; all the buildings looked more or less the same. In the darkness of night, it was entirely impossible for her to distinguish any difference, especially with her thoughts in disarray.

The Goddess must have smiled upon them, because they'd made it without encountering any other Guardians. Freya was glad. She wasn't sure what she would have done had they been stopped again – she was afraid of what she might have done.

Astrom and Bardan emerged from the shadows as soon as Olek drew up. Freya got down and they helped Makkyd descend.

She was on the threshold of unconsciousness and Astrom and Bardan all but carried her into the warehouse.

"Be seein' yer," Olek said in that coarse voice before he flicked the reins and the wagon pulled off. Freya watched him round a corner and considered the danger he had put himself in to help them.

"Ashtyn and the twins?" Astrom asked as Freya joined them in the warehouse. The tall woman's voice held enough fear to confirm that them staying behind hadn't been the ideal outcome. The image of Ashtyn as he reassured her he would return swam in the eye of Freya's mind. A coldness settled over her at the prospect that he may have been killed in allowing her and Makkyd to escape.

"They stayed behind to deal with Guardians who followed us out. They said they'd meet us here." Freya forced the words out, each one feeling like an ashen promise on her tongue.

"Did you have any trouble as you came here?" Bardan asked.

Freya's mouth was so dry that the words seemed to cut her as she spoke them. "Two Guardians stopped us, but we don't have to worry about them." The exact words to confirm their deaths refused to form on her lips.

They bundled Makkyd into the secret room and began the awful process of waiting. To distract herself from the prospect of Ashtyn's death, and the swell of regret and bone-deep sadness on which it was borne, Freya helped Makkyd drink and eat, watching as the redheaded woman seemed to recover her strength. All the while, she could feel the hum of Makkyd's body. It reminded her of the hum she had so abruptly cut off. Her mouth went dry at the recollection.

As the night stretched on and dawn went from a long-away possibility to an impending event, she knew she should go back to the Healing Centre, even to Symon. But she just couldn't find it within herself to move. Nobody spoke.

Finally, the warning system announced that someone was trying to access the warehouse. Bardan left to answer it, a knife in each hand, just in case. Freya hardly dared to hope, and instead readied herself to face Guardians. But Bardan returned with a sight that made Freya send fervent thanks to the Goddess: Ashtyn and the twins. They brought with them the smell of sweat, underscored faintly with the tang of blood. The thought passed Freya's mind that she now knew she didn't need to shed blood to kill. She shuddered, but nobody noticed.

The relief which all but choked her and the preoccupation with her deadliness made her deaf to the conversation around her. With a great effort, she tried to listen to what was being said.

"Well, everything's changed," Bardan said sombrely.

"Has it?" Ashtyn asked.

"I just said, this risks exposing everything," Astrom replied, an uncharacteristic bite to her words betraying just how thrown she was by the events of Makkyd's capture.

"So what do we do?" one of the twins asked. "Are we even ready?" His face was impassive.

Freya wondered how he felt about the people he and his brother had killed that evening. It didn't look as though he was concerned.

A sense of nausea swelled inside her. "I need some air," she said. She didn't wait to see if her departure was noticed as she left the room.

It was cool and dark in the warehouse. The rain, long-promised by the thunder, had started to fall outside. It drummed steadily against the roof of the warehouse. It was an unexpectedly gentle sound despite the violence implied by the thunder. Freya slid to the floor. She took deep breaths, trying to keep herself calm. Tears began to pour down her face despite her best efforts. She didn't sob, but the tears wouldn't stop.

When the door opened, she knew it was Ashtyn. He sat next to her and put his arms around her. She leaned into him, as comfortably as if he held her like this every day. He didn't say anything, he just waited for her to tell him.

"I killed her, Ashtyn," she whispered, tears dripping down her face. "A Guardian. She tried to stop the wagon and I killed her."

"It's not easy," he replied. The smell of his sweat and other people's blood still clung to him, but she didn't care. The solidity of his arms and the reassurance that he was alive was what she noticed most.

"But it was. For everybody else, killing means cracking bones or tearing flesh; blood and mess and noise. I only need to use my ability. I don't think Olek or Makkyd saw how I killed her, but I touched her and...I could do it. It was *so* easy. And now I know how easy it is." She stared down at her hands, almost wishing she could see blood on them – see some tangible remainder of the person whose life she had taken.

He ran his hand gently up and down her back, like he was soothing a small child. "You know you may have to do this again," he told her, the arm around her tightening.

"I'm not sure I can. I don't want to – I can't...hurt people, kill people. It's everything I was trained to fix." She lifted a hand to wipe the tears from her face. It was a futile exercise; they were unrelenting in the march down her cheeks.

She was glad he didn't tell her what they both knew: that despite her protestations, it was too late. She had killed someone. There was no going back from that. No unknowing that she could take a life.

"I wish..." she began, the paused.

"Yes?" he prompted.

"I wish we could just go and live on that farm and pretend this didn't exist." She said it in a rush, as if by saying it quickly, he may miss the vulnerability that she had just shown him, what she had really just confessed to him.

"Freya..." His tone was enough answer. It didn't matter; she had known before she spoke what his answer was.

"I know, Ashytn." She wrapped an arm around him and pulled him closer to her, just wanting the comfort of him.

Gradually, she came to suspect that perhaps at least some of the numbness that had seized her during the wagon ride had been out of fear that she may never see him again. That realisation, and the other implications it suggested, was far less shocking than she might have expected.

They sat together in silence for a long time and to Freya's surprise, it was a comfortable one. Finally, Ashtyn spoke.

"It gets easier, you know."

"What – the killing, or living with it?"

"Both."

"Maybe that's what I'm most afraid of," she replied into his chest.

His only response was to pull her closer to him, and she turned her head so that the arch of her cheekbone nestled perfectly against the swooping hollow underneath his collarbone. She wondered who he had killed, and under what circumstances. She was certain the Guardians who had pursued them tonight were dead, and that this was not the first time Ashtyn had taken life – he wouldn't have been on the expedition to rescue Makkyd otherwise. Perhaps it should have bothered her more that his hands were stained with blood. But so too now were hers. And she found comfort in his acknowledgement that the act of killing was one which he felt had left him marked. She found a comfort in the fact that she wasn't alone.

Freya didn't know how long they would have stayed like that. Something about being entangled with him outweighed the discomfort of the hard ground or the odd angle at which their bodies intersected. The patter of the rain outside eased around the time a faint lightening seeped through the cracks in the walls, signalling the arrival of dawn.

"I should go soon," she mumbled, pulling back from his embrace.

Ashtyn stirred as though he were awakening. "Will you be all right?"

"I should be." At some point, she realised, the tears had stopped. She rubbed her face blearily.

Ashtyn shifted so that she was leaning back against him and gently rubbed her shoulders. The tension his clever fingers eased from her stiff muscles almost made her moan. "Do you feel up to going back in?" he offered.

She nodded.

He helped her up and they returned to the hidden room together. The twins had left but the discussion continued. Makkyd was wrapped in blankets, looking so absurdly small that at a glance one would never have believed that she was the leader of the Resistance. But the tone in which she spoke left no doubt. "...people everywhere, but the question is whether or not they are ready.".

The conversation paused as Ashtyn and Freya walked in. Astrom filled the silence. "Given that the Kade now know Makkyd's identity, we've been put in a difficult position."

"Given that the Kade now know that I exist, they now know for certain that the Resistance exists," Makkyd interjected. Freya wondered how she had the strength to partake in the discussion let alone with such force.

"So it will make future operations far more difficult," Astrom continued.

"Yes, we established that," Ashtyn said, crossing the room to get himself a drink.

"So we either continue as we were and just keep Makkyd hidden or..." Astrom trailed off, looking uncertainly at Makkyd.

"Or we start," Makkyd ended the sentence firmly.

"Wait, start the uprising?" Freya asked.

"Well, we aren't going to start singing and dancing in praise of the Kade," Makkyd replied.

"When?"

"After the next day of rest. That's the time we'll need to get ourselves ready." Makkyd sounded so definite. Freya wondered if she had come to that decision through the course of the conversation of if it was a contingency that had been long planned. It was little wonder that the other members of the Resistance had wanted to rescue Makkyd immediately. She orchestrated everything. And there was something about her definitiveness that urged those around her to action.

"Are you sure? Are you even going to have your strength back by then?" Ashtyn looked her over, worry darkening the green of his eyes.

"Freya?" Makkyd asked.

Freya went to her side. She examined her once more, placing her hands on her arm. She pushed away the memory of the Guardian she had killed as she heard the hum of Makkyd's body, focusing on matters of life.

"You need maybe two nights of good rest," she said. "As far as I can tell there's nothing wrong with you aside from extreme fatigue. I can heal, but your body still needs rest. I can't give you that."

"There you go, Ashtyn. I'll be ready. Will you?" Makkyd's voice contained a note of a challenge.

Ashtyn raised his hands. "I'd follow you to the Gods themselves if you asked me. Just tell me what to do."

The streets were bizarre in their normalcy. Freya walked through them in the same healer's robe she had changed out of only a few hours before to go and rescue Makkyd. Maybe there were a few more Guardians than normal on the streets, but the city was by and large the same as it was every morning. The sun peeked over the rooftops, casting golden rays along the tops of the buildings and skating along the sheen of water which sat upon the pavers from the earlier rain. Street vendors cooked food, people chatted – more quietly than they once may have done, but they still took the time to dawdle and gossip as they made their way to work. The city was waking up as though nothing strange or violent had occurred within it the previous evening. People were as carefree as it was possible to be of late amid the recent severity of the Kade. It was a pale imitation of the city Freya had once known, but it was a world away from the shadows and knives of the previous evening.

Freya bought breakfast from a street vendor. She didn't think that she would be able to eat but she surprised herself, eating the freshly baked hana loaf in three bites; so quickly she barely noticed the interplay of spices as they danced across her tongue. She was still ravenous so she bought another, actually stopping to savour the warmth and flavour in each bite before tearing into the next hunk. In each mouthful, the flavours of the various fruits and spices practically exploded, demanding to be noticed, to be enjoyed. She couldn't imagine that anything could ever make her feel more alive, or more grateful for that fact. She even went back for a third, although she resumed walking as she ate this one. The rich, vibrant spices tasted just as good and filling as those mouthfuls of the first loaf. The warmth of the food spread through her, the simple pleasure exquisite.

The Healing Centre was, as ever, serene. Freya paused in the entrance atrium. The atrium, covered with a roof but otherwise open to the elements, was tiled with a beautiful swirling mosaic. She admired its delicacy as she walked across it to enter the main foyer. Inside, she paused, surrounded by the healers who moved purposefully around the room. The tranquillity and focus that suffused the area made Freya feel as though she had stepped out of a strange dream and back into the calmness of her normal life. As the healers moved past her, she wondered how they would react when the uprising began. Would they welcome the rebellion? Would they heal whoever needed help, or would they pick a side and take lives from the enemy, as she had done?

One of her assistants approached her. "My lady," he said with a deferential dip of his head. Freya had tried to stop the people in the Healing Centre calling her by the title of respect reserved for

Kade members, but while her every other order was obeyed, this one was consistently ignored. Today it felt especially odd to be called by the Kade title of respect.

"What do you have to report?" she asked, marvelling at the normalcy of her question. As every morning, she required some-one to meet her as soon as she walked into the Centre and provide her with a rundown of anything that had happened during the evening. She didn't like to miss anything, and people seemed to relax overnight. If she had learned anything, it was that night time was when people could be caught unawares, and the previous evening's events had only served to confirm this.

"Nothing untoward happened last night, although a few pa-tients did pass on, may the gods guide them."

"Do you have reports on them?" Freya asked, beginning to walk to her rooms. He trotted alongside her.

"Um..." He flicked through a stack of papers in his arms, creasing their surface as he did so.

"Careful, Flen. We import this paper from the Second Country and it's expensive. I don't want to waste money by having to get those reports copied," she warned.

Red brushed across the tips of his cheeks and he tried to rifle as quickly as possible without causing any damage.

Freya waited for two more minutes before her irritation took hold of her. "Don't bother to tell me what transpired if you can't give me the details of the incidents," she snapped.

He stammered an apology as he still sought the reports with increasing desperation.

She continued to walk, leaving him to run after her. She turned to look at him as he desperately searched. She sighed. "Don't apologise, just remember for next time, Flen." Even as she reprimanded him, she knew she should have softened her tone. But she just couldn't summon the energy to be kind, especially when she always requested this sort of information.

"They're from different wards," he explained as he leafed through pages, pulling out separate sheets and balancing them precariously on top of his stack.

"Was there any similarity of symptoms?" she asked, impatience simmering. At any moment she expected the sheaf of papers to topple to the floor.

"Uh—"

Freya exploded. "What is the point of you? Your purpose is to brief me. If I have to wait for you to read the reports, I may as well just go through them all myself."

He cheeks reddened further and Freya thought she saw his eyes glisten with unshed tears.

"Flen, I'm sorry, but this is a Healing Centre. We literally hold people's lives in our hands. If they die because we aren't the best we can be, we may as well kill them ourselves." She tried to be more gentle. "Go and organise your notes, come back and give me the reports at the lunch hour," she told him.

He nodded, scurrying away.

Sighing, Freya opened her door and went to her desk. She sat down, intending to begin the work for the day ahead. Vague guilt for the way she had allowed impatience with Flen to drive her to snap at him niggled at her. But she couldn't find it within herself to kindle that to fully fledged remorse. She could properly apologise to him later. However, the lack of sleep from the previous night all but overwhelmed her the moment she sat. She rested her arms on the top of the desk and placed her head on them. As her eyes became heavy, she was worried that if she went to sleep, she would dream of death and blood. The thought gave her pause but she was suddenly so fatigued she couldn't have stayed awake even if she'd wanted to. Regardless of whether or not she was going to dream of carnage, she was going to fall asleep.

She slept soundly, and dreamed of nothing.

ELEVEN

The bell that heralded the beginning of the lunch hour woke her. Even though she had slept only for a few hours, she felt rested. The spikes of ire and irritation that had seen her snap at Flen had resolved into something deeper that sat more comfortably within her – the coals of those emotions, burned low and hot with the knowledge of what would soon come to pass. A hesitant knocking on the door startled her from her self-examination. She ran her fingers through her hair, smoothed the creases out of her robe, and called for whoever it was to enter.

Flen opened the door barely wide enough to admit him. His trepidation was obvious in the way he slunk through the small opening into the room. "My lady, I have the reports you requested."

"Ah yes, thank you, Flen. I'm sorry about earlier, I wasn't feeling myself." She gestured for him to cross the room and approach her desk.

"It's my fault, I should have organised myself better. You were right to be angry."

"Yes, you should have done it," she agreed. "But that was no excuse for me to snap at you like that." She regretted the outburst for the lack of self-discipline behind it. Fatigue and the lingering sense of astonishment at her discovery of her ability's deadly capacity had driven her temper. But it wasn't an excuse for her behaviour. In the time that Flen had served as assistant to her, this had been his first moment of incompetence. An unfortunate matter of timing.

"It's good of you to say so, my lady." Flen couldn't quite bring himself to meet her gaze as he passed her the papers.

"Flen, I don't see a green band on your sleeve. Are you Pious?" Freya asked, noting for the first time the absence of the telltale band as he stretched out his arm.

"No, my lady, I'm Kade." He looked away as though embarrassed.

"You know that I am Pious," Freya commented.

He nodded.

"Does that make you uncomfortable?" she asked, staring at him.

"No, of course not." He answered too quickly, the words tumbling over each other in an effort to get out.

"You're a very poor liar, Flen," she told him curtly. He had the grace to blush. "Why does it make you uncomfortable?"

He was silent. "Flen," she warned, the slumbering coals of ire coming to wakefulness. His embarrassment at her origins seemed so unforgivably insolent, especially given her seniority.

He took a deep breath, the sound an unhappy one. "It's just...it feels odd, taking orders from a Pious."

"Why?"

He shifted from foot to foot. "We were told, during and after the takeover, that the Pious beliefs in the Goddess meant they wished harm upon the Kade gods..." He trailed off, obviously unwilling to elaborate any further.

"And are you a true believer, Flen?"

"Of course I believe in the gods." The thoughtless immediacy of his response told her that the words were formed by someone else and put into his mouth. It was obvious he didn't truly believe. It was dogma driving his answer rather than genuine belief.

"What else were you told about the Pious?" She leaned forward.

"That you...they, uh, that the Pious way of life was unstable." He blushed an even deeper shade of red.

"Unstable how?" she persisted. This was the version of truth that had led to the Kade uprising, and in the face of another uprising, it held particular interest. She had never had the opportunity to ask a Kade what they had been told to justify the brutal treatment of half their country's population. For a long time, that question hadn't seemed as important as the question of how to survive.

"The way the Pious behaved as a result of their traditions and behaviours was endangering the prosperity of the Third Country. It's why even now the Pious have to be treated carefully, because their ways run so deep that they may resurface and put the safety and prosperity of everyone at risk, and many of them can't ever completely let go of their old ways of thinking."

"What do you mean?"

"If you remember, the year before the Kade took power from the Dual Accord, a sickness came through the city."

She nodded. As an apprentice she had been tasked with all manner of chores to keep up with the wave of people who came into the Healing Centre, many of whom did not leave it on their feet.

"We were told that a Pious trader brought the sickness into the city and the Pious themselves made it worse."

"How?" She had heard screamed at her and other Pious that they had caused the epidemic that had seized Oranis, but she had discounted it as the accusation of the grief-stricken looking to their prejudice to offer explanation for the indifferent cruelty of disease.

"The Pious are communal and they bathed in a ritual fashion rather than to cleanse dirt or sickness from themselves."

Freya barely contained her snort of amusement. The first statement was true – while the Pious believed worship and prayer were largely solitary activities, they tended to form tightly knit groups of families and friends. One would often walk into the house of a relative or friend as if it were one's own. That may have exacerbated the spread of the ailment. But the comment about bathing was pure nonsense. Some Pious prayers required ritual cleansing, but it meant they cleaned themselves no less thoroughly than the Kade in their day-to-day lives. "I see. Anything else?"

"Some of our merchants struggled because the Pious gave one another favourable deals that created this impoverishment."

She kept her face carefully neutral. The hardest deals she had seen bartered and forged were often those between kin. But she supposed misfortune didn't much breed reason but instead the desire to find something or someone who was responsible for it, regardless of whether the culprit was actually guilty. That and the claims of god-killing spoke to how multitudinous the paths to inflaming a person's bigotry were – some obvious, some subtle. She wanted to believe in people's capacity for reason, but she found herself lacking. In her years as a healer, she had seen much of human stupidity in people's inability to take basic precautions against harm and she knew she had not plumbed the deepest depths of that particular well. That such prejudice could easily be inflamed meant also that it could be turned to the support of terrible things done to those who found themselves bearing the brunt of being born into the wrong religion.

"But I am Kade now, or don't you think so?" she said.

"You're right, you are. I just forget that sometimes I suppose," he said, obviously unhappy at having to answer these questions.

Freya knew he wasn't telling her the whole truth of his thoughts, but she suspected she wasn't going to get anything further out of him no matter how gently she cajoled or how forcefully she intimidated. Some things he would not say to her – out of fear or some deeper divide, she could not say. She let her hands fall to the desk, one hand running a finger up and down the green band sewn into her sleeve.

"What do you think of the Pious now, Flen?" she asked after a moment.

He swallowed nervously.

She took a small, petty delight in his obvious discomfort.

"I really couldn't say, my lady," he mumbled.

"Take a moment to think about it," she offered. A part of her felt bad for making him so uncomfortable. The other part of her enjoyed exacting a small revenge on him for his thoughtless bigotry. That bigotry, after all, was what the Kade governance had played upon to take power in the first instance.

"I think they've mostly seen sense, my lady. They've adopted the Kade ways. You're a shining example, if you don't mind me saying so."

"So you attribute my success to my obedience then?" A voice in the back of her mind told her to rein herself in, that this young man before her was not the true enemy. But a fire had been unlocked within her after the events of the previous evening and it would not heed this caution, it would not be extinguished.

He stammered and blushed again. "Not at all. Your skill is legendary," he spluttered.

"So why do you think that I must wear this band, if I am good at what I do, and am – as you say – Kade?" she demanded, pointing to the band on her sleeve. Recklessness drove her to ask him this question, to push him far beyond where she should have.

"To remind everyone else that your position is the result of your work for the Kade." His response had the cadence of one who has been told the line again and again.

"Do you think I should have to wear it, Flen?"

"My lady, it's not for me to say."

"Do you think that I deserve less, that I am less, because of my birth?" The look on his face – as though he had been caught stealing – was answer enough. She simultaneously felt a stab of triumph and an unbearable sadness.

"Never mind. You may go." She sighed the words out before he could answer, turning her attention to the reports in front of her. She knew she should have been concerned that he may report her for her line of charged questions, but she couldn't quite muster the willingness to care. Let him if he wanted. Soon enough, it would be irrelevant anyway.

She made her usual rounds through the Centre during the afternoon. Reckless she may have been in the questions she had asked Flen, but she wasn't entirely devoid of caution. To abandon the semblance of normalcy entirely would invite disaster rather than simply court it. It gave her a deep sense of satisfaction to see that everything was running as smoothly as possible. People were well taken care of, the wards were well organised. Yet that satisfaction was undercut by the question of what the Centre would look like in a few days' time. She couldn't possibly envisage that it would remain so orderly amid an uprising. Violence was guaranteed, and the braver or more desperate among people may make their way to the Centre for help. But would they be able to get the treatment they sought? Given the mix of Kade and Pious who worked in the Centre, how would an uprising largely supported by the Pious be responded to by those who worked within it? She knew from meeting Olek the previous evening that not all Kade were happy with the way their own people treated them. But surely many remained loyal. The carefully ordered and structured procedures she had spent so many cycles refining could likely be shattered when blood feuds were provoked – Pious may refuse to work alongside Kade, or Kade may resist the Pious attempt to seize control from the Kade government. Would people still be cared for?

Who would be treated and who would be turned away? How many people would forfeit their lives because they were caught in the crossfire or because they weren't able to get to a healer? And how many would be denied access to treatment because they worshipped the wrong god? If her conversation with Flen had been anything to go by, some prejudices and attitudes ran too deep to be denied. That wasn't to say that everybody allowed prejudice to subsume their decency, but enough – on either side – were compelled by blind belief that they would only ever see the other as lesser, as the enemy. Especially after the events of the history through which she had lived. Freya did not like the prospect that she may have to make decisions across lines of belief. Yet the more she thought about it, the more she realised it was likely. The prospect hung heavily over her.

She came across a young girl sitting on one of the beds, her arm heavily bandaged. Her parents sat beside her and the family was talking quietly amongst themselves, no real concern in their mannerisms. On a whim, Freya wandered over.

"How are you feeling?" She smiled down at the girl.

The girl shrugged. "It's sore."

"What did you do?"

"She was climbing and fell," her father explained.

It was such a mundane thing that it shocked Freya. Her world had been lived so completely in shadows and intrigue and tangled webs of control and power that she forgot that so many people simply lived their lives without really considering or worrying about such things, even when their lives were touched by them. A child climbing a tree was so completely and utterly normal that to Freya it seemed near mythical.

She gave a small laugh. "How did you fall?"

"I didn't grab on properly." The girl seemed reasonably resigned to her accident, even though she couldn't have been more than seven years old.

"She shouldn't have been climbing," her mother said, her lips a thin line of disapproval.

Freya saw the green band around the sleeves of both of the girl's parents at the same time she observed its absence on their daughter's clothing.

"Dannis, children will climb things," the girl's father said hurriedly, casting a worried glance at Freya.

Pious girls were encouraged to be graceful and elegant in their movements so as to reflect the Goddess. This meant that as a young child, Freya had often been scolded for climbing trees. Boys were allowed to get away with more, although only those who trained as fighters were truly encouraged to run, climb, and jump. The Kade were not so restrictive, allowing children of either sex to do as they pleased provided they prayed with the rest of the Kade community. Freya could only assume that the comment from the girl's mother was a slip, the old ways ingrained into her coming through – indeed, as they were in Freya, although she had hidden them for a long time. She knew too that the father's amendment was out of fear that Freya may think exactly what she did. Her stomach twisted as she realised it was very likely he thought she may inform on them.

She sighed. It seemed that even a girl climbing a tree was a part of this.

"Are you in pain?" she asked.

The girl shook her head.

"Are you sure?" Freya put a hand on the girl's arm. She couldn't help herself. She mended the bone a little. Not enough for it to be obvious, but enough for the break to heal quickly; to ensure that the family would be away from the Centre when the Resistance made their move against the Kade.

The girl nodded, beaming up at her with an innocent sincerity.

As she walked in the door of her home, the gentle dark of the just-fallen evening behind her, she realised Symon wasn't there. Despite her gratification at the respite from his presence, the house felt strange without him in it. Freya contemplated beginning on dinner but decided against it. To say that she didn't cook very well was a generous understatement. The only times she was of any use in the kitchen was when Symon directed her with the most precise of instructions.

So she went instead into her workroom – the part of the house that was truly hers – and busied herself by going through her notes and looking through her remedies to see if there was any room for improvement. She considered reorganising the Centre's work roster, something that nagged at her with the sense that it could be better but hadn't yet resolved itself in her mind, but she couldn't see the point of it. In a few days, everything was going to change anyway.

Sudden footsteps in the hall made her jump, then relax when she realised it was only Symon. She left her work to greet him.

"You're home early," he observed, giving her a quick kiss. The domesticity of it all made her feel strange.

"Late night last night," she said, trying to make her voice light and unconcerned.

"Have you eaten?"

She shook her head. "We should hire someone so you don't have to cook all the time," she told him. "Gods know we can afford it." Immediately, she wondered at herself, at the suggestion to make a plan for a future that she wasn't even certain would see her still in a position to afford a cook – or still be joined to Symon.

"I told you, I just don't like the idea of someone else being in here."

"But many Kade have people working for them," she pointed out.

"We *are* Kade, Freya," Symon said, a slight edge to his tone.

She stared at him for a moment, surprised yet again by his vehement insistence. "Of course."

"Freya, you are committed to the Kade, aren't you?" He stopped his trek to the kitchen to look at her.

"What do you think?" she snapped. "We've had this conversation so many times, Symon. It's almost as though you don't believe me."

His eyes widened slightly in surprise. "Freya—"

She cut him off as the coals that she had woken that day to find within her roared into flames. "I'm sick of feeling as though not only is the rest of the world testing my loyalty, but as though you are, too." Her voice rose, and a shrill edge crept into it.

"I'm not—" he protested, but again she wouldn't let him finish.

"I've done everything perfectly for the past six years. I've been promoted, I've worked hard. What more do you possibly want of me to prove my loyalty, to prove that I am the citizen you want me to be? I have done *everything*, Symon. *Why do you keep questioning me?*" She was all but shouting at him.

She expected him to shout back. But Symon didn't shout. Symon never shouted. He looked at her, his eyes so dark that they were like black pools, his face an unmoving mask.

"I'm sorry that you think that." His voice was so soft that it slipped into the echoes of her shout. "But you and I didn't choose for the world to change. We did choose to survive in it, and survive well. That means that we do have to live looking over our shoulders. The reason I keep asking you where your loyalties lie is because something's changed about you in the past year and I don't know what it is. But if the woman to whom I am joined isn't committed to this, it's my skin on the line. So maybe rather than getting angry at me, you should get yourself together." Throughout his speech, he did not raise his voice at all.

When she didn't reply, he reached out and grasped her wrist. She wasn't as surprised by the strength in his fingers as she was by the fact that he actually grabbed her. The idea flashed quickly through her mind that she could kill him with just a thought. It would be as easy as breathing. But the idea that had been evoked by her anger at him for daring to grab her receded as quickly as the anger itself.

"Freya, I need to know if you're still in this with me." He looked at her. There was an intensity on his face that wasn't of anger or desperation. She wasn't quite sure what it was.

Freya took a breath. "I'm still in this with you." She tried to pull her hand free from his grasp but he tightened his grip.

He looked at her for one more long moment then uncurled his fingers from her arm. She fought to not take the step back that she so desperately wanted. "Dinner," was all he said, moving into the kitchen.

Freya followed him in, silent, inwardly in turmoil. There was something deeply disquieting about lying so barefacedly to someone, even despite her anger with him. She wondered if Symon had seen the lie. Her suspicions about his status as an informant resurfaced as she watched him methodically prepare the food for dinner. She wondered if he would turn her in if he decided she had become a liability in his quest to curry a favoured position among Kade society. Regardless of whether or not he was an informant, though, she had told him something knowing full well that it wasn't true, knowing full well that her lie would very soon be revealed. And he appeared to trust her, even care about her.

"Symon?" she ventured.

He paused his chopping to look at her. "Yes?" He tilted his head to one side questioningly. In his gaze was none of the wariness that customarily preceded a fight.

Freya found herself unable to meet his gaze. "I'm sorry."

"What for?" He put the knife down and crossed the small distance between them, and she hated herself in that moment with a passionate intensity.

"I'm just...sorry." Freya hugged her arms around herself.

He took her face in his hands and gently kissed her – a display of tenderness that she had almost never received from him. Then he went back to making dinner for them.

TWELVE

It was with some degree of uncertainty that Freya knocked on the door of Ashtyn's shop two days later. In the moments between her knock and him opening the door, Zarech's face came into her mind, as it had many times in the past few days. She wondered what he would say to the guilt and nervousness that churned within her during the moments when the hungry flame demanding her rage be expressed was not burning her away from the inside. She wondered what he would say about a lot of things: lying to Symon who, like most in Oranis, was entirely unaware of what was about to take place across the city; what the Resistance success could mean for her and her relationship with Symon; and of course, the issue that had ignited the coals of anger and action within her, the fact that she could kill with her ability. For all the games he had played with her and the misdirected truths he had dangled in front of her, she had ultimately emerged from knowing Zarech with a better sense of herself and certainty in the choices she made. She didn't know how to think of herself: killer, fighter, crusader, or something far more murky than the crisp definitions attached to such labels, and she couldn't help but feel Zarech, who had gone from man of the Goddess to murderer, may offer some help in untangling the nuance the world required of those who passed through it. In short, waiting for the uprising to start had been hard, had given her too much time to think, and that had somehow driven her to Ashtyn's door. When he answered the door and saw her, puzzlement creased his face. She thought about leaving, but found no way to do so without looking as though she had lost all reason.

"What are you doing here?" he asked, stepping back so she could enter the store.

She walked into the shop, remembering that the last time she was there, she had been coming as Ashtyn's lover. "I just wanted to talk to someone," she said.

The store was almost unchanged: the table and chairs for Ashtyn's meetings with clients sat in the same place, the sharp smell of metal and polish permeated the air. Only the pieces on display had changed.

"Well, you know that I'm always here to talk if you need to," he told her, wiping his hands on his apron.

"Oh, sorry, I didn't think you would be working," she said hurriedly. She seized the excuse and prepared to leave.

"It's fine," he assured her.

"Please, don't stop on my account." She stood awkwardly, uncertain of whether or not she should simply leave. Part of her wanted to flee – the part that had only made itself known after Ashtyn answered the door. But part of her really wanted to stay.

"Freya, it's fine," he said firmly, ending all thoughts of departure. "Do you want something to eat or drink?"

She shook her head.

"Come upstairs anyway." He led the way to his living space on the floor above. It was as she remembered it: the large windows letting in the light, the beautiful furniture, the air of complete serenity. Ashtyn hung his apron on a peg near the stairs and, after moving aside some papers, sat down on a couch. She remained standing, looking around the room. Ashtyn regarded her expectantly. "Did you want to stay standing?" He sounded amused.

In response, Freya perched on the edge of the couch.

"Don't get too comfortable," he warned her, a half-grin twisting his mouth.

She smiled and edged down so that she was properly sitting on the couch. "I mostly just didn't want to be around Symon today," she confessed.

"That's...who you're joined to?" Ashtyn said slowly.

"I never told you his name," Freya said in sudden realisation. It wasn't guilt that seeped through her so much as a sense of the bizarre. Ashtyn and Symon belonged to separate parts of herself. She felt as though Symon and Ashtyn didn't live in the same world. In a way, they didn't.

"I never cared to find out," he replied. "Why don't you want to be around him?"

She was grateful for Ashtyn pushing the conversation forward. She didn't want to focus on the time in which they had been lovers. She didn't want to re-open the hurt of his betrayal, the hurt of not being able to trust her own judgement, especially when they seemed to be beginning to move past it.

"Because two evenings ago I lied so completely to his face. I told him everything was going to be all right and I know that it won't be. I know that tomorrow, everything changes." In truth, her rage with Symon had been caused by the collision of her two worlds. She hadn't really known what to do when she needed to lie to him, and the only way she knew how to respond was with anger at him for putting her in such a position.

"How do you feel about the woman you killed?" The bluntness of his question threw her more than anything else, but she was grateful he asked it.

"I feel as though I should feel more upset about it." She clasped her hands in front of her and looked down at them. She had been taught to view her hands as tools to fix people, to snatch them from death rather than send people to the divine realm before it was their time. But they looked exactly the same as they always had, just a pair of ordinary hands.

"But you're more upset about what happened with Symon." It wasn't a question.

"We've spent nearly seven years together, Ashtyn," she said softly.

"That's a long time."

"I feel like I'm betraying him."

"You are," he told her.

"Well, I'm glad we've settled that," she said, something akin to dry humour in her voice. "What about when you and I..." She trailed off, not wanting to explicitly reference their brief time as lovers. She didn't like the label, the connotations, or indeed the finality of using the past tense.

"He joined with you and together you did what really, no other Pious have done: you made it in Kade society. You did that because the two of you were of the same mindset. Now you've changed your mind and you know he won't join you. What happened between us was a betrayal, yes, but it's more of a poor reflection on you than him. Plotting to overthrow the leadership, though, that's something that, if discovered, throws a stain of suspicion and scorn onto him that would never go away. They're different kinds of betrayal," he said.

While not strictly true – the Kade penalty for infidelity was brutal – he did have a point. The penalty for plotting to overthrow the Kade was a lot worse.

"You aren't making me feel better," Freya replied.

He laughed. "I'm sorry." He put his head between his hands and laughed some more.

"It's not funny!"

"I know." He held up his hands in apology while he composed himself.

She waited patiently until he had finally stopped erupting into little giggles.

"You're right. And that's why I feel bad. You know, for someone who didn't even know Symon's name, you were quite insightful."

"I don't have to know him to understand his position."

She sighed. "Do you think we're doing the right thing?"

He raised an eyebrow. "It's a bit late to be asking this now."

"Don't worry, I made my choice." Freya reached out to fiddle with the papers strewn across the couch in the space between them, unwilling to look at his face.

"So why are you asking?" He gently tugged the papers away, forcing her to glance up. She found him looking at her. Something about it reminded her of the way in which Symon occasionally looked at her. Except Symon made her feel as though he was trying to know what she was thinking. Ashtyn made her feel as though he was trying to *understand* what she was thinking.

"I am doing this because of Her, because I can't live in service to a people that would let my Goddess die. The problem is that in saving Her, a lot of people will be hurt. I thought at one stage that, by rising up, we could make sure that fewer people would come to harm. But now I don't know which way leads to that outcome. I just don't know." The green of his eyes pulled the words from her. Speaking honestly felt good.

"So this is about the Goddess, then?" His voice betrayed nothing of his thoughts and the snare of his eyes distracted her from being able to notice how his face might give him away.

"Yes. No. It's not that simple." She put her head in her hands. Once she had thought for a moment, she looked back up to him. "As a healer, I'm bound to save whoever comes to me needing help. If I must stand by while my own people are eradicated, I feel as though I may as well slit the throat of every sleeping Pious myself."

"And the Goddess?"

"She only lives while we live to worship her. She's our *god*, Ashtyn, and the Kade and their gods want her to die." Freya lightly slapped her hands on her thighs for emphasis.

"What if you didn't know that she exists?" he challenged.

"But I do, and that in some ways that makes all the difference. That's my cause, to protect her and her people. Pious and the

Goddess, they're linked – if one dies the other may as well. That's what I'm willing to risk my life for."

"I can't argue with that." He stood up. "I want an infusion. Would you like one?"

She nodded.

He came back a short while later and handed her a ceramic mug. Companionable silence coated the room as they sipped. The last time she had felt so comfortable with someone had been with Ashtyn, too.

"Why were you working?" she asked eventually.

"What do you mean?"

"Why were you working when everything changes tomorrow? I mean, all this—" she gestured to the room around her " —may be lost in the fighting."

He smiled and it lit up something inside her. "You aren't the only one who's scared about tomorrow, you know."

He laughed at the expression his comment brought to her face.

"I thought this was what you'd been waiting for."

"That doesn't make it less frightening," he said. Nothing about his demeanour would suggest he felt any trepidation about what would happen the next day. But, she supposed, he would have to be a fool to not be at least a little afraid.

"I'm glad you understand." She gave him a shy smile.

"Wait here one moment."

He left the room without waiting for her to answer and re-turned holding the laastram he had made for her. She stared at the series of metal bands joined by the fine chain.

"You should wear this tomorrow," he said.

She held her hand out and he gently deposited the delicate work in her outstretched fingers. She turned the beautiful rings over in her hands, looking at the craftsmanship as she had done so many cycles before. It was as beautiful as she remembered.

He cut her off as she opened her mouth to say she couldn't accept it. "I made it for you, I want you to have it."

She ran her thumb over the smoothness of the metal. It had begun to warm in her hands. She would have expected it to drown her in sorrow and the regret of remembering how desperately she had loved him, but instead the laastram only seemed to resonate with a sense of rightness within her. Even so, she wasn't certainly she could accept his gift. "Are you sure?"

"I wouldn't want anyone else to have it. And it may come in use tomorrow. I like the idea that it may help you." The laastram's dual use as a meditative device during Pious prayer and as a form of protection in battle had made it a symbol of Pious defiance during the Kade takeover. There was something poetic about Freya wearing one during the uprising.

"Do you remember what we need to do tomorrow?" Ashtyn's question moved the mood on, reminding them both of the task ahead. To become mired in sentiment would not serve them.

Freya nodded. Makkyd's instructions had been relayed to her the day before by a runner. They were as cryptic as ever, but she knew Makkyd had created a part for her to play that would be explained when the time was right. Besides, she knew enough about her intended purpose in the world after the uprising: to organise the healers, to keep that aspect of daily life running as smoothly as possible.

"Ashtyn?" she ventured.

"Mmm?" He looked at her over the rim of his mug with a lazy docility.

"Would you mind if I stayed here tonight?"

Surprise seized his features. "Why?"

"I don't want to be in my house tonight. It just doesn't seem right." She looked at the laastram in her hand rather than at him. She was too scared that he may say no.

He spoke so quietly that she almost didn't hear him. "Of course you can stay."

They spent the rest of the day together. He showed her what he was making, they talked, they ate. The time melted away and, under different circumstances, Freya would have been intoxicated by the ease and comfort of his presence and the way she felt so known and seen by him. She didn't need to put on any version of herself. She didn't need to worry about what she said or did because he would never judge her for a careless word or gesture but instead liked all of who she was.

Night fell. Freya felt a stab of guilt as evening cloaked the city. Symon would wonder where she was. But she couldn't face the idea of being with him, of pretending that everything was normal, when she knew everything was about to change. Especially not when he may be harmed in the rebellion. Or really, when he learned of her part in it.

It was only when Freya yawned that she realised she hadn't actually thought about how they would sleep. The possibility of them sharing a bed, even simply to sleep, made her blush.

"You take the bed, I'll sleep out here," he told her as she stifled another yawn.

"No, it's fine, I'll sleep out here. I've done it before." She smiled at the memory of falling asleep on his couch, forced there because of a curfew. It had possibly been the first time since the takeover that she had felt safe.

"Really, it's no bother, Freya," Ashtyn insisted.

A part of her regretted that he was so insistent about it. Only when he effectively said no did she realise that she would have said yes.

He loaned her a loose shift which she changed into.

"Is everything all right?" He peeked cautiously around the door to make sure she'd finished changing into the shift. When he saw her sitting on the bed, he stepped into the room.

She smiled, only finding herself slightly self-conscious of her state of undress. She wondered if he noticed the thinness of the material or the way the shift barely covered the tops of her thighs. "Yes. Thank you, Ashtyn."

He leaned down to press a kiss to her forehead. His lips lingered against her skin as though he were trying to press into her feelings for which words were inadequate. "For you, Freya, anything," he told her before he dimmed the gas flame and left her to fall into a deep sleep.

The bells woke her. A few moments later, Ashtyn came into the room, cautiously tiptoeing in case she wasn't yet awake. She stretched and waved a good morning at him, her mind still clouded by sleep.

She dressed slowly in his bedroom, putting on the laastram first, then pulling a long-sleeved over-robe on so that nobody in the street would see it. Her fingers traced the outline of the laastram underneath the cloth. Putting it on made what was about to commence feel real. When she came out to the main room, he handed her a plate of food. They ate together in silence. She wondered if he was as nervous as she was. She didn't know if he was normally silent in the morning or if usually he would chat and laugh. It was once something she had assumed she would learn over the course of a life with him.

"Are you ready?" he asked her once they had finished eating.

She didn't answer. Her throat was too tight. She had only managed to eat because she knew he was watching her and she needed strength for the day ahead. Her response was to lead the way down the stairs and outside.

They walked through the streets together, their pace just a touch slow, as if they wanted to stretch out the moments in each other's company. Freya was all too aware that one or both of them could be killed in the events that were about to begin and she wanted to grasp every moment she had with Ashtyn. Freya wondered if anyone she knew would see her walking so companionably with a man who was not Symon when she should be in the Kade district at the morning prayers. An informant would greedily seize upon this, or Guardians would likely take her for further questioning. There was a certain lightness to how freely she defied the need for the care and consideration that had hung over her every day for the past six years. Such things didn't matter anymore.

As they walked, Freya couldn't help but notice the city anew as she sometimes did. Love for it swelled within her. The older, elegant pink-stoned buildings made from mezite stone, which could no longer be safely mined from the mountain on which the Followers of the Dark Gods had called their home, gave the city a warmth. The contrast between the white stones of more-modern buildings and the mezite made it visually delightful to walk through the city. The flourishes on the more-recent buildings – carvings on the peak of doorway arches, or the sculpted motifs on corbel tables that supported gutters on the rooftops – made it easy for the eye to slide along the buildings of Oranis. The soft early-morning light, when dawn had only just graced the world, brushed the buildings in the most tender illumination. Freya loved her city. Enough to fight to make it a better place.

They reached the building where they had been told they would receive their final instructions. Standing outside it, Freya took a breath. Ashtyn had asked her if she was ready and she hadn't answered because she wasn't certain that she was.

Ready or not, though, the uprising was about to begin.

THIRTEEN

Freya's group made good time through the streets on their way to the Healing Centre. Just as Freya was beginning to think they would reach their destination without encountering any obstacles, they rounded a corner to find a troop of Guardians waiting for them. There was no opportunity to run or hide. But those thoughts didn't cross her mind. There was only the urgent, pressing need to fight for her survival. To her surprise she wasn't cut down in the first few exchanges. Astrom's endless training was proving its worth, as was the laastram on her left arm. She was struck there twice. Both times the bands saved her from the bite of a blade's keen edge. She ducked underneath a Guardian's swing, using her momentum to hook her staff around his legs and dump him on the ground. A quick rap to the head left him unconscious.

She turned, raising the staff in the expectation that someone else was coming at her, but nobody did. Stillness and silence returned to the street.

The fight had lasted only a few minutes, but Freya felt as though it had dragged on for hours.

"Is everybody all right?" she called out to the rest of her group. In the sudden quiet, her voice echoed off the stone buildings and streets.

Two of the company escorting her had sustained injuries serious enough to warrant taking a moment to attend to them. She pulled bandages from the healer's bag strapped to her back. The use of her ability around anybody who was unaware of the abilities of the faithful was strictly prohibited on Makkyd's orders. It was why she hadn't used her ability to incapacitate the Guardian she'd been fighting when she there had been an opening for her to do so. Makkyd said ensuring the Kade did not know what sort of advantage the Resistance had was vital. But that wasn't the only reason.

"I don't want us to rule by fear," Astrom had said to Freya after Freya asked her about the order.

"Do you really think people would be afraid of us if they saw us using our abilities?" Freya had asked, listening with half an ear as Makkyd gave instructions on how she wanted the food in Guardian headquarters to be dosed with barat to incapacitate as many of them as possible.

"You think if we display what most would call magic gained by some deal with a dark god while we, the Pious Resistance, take the city, the Third Country people will find us unthreatening?" Astrom punctuated her question with a stare that inferred she had a very low opinion of Freya's intelligence at that moment.

She held Astrom's gaze until they both broke into poorly muffled snorts of laughter.

"I see your point," Freya said.

Any further discussion had been terminated by a glare from Makkyd, who waited until they fell silent before she continued outlining instructions for how she wanted the aqueducts to be secured.

"While I'm tending to Mish and Selim, what are we going to do about them?" Freya asked as she bandaged a wound on Mish's shoulder, inclining her head toward the Guardians who lay either sprawled on the ground or held down by Resistance members.

"We have our orders," Sek, one of the weaver twins who had participated in Makkyd's rescue, said. He removed a length of rope from a bag slung across his back and began to tie up the Guardians. The winces of those who were still conscious led her to suspect that Sek's knots were viciously tight. Her empathy for their discomfort was overridden by the security of knowing there was little chance they could escape. He tied them together in a line, even securing the unconscious Guardians. Two were left on the street, pronounced dead. A sharp tug on the rope jerked those who were awake to their feet. "You can carry your fallen comrades," Sek told them.

It left the Guardians unable to fight back, as every unconscious Guardian needed at least two of their comrades to carry them. Freya had to admire the vicious efficiency.

"I should examine them," Freya said, looking at the congealing blood on the face of one Guardian. Brown eyes stared back, shining with anger despite the pain that carved lines into the skin around her eyes.

"If you really want, once we've taken control of the Centre. But not here in the street," Sek replied.

If she had really wanted to, Freya could have overridden him. This was her mission. But he was right. They didn't have the time to waste. Makkyd's plan required as much of a simultaneous strike as was possible, with groups flowing out across the city to capture key buildings or structures. Freya's task was to take her own Healing Centre. From there, once the Resistance captured the city, she could viably claim control of the healers across the city. She felt a small thrill of unease at the prospect of walking into the building and announcing to everybody within it – everybody who had worked underneath her – that she was seizing the Centre for the Resistance. She stopped herself from speculating on how her people would react. They had to get to the Centre first and it was entirely likely they'd encounter more Guardians along the way. Of course, coming across Guardians meant fighting them. It was by no means a guaranteed path to the Centre, especially as the bells signalling a curfew had already rung, presumably as the Resistance's first attack had been discovered, before falling quiet. Makkyd had outlined a plan for seizing the bell towers, sending people ahead of time to silence them. "I'm so sick of those stupid things," Makkyd had admitted. Freya grimly agreed.

It was unfortunate that not all the towers had been seized in time to stop any warning being sounded, but such things couldn't be helped. It just meant they had to be even more careful as they moved across the city.

Few people were on the street. The sounds of fighting reinforced the bells' message – both their earlier sounding and the way they had been so ominously cut off – and there was something about the atmosphere in the city that dissuaded people from coming out onto the streets. The air was too still, too tense. Certainly the whole of Oranis seemed to be holding its breath. Freya wondered how many people had been waiting for this, expecting this, and for how many an uprising was a complete surprise.

The Healing Centre was open. Of course it was. Not only was keeping it open a testament to the power and authority of whoever controlled it, but it was a place of healing. There was an obligation incumbent upon any healer within it to help the wounded. And there would be plenty of wounded today. Freya just hoped that the healers in the Centre would remember that obligation.

Two Guardians stood by the front entrance, tense and alert. Each looked nervously down the stairs that led to where they stood. The group of Resistance members huddled together in a narrow alley nearby, off to the right of the entrance. It was the perfect place for someone to stand if they wanted to see the entrance but didn't want to be seen themselves. In the many reports that Freya had been asked to write detailing the Healing Centre's points of vulnerability in the event of an attack, she had never identified the alley. Mish, who had been designated her second-in-command, held a knife to the throat of one of the Guardians.

"If any of you speaks..." She left the threat hanging in the air.

Freya had always thought the Guardians' loyalty to the Kade was absolute, that they were utterly, dogmatically, willing to sacrifice themselves without thought if it meant protecting the Kade. But she wasn't so sure anymore. None of them spoke. Some looked down at their feet, some simply glared at the Resistance members around them, and some looked at them with expressions that could have been curiosity.

"How do you want to do this?" Sek asked her.

She chewed her lip, thinking for a moment. Over the cycles she had run the Centre, she had contemplated all the ways in which it might be taken. In the back of her mind, whenever she conducted her rounds of the Centre, had always been an appraisal of the places an invading group may easily pass through or be slowed, of how the building full of people might be quickly taken, and how those people could be moved to one place. The insistence on her daily rounds had been to ensure everything ran well, yes, but it had also been done in service of a darker purpose that was now coming to the fore.

"Let me go first. They'll hesitate to attack me." She handed her staff to one of the others. Any weapon was too conspicuous. She would never get even halfway to them with it.

"And then?"

"Remove them. Two of us should be enough." The coldness of her language surprised her. No, not the coldness, the ruthless-ness. "If you can, please don't kill them," she added, her gaze fall-ing on Mish's knife.

Sek's lips pursed in what she could only take as disagree-ment. She chose to ignore it. He could disagree with it all he liked, the directive needed to be given. She would not have lives need-lessly taken, especially not near a place of healing. And certainly not near *her* place of healing.

"Count to twenty-five." She straightened herself, pulled her sleeveless tunic so that it sat slightly straighter on her, and walked out of the alley toward the Centre. She wore the laastram on her left arm, a brown sleeveless tunic rather than her healer's robes, and her hair was fully pinned up. She could not have looked any more different from a member of the Kade leadership. But she walked with authority and that was a powerful thing.

The Guardians turned to regard her as soon as she walked into their field of vision.

"Is the building secure?" she called out to them as though nothing were different about her appearance, as though she had every right to be there.

The authority in her voice had them responding before they even had time to consider that her clothing signalled something was wrong.

"Yes, my lady. We have people on every floor and two at every entrance." Exactly as her own plan had directed in the instance of a threat to the Centre or the city.

As she drew nearer, she realised one of the Guardians was the sweet-faced Sord. A knife entered her heart as he looked at her and smiled. How he was able to smile at her so openly, despite the events of the day, she couldn't fathom.

"My lady, you should come inside. The streets aren't safe," he called, the familiar furrow of concern appearing across his forehead.

She couldn't help herself. "What about your family, Sord? Are they safe today?"

"They should be. I sent a runner to my sweetheart telling her to stay indoors."

His companion looked at Freya closely. "Why are you wearing..." The end of his sentence was cut off as his gaze shifted to focus on a point behind Freya. She didn't need to look behind her to know that two members of the Resistance were hurtling toward her. She didn't stop to speculate on who it was, but instead broke into a sprint herself, launching herself at the Guardians.

Sord and his companion – Freya knew him by sight but had never chatted with him like she did with Sord – were too surprised to do much. Her arrival had made them relax, distracted them so that it required a few extra, vital seconds for them to reach for their weapons, let alone draw them. Even though there was still several lengths to go between them, she reached the top of the stairs only just as their positions had shifted and their hands had wrapped around the weapons at their waists. She didn't so much aim as crudely launch herself at Sord. Her ascent had left her without a clear stance on the ground, so she didn't knock him from his feet as she had envisaged in the half-formed idea in her mind. They went stumbling backward together.

A moment later she heard the thud of contact as the second Guardian was taken down.

Despite his innocence, Sord was a trained Guardian. And that meant he was quick and dangerous. He turned so that she fell past him and he could free his weapon. Freya dropped down so that she didn't fall flat on her face and pivoted, her palms slamming into the ground so that she could spring back up. The first thing Astrom had taught her was how to fall. Sord brought his weapon up and stood over her, his stance wide, ready for an attack.

"Get inside, my lady," he said.

Freya realised he still didn't think she was a threat. A bitter taste settled around her tongue.

"Sord, put down your weapon," she told him quietly.

She couldn't quite see past him but she could see the legs of the two Resistance members as they faced Sord.

"I must defend you and the Centre," the young man said obstinately. He bent his knees, preparing for action.

"There are three of us, Sord," she said.

It took him a moment to comprehend what she was saying. She saw the way the shock made his knees sag, the way his body slackened, then tensed, as he processed this news. It was without thought that she reached out and touched his leg, hearing his life-song flow into her mind as she did so. It only took only a moment to dim it enough and she pulled her hand back as he crumpled to the ground so that nobody would see she had touched him. She knew that she shouldn't have used her ability but the thought of Sord being killed was too much to bear.

Sek stepped over to look down at Sord's form. "Neat," he said simply, turning and waving to waiting Resistance members.

"Is he alive?" Enna, one of the other Resistance members, asked. She looked curiously down at the Guardian who looked even younger in unconsciousness. As a more junior member of the Resistance, she wasn't aware of the abilities of the faithful and was obviously trying to determine how Freya had incapacitated him.

Freya's nod was the only answer she gave, declining to respond to the unanswered question of what she had done to render Sord unconscious. She placed a hand on the young Guardian's brow to ensure he hadn't hurt himself in the fall. "He won't stay asleep for long," she cautioned, relieved by what she heard.

Sek grunted, hefting the young man's prostrate form as the rest of their group, complete with captive Guardians, finished their trek up the stairs. They paused to allow him to take the trailing length of rope from the line of Guardians and tie up Sord with it.

Freya went over to the other Guardian, but there was no need; he was dead. Sek had obviously felt he had to kill the Guardian. Irritation flashed within her at the carelessness of the killing, but she knew he would point out it was better than losing one of their own, and she definitely agreed with that. The body was quickly pulled inside the atrium out of sight of anyone on the street. From there, the group pushed open the doors to the main foyer of the Healing Centre.

As they strode in, everybody in the foyer turned to look the twenty Resistance members and their Kade prisoners. Freya stepped into the centre of the space before anyone could break the stillness which surprise had spun. All eyes turned to her and anticipation fell on the area like darkness. She knew every single worker there. She knew whether they had families, their specialties, the tasks they hated doing. She had made sure that she knew. And now she knew what it looked like when they realised that she wasn't who they thought. But she didn't have the luxury of unease. Ignoring their stares, she nodded to the Resistance members. In twos they silently peeled off, each duo going to a different point in the Healing Centre to secure it. She had told them where to go, showing them a plan of the Centre. They knew what to expect when they reached their destinations. Two Resistance members took up a guard inside the foyer, and Mish remained a few steps behind Freya. Even as the Resistance members slipped through the foyer to take the Centre for the Resistance, the people watching Freya said nothing, waiting for her to explain. She had worked hard to earn their respect – even if it was begrudging in some cases – and that respect had kept people still while they awaited an explanation.

"We don't want to hurt anybody, but I am afraid that we will if necessary," she said, her voice carrying clearly through the stillness. "Please do not attempt to leave the building." Despite her own uncertainty, her voice was perfectly even. She was grateful for that.

"So what should we do?" a healer named Myrv asked. There was a hint of challenge in his voice. He was Kade. Suddenly he was the enemy, when only the day before, he had carried out her every directive without question. Then again, perhaps he had always been the enemy, she just hadn't known.

"Are you going to try to cause trouble?" Freya locked eyes with him, her face an uncompromising mask. She willed him to drop his gaze. He held her stare for a long time but finally he looked down.

Only when she was sure he wouldn't say anything did she answer his question. "You will need to stay here. Once they have secured the building, my people will bring everybody into the foyer. I'll tell you more then." She didn't wait for his reply, instead walking straight to the string of bound Guardians who had been stood against the wall nearest the door. Freya could only assume it was the sight of these disarmed Guardians that had prevented anyone from trying to overpower her group. The spectacle of authority figures so clearly neutered was powerful enough to keep people from violence even though they outnumbered Freya and her people. Sek and another member of the Resistance whose name Freya didn't know watched over them. She wondered what they would do if the Guardians made a threatening movement. Would they be swiftly executed? Knocked unconscious? The idea of any brutality being exacted in front of the foyer full of people was not one with which she was comfortable, but she knew Sek would justify such violence with the claim it ensured no others were hurt. She hated that the claim had merit.

Sord was awake, looking around the foyer groggily. She crouched down next to him and peered into his face. She hadn't really known what to expect when she had thrown him into sleep, as she'd never done it before. But she had needed to do something before Sek could justify killing him, too.

Sord's eyes gradually gained more focus.

"Can you hear me?" she asked, putting a hand on his arm. She could feel his lifesong, strong and vibrant. It surprised her how glad she was to know he was all right.

He blinked twice more and then his gaze cleared. "Healer Kuch...what happened? Why am I tied up?" His use of her formal title made him seem even younger. It sent a knife of guilt through her.

"You're tied up because you're a Guardian." She spoke in the tone she reserved for patients who didn't realise just how sick they were.

"But why? We haven't done anything wrong."

"Sord. There's an uprising going on. Pious are reclaiming the city." She watched as her words trickled into his comprehension. Before he could say anything, she added, "And I'm a part of it." It was a terribly painful thing to tell him just how deep the extent of her betrayal went.

His face transformed into a frieze of hurt. He even recoiled from her.

"Sord..." She felt helpless, uncertain of what she should say.

He turned his head aside – the only definite movement he could make given he was tied up.

"I'm sorry," she said softly.

"Me too," he whispered, still refusing to look at her.

FOURTEEN

The Resistance quickly secured the Healing Centre. The information Freya had provided gave the Resistance members the upper hand, taking the routes she directed to quickly and quietly sneak up on the Guardians at their posts. Rendering the Guardians unconscious from behind or putting a knife to their throats before they even realised they were being attacked saved their lives as well as the lives of Resistance members.

People began to trickle into the foyer as the wards were secured, all in accordance with Freya's plan. Very ill patients were permitted to stay in their beds, watched over by Resistance members who replaced the Guardians across the building. She had considered for a long time how to deal with the sickest patients and concluded that she couldn't move them if they were unconscious or very frail. It was the only serious weakness in her plan that she could find, but she would not compromise on this.

The people in the foyer sat on the floor, various states of resignation and boredom in their postures. When they spoke, it was to each other, and quietly. Someone produced dice from somewhere and started playing with the person next to them. Occasionally they scoffed or laughed at each other as the dice favoured or frowned upon them. Freya was amazed at their placid acceptance of the situation and the lack of concern they appeared to be showing. The resilience of the human spirit to take simple enjoyment in the moment touched her. Although, she supposed, it looked as though they may be in for a long wait. They may as well do something to pass the time.

As new people arrived from other parts of the building, a stir went around the room, but it quickly petered out. The assembled group milled uncertainly, casting glances at Freya, the other Resistance members, and the trussed-up string of Guardians.

As more people crowded into the foyer, Freya couldn't help but put a hand to her staff for reassurance. She shook her head at the reaction. Here she was in a place of healing – *her* place of healing – and her first response when feeling uncertain was to ready herself for violence. She wondered what dark purpose rebellion was curling around her heart.

Her position next to the three Resistance members and the captured Guardians meant that while almost everybody who entered the space looked at her, nobody approached her. The space began to fill despite its cavernous dimensions. Much of the crowding was due to the wide berth people were giving Freya and her entourage. Some gave her approving nods, some glared at her; many just looked at her with curiosity. All of them stayed well away from her. She had always felt somewhat separate from other healers due to the manner in which her skill was regarded and sometimes envied. That had only become worse as she had been elevated through the ranks of healers to become a Master and then again to the position of running the Healing Centre. But the distinction had never felt so real until this moment. She did not speak with Sek or the other Resistance fighters but instead watched those who came in, noting their reactions, remembering what she knew about them all. She wondered what they thought about the Kade leadership and the downtrodden Pious. She wondered what they thought about rebellion. She wondered what they thought about her. But while the body and all its secrets were known to her, the mind was an entirely foreign land.

Finally, the trickle of arrivals slowed to nothing. The final Resistance member returned to report that they had secured their area. Satisfaction glowed within her at the fact that the Healing Centre had been taken with barely any bloodshed. She stepped forward, the action immediately pulling everybody's attention toward her. The relative silence of hundreds of suddenly attentive people within the small space, punctuated by occasional rustling, coughs, and throat clearing, descended.

Freya stood as tall as possible. Whatever uncertainty she felt, she would not allow herself to show it. This was *her* Healing Centre; she had addressed the same group of people before to give out instructions that she expected to be followed. This should be no different.

"Some of you may be aware of the discontent that has been present in the city recently." She used the same manner as when she was outlining a new procedure: detached, clear, calm. "Everything good that the Kade has done to which you might be able to point has been achieved through fear and bloodshed. And it hasn't even benefited that many people. Those of you in here who are Kade, can you remember what your lives were like seven years ago? Were they that much worse? I know that you used to be freer, that you didn't have to live in fear of what unknown brutality you may face for breaking laws and edicts based on your religion's guidelines. Are you truly happy living as we do now, in a city where everybody is afraid to linger on the streets? And my Pious brethren, how many of you are truly happy to worship gods that we did not choose but were instead forced to worship? To live a way of life that is not of your choosing or face the consequences not only to yourself, but to those you love the most dearly?"

She paused, giving time for her point to be considered but not so much time that someone may jump into the breach of silence and offer a rebuttal.

"We are taking back the city, nor simply for the Pious, but for every citizen of Oranis and the Third Country. We have taken the Centre and other parts of the city are even now being claimed by the Resistance. Anybody who wishes to join us, we welcome you.

For those of you who do not support the uprising, we understand. We will, however, have to ask you to not resist. I don't want any violence in here if it can be avoided. Any more violence." She glanced back at the captured Guardians to underline her point: violence would be met with violence. The Guardians glared back at her with impotent rage. All except Sord. He was looking resolutely down, his shoulders slumped in a posture of defeat and sorrow that tugged at her heart. She pushed the feeling aside and turned back to the crowd.

"Until the city is secure, the Centre will be locked down. Anybody who comes to our doors seeking aid will be admitted. This is a place of healing and I will never turn away anyone who asks for help. But I'm sure you understand why we can't allow you to leave.

"We want to create a better place. Nobody wants violence. But we can't keep living like this."

A ripple went through the room at the finality in her voice and she prepared herself for the questions that she knew were about to come. She had already decided she would only answer the first one. All engaging in a back and forth would do was weaken the authority she had only just created.

"What are we to do here, then?" a voice shouted.

"I'll have to ask you to stay here for a little while," Freya responded, her voice calm and soothing. She didn't wait to hear if there was a response to her words, or for someone else to press her. She strode out of the room, gesturing for Mish to follow her into the corridor.

Once she had gone far enough that she was certain nobody from the foyer could hear, she asked, "Do we have enough people to ensure the building is secure?"

"We could have fifty people, and if these people decide they really want to get out, we'd be in trouble. There's at least seven hundred people in this entire building – that includes patients, family members, and healers. That's a lot of people." Mish did not sound particularly concerned, although she definitely had a point; obedience was only created by the semblance of control and the ability to enforce it. As the Kade was learning now, if people were unwilling to submit to the authority their leaders claimed to possess, they had no power. There were a great many more of the people over whom they were trying to assert control than those seeking to do the controlling.

"That's not a great comfort." Freya frowned. She considered several possibilities, all of which had been envisaged over the time of her tenure in the Centre. Then she selected the one she had been favouring all along. "Let me speak with my people. There should be a hundred or so healers in the building – some will still be here from the previous shift – and fifty administrative workers. Once I'm in my rooms, send them to talk with me one at a time. I imagine that at least a few of them will be willing to support us. Those who do may be surprisingly helpful."

Mish's face betrayed nothing of whether she thought Freya's decision was too risky. Freya didn't know her well – they had trained together a few times and spoken enough for Freya to determine she was competent and someone she could envisage trusting. She liked that Mish didn't bother to question if she was certain. For as long as Freya had supported the Resistance, she had marked the staff at the Centre who she thought may be willing to support an uprising and those who would likely oppose it; often that was determined by whether they were Pious or Kade. But those were unconfirmed suspicions. Aside from her interrogation of Flen a few days earlier, she hadn't dared even hint at such questions when speaking to her people. So she needed to verify those guesses.

The entirety of the day slid by as she spoke with her people. Daylight fled the sky outside her windows and the city beyond was silent as night fell; the bells evidently remained in the hands of the Resistance. Freya was glad of it. She had grown to hate their sonorous invasion across the very air. She hated that they determined the beginning and end of the day. She hated that they called people to mandated the prayers. She heard from the people who came to speak with her that some of the Kade within the foyer chanted together as the last rays of light bled from the slice of sky visible from the high windows. Some of the Pious joined in. Most did not.

Food from the storerooms was brought out and distributed across the Centre. There was enough to last for at least a few days if necessary. Freya had prepared in that regard, too, ensuring the Centre had a significant store of preserved fruits and meats for this very moment. Mish offered her food but she refused it. She did not want to take any pause from speaking with the people who worked under her in the Centre. She wanted to continue through until the task was done. The unique type of fatigue which accompanied sitting for a protracted time seeped through her, but she pushed it aside as dusk turned into true night.

She was surprised by the number of both Kade and Pious who were eager to offer their support to the Resistance. She chose not to pry into their motivations – time alone did not permit it – but she nevertheless gained an impression of deep and vehement dissatisfaction with the Kade from far more people than she had expected. Makkyd had hinted at it but Freya had never truly believed her claim that a great many people did not wish to be ruled by the Kade, until now. Still, most were unwilling to cast their lot either way until the uprising's outcome was determined. She couldn't really blame them for that.

A few people refused outright to speak with her and some, but not as many as she expected, told her they would not co-operate with the Resistance. She was not surprised that Flen was among the latter.

Everybody who entered her rooms looked at her warily, as though she were a dangerous animal that would maul them at any moment. Her status as the arch-collaborator and the knowledge of her skill as a healer had always ensured distance between her and others, but this was something different. Now she was the twice-turned traitor.

For the most part, she considered the discussions a success. She had feared everybody would adamantly vow to oppose the Resistance and try to kill her.

Once she was finished she stood and allowed herself a moment for the exhaustion of all the day had asked of her to weigh on her. Then she sloughed it off and left the solitude of her rooms to continue the work still to do. Mish was waiting outside, a new plate of food in her hands. Freya accepted it with a murmur of thanks and listened to Mish's report of all that had transpired while she had been speaking to her people. Scuffles had broken out once or twice, but each time, their people had been quick and efficient in incapacitating the perpetrator. Those who were deemed a threat – which of course included the Guardians – were placed in unoccupied rooms in the contagion ward. It was on Freya's orders that the contagion ward be used for truly dangerous prisoners, but at Mish's report that they had been carried out, she was nevertheless reminded of the time she spent in such rooms tending Zarech.

She did not allow the emotions which the memory called forth to claim her but instead strode to the next task: going to look over those patients who couldn't be moved. They were being tended by those healers Freya believed were either true supporters of the uprising or who would never engage in any act of violence. Not only did she want to check the quality of care being given to the patients, but she also wanted to be seen engaging in the familiarity of her rounds among the wards. It was just one small way she could remind people that despite everything, she – and the Resistance – were committed to the citizens' wellbeing.

She found the quality of care not diminished at all, and allowed pride at her healers and their ability to not allow the circumstances to affect their work to swell within her.

She returned to the foyer which was now dark, the only light provided by the gas flames in the corridors outside, and the cool night sky flooding in from the high windows. Pillows and blankets had been brought in from the wards so people were comfortable sitting or lying on the floor. Freya looked out among the people and relaxed just a tiny bit. The Centre was secure; of that she had no doubt. As some people drifted off to sleep the eerie silence of the city at war with itself was even more obvious. It was hard to be stuck inside the Centre not knowing what was transpiring outside, but this was the part she had to play and she had done it well.

Freya sat on the floor near the front entrance. Two members of the Resistance sat on either side of the doorway, comfortably alert. Not for the first time, she considered how much training they must have undergone. Makkyd's penchant for secrecy left her ignorant of how the Resistance had recruited and trained their best fighters or for how long they had been training for this. Their skill suggested they had been training for many years.

The dark hours passed. Freya didn't – couldn't – sleep. Finally, she stood and walked along the narrow paths between the settled forms. She wasn't sure what she was hoping to achieve, but she was overwhelmed by the need to feel surrounded by people rather than alone up the front of the room. Her clothes snagged on something. Stopping, she saw that a child had tugged on her jacket as she passed by him. She crouched down.

"Are you the lady in charge?" the boy asked.

She nodded.

"How much longer will we be here for?"

In the darkness she couldn't tell his age but she was reasonably confident that he hadn't seen ten years. If he had been alive during the Kade takeover, he wouldn't be able to remember it.

"Where are your parents?"

He pointed to a sleeping form beside him. "She wouldn't tell me why we're here."

"It's complicated."

He bristled. "I'm nearly seven."

She smiled. At least he wasn't afraid of her like everybody else seemed to be. "Do you know who the Kade are?"

He nodded solemnly.

"And the Pious?"

He nodded again. "They used to worship the wrong god but now they don't."

"Well, not quite." Freya sat down. He moved over to make space for her. "Kade worship one group of gods. Pious worship a different god."

"Why?" Even in the darkness, she could see his eyes wide with the sort of curiosity unique to children.

"It's a long story. Are you sure you want to hear it?"

He nodded again in earnest.

Freya settled herself so that she was a little more comfortable and delved into the recesses of her memory to recite the story she remembered from her childhood. Her voice was soft, the cadence of her words falling along the way she remembered her father telling it to her. She hadn't felt so close to him in years. "Before our countries were formed, when the world was a place where fear and survival were the only concerns in the minds of people, the gods came and spoke to us.

"They showed us a great many things, and as they touched us, we touched them. We learned so much from them. We clothed ourselves, we armed ourselves, and we built cities to protect us from the terrors of the world. Life became more than simply blind survival. It became about enjoyment, about pleasure, and beauty, and laughter – things also shown to us by the gods. So we lived in accordance with the ways they taught us, and life was good.

"It is said that during this time, there was unprecedented peace between people, and between the gods, too. Then the gods looked at how good life was for us and hungered to be a part of our world, for while they are many things and very powerful in their own way, they don't have the same form as us. They wanted their own bodies to walk among us, to touch us, to feel the sunlight on their faces, the rain on their skin, and the wind in their hair. But to form their own flesh – flesh that can house the power of a god – is terribly difficult. The gods discovered that such things need a great deal of strength. So they began to gather their energy to try and take on a single form. They formed alliances amongst themselves, they ordered people to worship only them.

"Time passed, and people began to separate themselves depending on which god they worshipped. They still lived together but they began to live in ways that were different to one another. The gods picked their chosen few to speak with – they became the Ordained of each group. The differences in how the various groups lived became so different over time that the countries were formed according to these divisions. Then even the countries themselves became divided. Here, in the Third Country, we are the Pious and the Kade. Some people worshipped the gods of the Kade and some people worshipped the Goddess. For many years, we lived together, different but peaceful." She faltered, unsure of how to explain the next, terrible part of the story to this child.

A voice from nearby chimed in. "And then one day, the Kade wanted more power. So they told the Pious they would have to live as the Kade did and worship their gods." Startled, Freya looked up. The figure of a man was sitting up, his posture intent in the way he was faced toward Freya and the child. The colourless shadows of the foyer robbed her of the ability to see if there was a green band on his sleeve or not. He nodded as she met his gaze.

"And now the Pious are unhappy with this," she said carefully.

"Because they think that their Goddess should be the one to become real?" the boy asked.

She hesitated. He was, of course, correct. But the truth of the story had long been forgotten by most of the world and made into mere myth. There was no certainty that it was all true, but without doubt there was more truth than many thought. "Well, in a way. Mostly it's because they want to be able to choose who they worship. But there are other reasons, too," she said.

"Like what?"

The same man chimed in again. "How the Pious and the Kade live is slightly different. But those small differences are significant to us. When we worship, how we worship, how we work, how we love. Even how we dress. It's not right to tell us to change all those things to worship gods we didn't choose."

The boy was silent. He bit his lip and looked down at the ground, clearly thinking. "Are people going to be hurt?"

Freya thought of the dead Guardians left lying on the ground that morning. They were somebody's family and they had been left unceremoniously on the street. Unable to find the words, she nodded.

"People shouldn't be hurt," the boy said.

From the dark again, the unknown man's voice came. "People have been hurt by the Kade for not living in accordance with their edicts. People were hurt when the Kade took over. People are always going to be hurt. It's about how many are hurt less by which action."

Another voice murmured an agreement.

From nearby, a woman spoke up, quietly but angrily. "Tell me that life isn't safer under the Kade, more prosperous. The Dual Accord got nothing done. We need one definite governing body to make decisions on behalf of the people. All the Accord achieved was incoherent laws and bad trade agreements with the other countries."

People began to wake at the sound of the talk and add their own opinions. Perhaps the shroud of darkness made those supporters of the Kade feel as though anonymity meant they could safely offer their perspective. Freya listened as quiet squabbles ebbed and flowed around her. The child looked around, not really listening to the content of the disagreements. She placed a hand on his shoulder. "There isn't one right way or decision," she told him. "But I had to do what I thought was right."

She stood up and spoke loudly enough to be heard above the rising volume of the whispered arguments.

"That's enough. It's done. There's no need for more discussion."

The room fell silent and she realised just how much she was feared.

She made her way back through the mass of prostrated forms to stand once again with the members of the Resistance by the door.

"You shouldn't have walked among them," Enna admonished her.

Having no real argument as to why she should have, Freya shrugged. "You can't regret what you've done – it's done," she replied. "You can only learn from it."

Day broke. Tendrils of light began to kiss the high windows, lightening the foyer. The pale gold of the sunrise bathed the room in hazy streaks. Even with several hundred people in the room, Freya was struck by the beauty of the building with its cream-coloured walls, high ceiling, and pink flooring. Oranis's reputation for having such beautiful buildings was well deserved. Freya just wished that the beauty of the city wasn't marred by the violence of its people.

"I'll go and check on the patients in the wards," she told Trush. She had wanted to at the very beginning of the evening, but the darkness could have concealed too much and nobody wanted to spare a guard from the foyer to ensure her safety.

As she left the room, she tried to find the child with whom she had spoken but he was lost amid the sea of people on the floor.

FIFTEEN

The tedium of waiting brought Freya's thoughts to places she would rather they not go. She wondered how the struggle for the rest of the city was unfolding. The lack of any attempt to take the Centre suggested the Kade had their hands full trying to keep themselves alive. But she had no way of knowing. She wondered how Ashtyn was faring. He had been tasked with securing the gildsmiths' district. That meant keeping people inside their homes or workshops so they didn't cause extra confusion. From the instructions Makkyd had given him, Freya discerned there was quite a bit of danger involved. Ashtyn couldn't round up all of the people scattered across the area rife with little alleys and countless workshops and stores; there was no single space large enough to hold them all, even if he did manage to locate them peacefully. It meant that he would be facing the possibility of assailants from every doorway and alleyway.

When her thoughts weren't occupied with worry for Ashtyn, they churned unpleasantly over Symon. She had no idea where he was – she had deliberately kept herself away from any way of knowing. She could only assume he would not greet the uprising with any joy. He had created a life in the Kade world and any change would threaten that. She wondered if he was worried about her – after all, she hadn't come home the night before the uprising. When she had gone to leave the Centre, she had paused on the steps as she was about to head home, and then her feet had simply taken her to Ashtyn's door. Even though Symon might not have

159

initially worried about her due to the many times she stayed in the Centre overnight, he surely would be worrying about her now. Even though she couldn't have in any way tipped him off about what was to happen, that she had not returned home the night before made her feel all the worse for her deception – all of her deception. The guilt left her feeling ill. Her thoughts and worries refused to resolve themselves, which only made her feel worse.

Freya tried to keep her mind busy by checking on the patients in the wards, but she didn't want to spend too much time there – it was good for the healers who she assigned to tend to the sick to feel as normal as possible so that they accepted the new leadership. So instead, she watched the people in the foyer as they lounged, spoke quietly to each other, or slept – many of them were, after all, sick. She moved listlessly, unable to speak with the people who were – for want of a better word – her prisoners, and unwilling to speak with the other members of the Resistance. By the end of the morning, she caught herself hoping that a scuffle would break out to disrupt the monotony. Waiting with nothing to do was something at which she was terribly inept. In truth, she hadn't expected there to be quite so much sitting and waiting associated with an uprising. She wanted to forget the thoughts that troubled her, not have time that made them seem all the louder.

It was a relief when the message came for her late in the afternoon. She was halfway through another round of the wards, undertaken out of desperation to actually do something.

She stepped into the corridor to speak with the runner. The deep yellow afternoon sunlight came in through the windows which faced the Centre's internal garden and made the entire corridor luminous.

"Astrom's been injured," the runner said without any preamble.

Freya swallowed her first response of unpleasant surprise. Makkyd had warned her that she may be called upon to heal the Resistance's leadership. Her value to the Resistance lay not in her ability to be a fighter who would win great battles but her capacity to put those who had fought back together again. For the Resistance leaders, Freya's abilities were to be used without reserve. Each of them, including Freya herself, was to perform particular roles in the aftermath of their victory. If any of them were to die they could certainly be replaced, but it would be unideal to say the least. So Freya's responsibility was to keep them alive. Still, she had hoped if any of the Resistance leadership did need her help, it was someone who wasn't a friend.

"I can leave right away," Freya said. She wasn't comfortable with the prospect of leaving the Healing Centre; it was hers and she couldn't believe it would be quite as secure without her in it. But she was glad to be given the excuse to leave the tedium of waiting, and her unwelcome thoughts.

Mish stepped forward, a healer's bag in her hand. Freya had no idea from where she procured it. "Take two of our people with you," she said.

Freya nodded. She didn't think she really needed three people – including the runner – to escort her, but she didn't want to waste time arguing.

Oranis was empty. Walking through the deserted streets felt as though she had been transported to a foreign land. She thought the tang of smoke tickled her nose, but she couldn't see any evidence of it in the sky.

Freya's eyes tracked the buildings they passed, her gaze lingering on the shuttered windows and closed doors. The buildings seemed unoccupied but Freya knew better. Almost certainly, a great many eyes were surreptitiously watching their passage through gaps in shutters. Oranis's inhabitants were waiting to see what the outcome of the uprising would be. It was exactly what most people had done eight years before. Freya had long since learned most people simply wanted to live their lives in peace, not die for some great cause. For a time, she had been one of them.

When the Kade had taken power, she had stayed indoors with the rest of her family, huddled with her sister as her parents spoke in worried murmurs. Her father hadn't been a hero who charged out to try to protect the Goddess' Children who were slaughtered, her mother hadn't run out onto the street to almost certainly sacrifice herself in one glorious show of defiance. Her parents had been ordinary people, worried about their safety and the safety of their two daughters. They locked their doors, shuttered their windows, and hoped they would be left alone as the Kade groups moved through the streets, claiming the city as theirs. The only reason Freya's family had died had been her sister, Rohana's, childish defiance many cycles later – an impulsive act made with a child's lack of understanding as to just how brutal the reprisal could and would be.

The emptiness changed the feel of the streets. Normally, they often seemed too narrow, filled with people and carts competing for space. Even when she walked home from the Healing Centre long after the sun had set, there was the occasional soul out – a night worker or a Guardian troop. Now, there was only the sound of their journey. It created a sense of malevolence which impressed upon her that if everybody else was too afraid to leave their buildings, then she too should be seeking shelter rather than walking so brazenly through dangerous streets.

The buildings seemed less beautiful without the bustle of people. She was forced to conclude that the city truly was only made wonderful by its inhabitants. Without them, the buildings were undeniably still a visual spectacle but they were lifeless, with none of the vitality and glow that the sound of everyday life lent to them.

"How much of the city have we secured?" she asked the runner.

"We definitely have the Pious district. On top of that, we have the artists' district. We have about half of the market, weavers' and the merchants' districts – including control of the merchants'

gate. In those areas, we've removed all Guardian patrols and secured borders."

"Borders?"

"Mostly we've blocked off the streets with whatever we can
find – dirt, rubble, even parts of buildings where necessary.
Should make it hard for a large group to get into the areas we control."

"How do we take the rest of the city?"

"If we take the governance district, we figure the rest of the
city should more or less fall – we may need to make an incursion
into the Kade district, but we'll see. That's where the fighting's
taking place now – near the halls of governance. The Guardians
and the Kade's elite forces have drawn back to buildings where
most of the Kade officials are holed up. We're working to keep
them isolated, break through the ranks. You know."

Actually, Freya didn't know. She wasn't a soldier, she knew
nothing of combat or of how to break through a building that was
under siege. All she really knew about was healing.

"How many of our people have we lost?"

"Not as many as we could have."

"Have we had any trouble within the areas we've secured?"

"For the most part, no. People are staying indoors, although
a few brave souls have tried to rush us."

"What happened to them?"

"From what I know, all were neutralised."

"What does that mean, exactly?"

"It means that our position is secure."

"Are we going to be attacked on our way to Astrom?" she
asked, casting a wary glance at the buildings. She could have sworn
that she glimpsed the fleeting adjustment of the shutter across one
of the windows. Her hands tightened around the staff she had
taken up on the way out. Suddenly, Mish's insistence on two
guards didn't seem so trivial.

"If we are, we fight them off."

Fortunately, Astrom had been fighting near Freya's Healing Centre. She had been tasked with overseeing the Resistance's incursion across the southern districts of the city; the merchants', builders', and artists' districts. Makkyd was coming in from the north, overseeing the attempts to secure the gildsmiths' and weavers' districts, as well as the Pious and Kade districts. Freya wondered what would happen if Makkyd were wounded. How would she get across the city to treat her, let alone reach her in time? The only thing she could assume was that Makkyd had a plan for that, too, and if Freya was needed, there was a way to get her safely through the city.

Within a short time, Freya and her escort reached the building where Astrom had been taken – a mason's workshop. Resistance fighters guarded every entrance, weapons drawn, wariness and even jumpiness evident in the way they scanned the streets. Freya knew many of them by sight as Astrom's employees. From what Freya had observed, they adored Astrom. She noted the splintered door and deduced they had broken in to get Astrom off the street.

The inside of the building was dark; the bright afternoon light did not penetrate the shutters and none of the gas flames had been lit. Items inside the workshop had been obviously pushed roughly aside as Astrom had been carried in. Incomplete stone pillars and tools were strewn about. One pillar lay broken in two. Freya was shown to a small back room, presumably a place for rest or refreshment. The door was closed and guarded by two people, both with weapons drawn.

"She's in here," one of the guards said, opening the door. "We bandaged her best we could. Her side..."

At her gesture, the guards moved aside for her to enter the small room.

"If I need anything, I'll call," she told them, shutting the door behind her. She could tell they would be of no help, even if she were working like any other healer; in such instances, a hovering audience was only unhelpful. But of course, she needed them out of the room to keep the miraculous healing she was about to perform on Astrom a secret.

The first thing which drew her attention was the ripped fabric on the floor. Presumably, it had been torn to form a makeshift bandage. Astrom was sitting on the ground, propped up against one of the walls, looking at her expectantly. A film of sweat coated her brow, but her eyes were alert and keen.

"Ah, you've come to visit me," Astrom said.

Freya knelt beside her friend, casting a professional eye at the bandage – if it could even be called that. Blood seeped through in an ugly brown-red splodge. "It was a little dull in the Centre," she replied. Lighthearted exchange was a healer's tactic of keeping patients distracted from their own pain and fear. Freya slipped into it with practiced ease.

Astrom's heavy breath might have been a chuckle. "Glad I could give you an excuse to leave."

"Did someone clean the wound before they wound this drapery around you?" Freya asked, trying to keep the disapproval from her voice.

"They wanted to, but I told them to leave you something to do. You know how I like to challenge you," Astrom replied, her words forced out on panting breaths.

"How kind of you. I'm going to have to take it off and it's not going to be comfortable," Freya warned.

Astrom nodded once to show she understood. She hissed in pain as Freya peeled away the dirty cloth from her friend's side.

The gash in Astrom's side was huge. The way her leg sat was, to Freya's trained eye, obviously broken, but it wasn't going to kill her. The wound in her side however... Her ragged breathing was the sound of a woman in a tremendous amount of pain, but Freya ignored it as she took inventory of her friend's condition.

"How on earth did you do this to yourself?" Freya asked.

"Tripped and fell," Astrom joked, her chest heaving with the effort of speaking.

"Clumsy of you."

She fell silent as she contemplated the extent of her friend's injuries. For a moment, the idea of healing one of her only friends filled Freya with panic. But then her training flowed through her, shutting down all emotion, and she focused on the body that was in front of her rather than the person inhabiting the torn and battered flesh. Freya put a hand near the wound in Astrom's side. She winced as the atonal sound of Astrom's lifesong struck her. The wound was long and deep, the largest that Freya had ever been required to heal with her ability. But the Resistance couldn't afford to lose Astrom, so Freya couldn't afford to fail in healing her.

It took her a long time. She carefully exerted her will over Astrom's damaged body, stemming the bleeding, healing the tissue, and sealing the wound. The extent of the damage was breathtaking and the delicacy of the work involved was beyond anything she could have envisaged.

Finally, Astrom's side was healed. Freya rocked back on her heels as she breathed deeply, recollecting her focus so that she could tend to Astrom's leg.

"That feels better," Astrom said. Her voice had smoothed out, the pain which bit through her words no longer there.

"What happened?"

"A group of Guardians managed to make it past our barriers. They jumped our patrol. Stupid of me not to expect that there would be at least a few Guardians who hadn't been poisoned by the barat we put in the barracks food. We lost two people. I had to fight two at once." Astrom put a hand to her side as she answered, probing the area that had until recently been a gaping wound.

"Only two?" Freya joked.

"I was doing a good job, but one of them managed to get me. I fell down and then some cheeky bugger stepped on my leg. I blocked a blow that was meant to take my head off – I don't think it did my wound any good." She lifted the bloody rags of her tunic to examine the now-unblemished flesh and shook her head.

Freya was struck by the strength of the woman before her, that she could still fight with a broken leg and grave wound in her side.

"Better a hole in your side than your head," she said.

"Right you are. Anyway, lucky for me, I cut his legs out from under him. But I would've been killed by somebody else were it not for Malik."

"Malik?"

"An apprentice of mine. A handy fighter, too. He finished off the Guardians. I don't know how he did it, he was so wounded, but he saved me for sure."

"He's wounded? I could look at him." Freya's instructions from Makkyd had been strict: her abilities were to be restricted only to the Resistance leadership. The consequences of people finding out what she could do were too unpredictable. She understood, but she could still try to heal him the old-fashioned way. It sounded as though he deserved her help, too.

Astrom's face tightened. "He's dead."

"Oh." Freya started to work on Astrom's leg, unsure of what else she could say in the face of her friend's obvious grief.

Moments passed as she wrestled the bone back into its rightful place. Astrom remained silent, either giving Freya space to work or consumed by her own thoughts. After long minutes had passed Freya gave herself a pause to collect her focus. Her thoughts were scattering as she tried to focus on healing Astrom's leg. As she waited for her focus to recollect, almost of its own accord, the question tumbled from her lips. "Is there any news of Ashtyn?" She tried to sound as casual as possible, and was certain she failed abysmally.

"Last we heard, he was still in the gildsmiths' district, keeping things calm there."

"Like you were here?" The question pushed its way past Freya's lips before she could help herself.

"Well, yes," Astrom admitted.

They fell silent for a while as Freya concentrated on Astrom's leg. It was difficult. She found that she had to *want* it to heal far more than she had the wound in Astrom's side. She had never pushed herself to the limit of her healing ability, but she could now feel the strain the effort was taking on her, and the manner in which it sapped her capacity to concentrate. It didn't help that fear for Ashtyn was insidiously creeping around her thoughts.

"I'm sorry about Malik," she said softly.

Astrom squeezed Freya's shoulder. "Thank you. I recruited him myself, you know." Guilt flavoured her voice.

"We all know the risks." Freya knew it wouldn't make Astrom feel better, but it was important to say it nevertheless. It's what she told herself about Ashtyn, about the possibility of her own death. She leaned back, rolling her neck to ease the crick in it. "There. Done."

Astrom heaved herself up. Freya followed suit quickly in case Astrom's balance was still off. She carefully put her weight on her leg. She barely wobbled.

"You really are touched by the Goddess," she remarked. "If I didn't believe before, I certainly do now."

Astrom's comment harked back to the reason so few people knew about what abilities true faith could provide. She had given Freya perhaps the best reason for the continuation of the secret. Belief brought on by a desire to acquire abilities for one's own purpose led to events like the Kade takeover – a bid for more power and for self-enrichment.

"It feels all right?" Freya asked, carefully watching Astrom as she moved.

She nodded.

"Be careful, you'll probably still feel tired for a while. No more fights, ok?"

Astrom laughed. "If we come across another troop of Guardians, I'll just ask them to go easy on me because you said I wasn't allowed to fight."

Freya couldn't help but smile. "I have to at least say it."

"True. Hopefully we won't face too much further trouble. Things are otherwise quite calm here."

"I'm surprised we've taken so much of Oranis so easily," Freya replied.

Astrom strode over to a chair that had been knocked over and righted it. "We have a lot of support – especially in the warehouse and builders' district. There are a great many people that the Kade has alienated in its years of heavy-handed rule. All we had to do was promise to actually consult with people from time to time, not take their goods without adequate payment, and to not institute the extreme punishments of the Kade for lawbreakers." She sat down. "You're right, I am a little tired," she added, her breathing ever so slightly heavier.

"Don't overstretch yourself," Freya cautioned.

"It's the middle of an uprising, Freya. I'm not sure that I can follow that order."

"Well, my work here is as done as it can be. I should get back to the Centre." Freya shuffled around the room, idly looking at the mismatched collection of mugs on the shelf, the loose leaves for an infusion in a jar. She was already feeling nervous at the thought of the Centre without her overseeing it, even though returning to it likely meant a return of the doubts and fears she didn't want to face.

"Yes, of course. I'll get someone to escort you." Astrom stayed in the seat for a moment. She briefly closed her eyes in a visible act of collecting herself. "I suppose I'll have to fake a limp and some kind of hurt to my side, won't I?" she muttered, half to herself.

Freya said nothing. She had thought a similar thing. Astrom stood and took a couple of experimental steps with a stiffened leg.

Once she was satisfied she had the gait correct, she walked to the door and opened it.

A small group faced them, grim relief moving across their features when they saw Astrom was alive and walking. Freya expected a stronger reaction from them, given the severity of Astrom's wound, but perhaps Astrom had hidden from them just how gravely she was injured to try and keep the secret of Freya's ability.

"Don't worry yourselves, Freya's patched me up," Astrom said in response to the silent examination. She limped into the workshop. Freya followed.

"Yen, you have news?" Astrom asked a woman who had been drinking deeply from a flask, her face red and sweaty. She looked haggard, as though she had come here at a full sprint.

The woman wiped her lips. "I've been sent to tell you – the Followers of the Dark Gods have started attacking the city."

"What!" Astrom exclaimed in unison with Freya.

"Who are they attacking? Have they taken a side?" Astrom continued.

"From what we know, their attacks are indiscriminate. We think they're taking advantage of the chaos."

The grim mood of the room which Freya had initially taken as the after-effect of worry for Astrom suddenly made a lot more sense. To have nearly gained control of the city to see that threatened left Freya feeling devastated.

Astrom turned back to Freya. "Sorry, Freya, it would seem you have to stay here a while longer."

SIXTEEN

Astrom's people fortified the mason's store and transformed it into a command centre. As the night marched across the city, messengers came in and out. Astrom based herself in the workshop where a table was set up. She gave orders, approved plans put before her, and received news – good or bad – with a lack of reaction that would have made Makkyd proud. There was little Freya could do to assist Astrom, so she had plenty of time to inspect the workshop and the clues it contained to the work it produced and the kind of people who worked there. She noticed the personal differences in style across the pillars and the way the workers had made their piece of the workshop their own. Some had sketched rough guiding designs on the wall in chalk, some had left wax tablets with notes to themselves strewn on the floor. On one bench, unmolested by the Resistance, tools were laid out as though the owner were about to resume work at any moment. The abandoned pillars which were pushed to the edges of the room seemed eerie in the way they lurked in the corner of the eye as shadowed figures. They seemed to Freya's mind silent observers to the drama going on around them.

Mostly, Freya listened to the conversations and formed a picture in her head of how much of Oranis was under the control of the Resistance and where residents were pushing back, where the Kade had deployed guardians to hold territory, and where the Followers of the Dark Gods were seen and what they were doing.

True to their nature, the Dark Gods' Followers acted in small groups, randomly causing anarchy: looting, destroying, and killing with a relentless viciousness. Resistance fighters were attempting to stop them where possible, but Astrom noted that very few were skilled enough fighters to pose a threat to the Followers whose own lack of skill was more than made up for by their zealotry. Moreover, most of those Resistance members were guarding important buildings across the city which they now held, such as Freya's Healing Centre. Certainly, Astrom expressed relief that the Followers seemed to be moving without purpose rather than targeting vital buildings and structures –perhaps those sites were too strongly defended to tempt even them. The groups Makkyd had ordered to hold the access points to the city's aqueducts suddenly seemed a very good idea. Freya wouldn't put it past the Followers to poison Oranis's water supply – they had poisoned a shipment of barat, after all. She wondered about this lack of purpose. Under Zarech's command, the group had acted with a purpose and coordination that seemed to belie their pursuit of a state of perfect anarchy. What they were doing now seemed opportunistic, entirely at odds with the consideration and planning they had previously demonstrated. She wondered if Zarech's demise had left them without order. Yet somehow she couldn't quite believe it. She felt that there was some greater plan at work.

The night passed at once slowly and fast. Although the reports at the beginning of the night suggested the Resistance's position was quite strong, Astrom's face grew more and more grave as reports of the Followers' actions continued through the night. They were inflicting a lot of damage. As the hours passed, a few people came in bearing injuries from skirmishes with the anarchists. Freya tended to them, using her ability where possible to lessen the extent of the wounds without drawing notice to what she was doing. She was grateful for the wounded; they gave her a way to feel useful. Against Astrom's strategic knowledge and clear-sighted tactics, Freya felt decidedly useless.

Dawn was approaching when Astrom ordered the latest messengers to rest in the back room where Freya had tended to her. Guards prowled outside, leaving Astrom and Freya alone together.

"This is a bit of a mess." Astrom's voice was weary with exhaustion and glumness. Freya could tell she was fatigued but knew it was pointless to say anything. Astrom would not rest while she was still required. Freya could relate to that.

"It's not all bad. We still have the Healing Centre and the merchants' hall very securely under our control," Freya pointed out.

"Oh, we're unlikely to lose the city. But it's about how we're perceived. How can we be a legitimate governing body if the Followers of the Dark Gods make an incursion into Oranis itself the very day after we rise up?"

Astrom paced with restless annoyance.

"Sit down. You'll tire yourself out," Freya said.

Astrom obeyed the healer's command, planting herself back down in a chair. She ran a hand across her head. The tight braid into which her hair was pulled had survived even her injury.

"They're attacking the Kade," Freya pointed out. "Surely that's an advantage."

"Freya, you've missed your calling in life as a strategian," Astrom said, lifting her hand from her head, a thoughtfulness crossing her face. "It's still bad for how people will perceive us, but far less than it could be."

"So what will we do?"

"Ask them *really* nicely to stop," Astrom suggested with a wry grin, making Freya laugh. "What I will do, once I've stopped feeling sorry for myself, is form a plan to sweep through our areas and isolate the Followers. Then we'll stand a chance of getting them out of here. The problem is that we never planned for this, so we're going blind. We should have, but we didn't. We never even thought those anarchist scum would make a move."

"You know, I still don't understand why they actually want anarchy," Freya commented.

"Oh, it's mentioned in some of the holy writings we found. They believe that anarchy will lead to their gods coming into our world," Astrom said.

"How? Why would they want that?" Freya asked, aghast at the thought that anybody would ever want to stand alongside a god that sought anarchy.

Astrom shrugged, the faraway expression of someone in the throes of planning on her face.

"I wish the Goddess' Children hadn't all been killed," Freya muttered.

Astrom snorted, focus returning to her eyes. "Even if they were still alive, they'd probably keep things from us. They did before. In the name of preserving true faith. Or whatever."

Freya shook her head, overwhelmed by the intrigue that accompanied faith. She understood its necessity but it didn't sit comfortably with her.

"When did you start believing?" she asked, curious about how her friend's faith sat alongside this cynicism.

"I don't think I've ever not believed," Astrom replied thoughtfully. "I guess small children do naturally believe, though. It's something they've always been told, so up to a point they accept it as the complete truth. So it's a question of how old I was when I realised that it may not be true. I do remember it, actually. I was about twelve. I was messing around in my father's workshop – he was a gildsmith, almost as good as Ashtyn in fact – and I put this assortment of scraps together. It was so beautiful, this random collection of material that I'd put together with absolutely no purpose. I thought that if this beauty could randomly exist, then there must somewhere be a power beyond me that understood more than I did."

"But you don't look with much kindness on the Goddess' Children," Freya prompted.

"I can have faith in a higher power while not having faith in people who claim absolute understanding of what that power wants," Astrom replied.

Freya sat silent for a moment. "Are you scared that we may not succeed?"

Astrom looked up, regarded Freya for a moment, then nodded.

"Me too," Freya whispered.

"But I'm not just scared we won't succeed. Really, this is the easy part. The hard part comes after we win. Actually living in peace with the Kade community. I'm mostly scared we'll be just as bad as the Kade."

Astrom's point rendered Freya silent. She had been so focused on the burning need to remove the Kade from power that she had paid very little thought to how she wanted to live alongside them in a world in which the Kade governance had been overthrown.

She looked around the dark workroom, at the silent shadowed oblongs of the incomplete stonework. The darkness had a way of drawing forth reflection in a way that light did not. She wondered if she would be able to let go of the anger that burned within her at what she and her people had endured for seven long years. She wondered if she would be able to let go of the anger at how she had turned away from her outrage and desire for something better in a bid for self-preservation.

"How do we stop ourselves from being like them?" she asked, her eyes still fixed on the shadowed part of the room.

Astrom's sigh was world weary. "I guess we start by creating a society in which we can be happy. Where we build our lives in a way that we want rather than the way we need to in order to stay alive and safe."

Freya's thoughts flew to Ashtyn. If the Kade hadn't taken over the Third Country, she wondered if she would have become bound to Symon. Likely not. What choice might she have made then? A man with green eyes and a disarming smile? It was possible she'd never have met him, though, or he'd have become bound to the woman of whom he had once spoken. Or that he would have been the person with whom she fell in love. Yet he may not be a choice she could make in the world where the uprising succeeded, either. So much lay between them, left unsaid, unresolved, possibly unsurmountable. Her chest felt constricted, as if the emotion such thoughts aroused were squeezing the breath from her.

"But anyway. Being scared is a luxury we can't afford right now." Astrom's brisk tone cut across Freya's musings. She bent over the map of the district that had been unrolled on the table hours before, when the reports were streaming in. "If we place blockades in the streets here, here, and here, there won't be any way someone can get past them. That would allow us to restrict where the Followers could go."

"But how can we do that?" Astrom's emergence from her own despair pulled Freya from the melancholy and sorrow in which she had been wrapped.

Astrom smiled humourlessly. "Makkyd informed me two days ago that one of the warehouses near here is packed with debris and dirt in preparation for that exact purpose. Why she thought this needed to be kept secret until the very last moment, I'll never know." She shook her head.

"I worried we were tearing apart buildings to create those blockades." Freya was again amazed by Makkyd's forward planning. The sheer scope on which she had considered nearly everything was intimidating.

"No. We don't want to be known as the movement that tore down Oranis while we tried to claim it," Astrom replied.

She crossed the room and opened the door to where people were resting. Astrom told them what she wanted and to whom they should give their messages. She was direct in her instructions, but also somehow conveyed she would rather nobody else be given the task. The messengers left imbibed with a vigour Freya felt had little to do with the rest they had taken and more to do with the determination Astrom effused.

They had only been gone a few moments when a man entered the room bearing a covered basket.

"Pardon me, but I thought you may want something to eat," he said, staring at Astrom with a something akin to reverence.

"No pardon needed, Tomash. People like you are what the uprising turns on. Goddess bless you for thinking of it." Astrom smiled at him.

He left, smiling from ear to ear.

"You're very good with everybody," Freya observed. "You make people feel important."

"You are too," Astrom replied, offering a loaf of hana to Freya. She took a bite of her own and grimaced. "Stale, I'm afraid," she said apologetically.

"I don't know the names of anybody in the Resistance," Freya said, then nibbled on a corner of the loaf. It was as hard as a rock.

"You haven't exactly been in the centre of things, or indeed us, for very long. Most of us, especially those of us in the leadership, have been around almost since the beginning," Astrom pointed out. She bit into a piece of fruit. "Mm, this is better." She handed one to Freya who put the hana down, conceding defeat to preserve her teeth.

"Exactly, I don't understand why I've been placed so high when I barely know anyone." Freya said before she took a bite. It was indeed far better than the hana – easier to chew and it didn't even leave an unpleasant taste on the tongue.

"We needed someone who could take over the healers. Nobody else was even remotely able to do it. The fact that you have true faith was enough for Makkyd, which was enough for the rest of us," Astrom said around the final piece of her fruit.

"Even Lyssa?" Freya couldn't help herself.

Astrom laughed. "Of course. It doesn't mean she had to like it, though."

"Why *does* she dislike me?" Freya tore off a piece of the hana and idly crumbled it between her fingers.

"I refuse to become involved in this. That's a matter between the two of you." Astrom held her hands up to emphasise the point.

"She started it," Freya exclaimed. As soon as the words left her lips, she looked at her feet, abashed by the childishness of her outburst. Astrom's only response was to raise an eyebrow. Freya felt herself blushing.

"Remember, we've also had to keep you secret," Astrom added, generously overlooking Freya's moment of petulance. "Our people who know or know of you already look up to you. Give it time. You'll meet everyone and learn their names."

"But people already know me as a traitor. You remember how Olek treated me when he realised who I was," Freya said.

"And you remember how he accepted you?" Astrom threw back. Her voice turned gentle. "You have to learn to stop being so scared, Freya."

"Easy enough to say," Freya said glumly.

"Well, you came to us. That took guts."

Freya sat silently with her thoughts while Astrom returned her attention to the map. Cracks of light began to ease their way through the shuttered windows. "We should be able to get you back to the Centre soon," Astrom commented, glancing at the window.

"I must admit, a part of me isn't certain about going back," Freya admitted. She was torn about the prospect of returning to the Centre. On the one hand, she wanted to return somewhere it was possible she could be useful. She could offer no opinion or expertise in the matters with which Astrom dealt so confidently. If need be she could at least attend to the sick within the Centre. However, the prospect of facing the judgmental eyes of the people there, many of whom she had implicitly lied to for several cycles, was one she wanted to avoid.

"I can understand that in some ways your role is tougher than most of ours. You're quite well known, so you'll probably get more anger from people than the rest of us," Astrom said. Freya found comfort in Astrom's understanding even if she failed to make her feel any better about returning to the Centre. She could see Astrom's face quite clearly now. Dawn had well and truly broken. Freya wasn't certain, but she thought she could discern new lines around Astrom's mouth and eyes.

"All right, let's get you back to where you need to be," the older woman said. "I'll escort you."

"You should rest," Freya objected.

"Not an option, I'm afraid. Besides, I want to see the streets, make sure our people have done want I told them to do with the blockades."

Freya knew this was a battle she couldn't win. She wordlessly stood, firmly pushing the fatigue in her limbs aside, and accepted the staff Astrom handed her.

SEVENTEEN

The streets were as empty as they had been the previous afternoon. The city didn't feel alive, it only seemed like a collection of abandoned structures. The smell of smoke was stronger, permeating the air with a tang that lingered in the nose and on the back of the throat. It dirtied the sky, making a brown haze above Oranis. The emptiness of the streets made the slap of their footsteps echo with a loudness that Freya would not have thought four people could make. If not for the smoke, she could have pretended the city was deserted. How long, she wondered, would it take until the city began to be reclaimed by the natural world? She could envisage grass pushing its way through the smooth slabs of stone which paved the street, tearing them apart with patient persistence. What shrubs or trees would invade the spaces occupied by buildings, pressing without relent until the walls crumbled? Surely without being continuously repelled, dirt would cover what remained of the paving stones, insidiously invade the buildings and bury much of what was left. She wondered how much time it would take until the city was entirely reduced to the stones and earth it had once been. If fighting continued for long enough, she wouldn't be surprised if that was exactly what would occur.

Everybody kept their weapons drawn. Every sense told Freya she was traversing danger. The smoke thickened overhead, more blue-black than sepia, and the smell intensified. It was no longer an irritating hint of sharpness high up at the back of the throat, but a discernible taste that filled her mouth and nose and urged an instinctive response of panic which was resisted only by a force of will.

She wondered where Symon was, if he was all right, if he was worried about her. Once more, guilt punched her for her thoughtlessness. He seemed like another world away from her, only a concept rather than someone beside whom she had slept for nearly every night for close to seven years.

Her thoughts were cut short by a feral yell. Three figures clad in mismatched garb ran at them from an alley. The two Resistance members and Astrom moved immediately, putting themselves between the attackers and Freya. Their weapons snapped up, bright in the hazy light.

As she raised her staff, she saw one of the Resistance members viciously cut down by a woman whose grin spoke of madness. The attacker came at Freya, blade outstretched, an animalistic snarl issuing from her mouth. Freya had just enough time to assume a fighting stance before the woman lunged at her, not so much trying to stab her as to ram her. Surprised by this unorthodox approach, Freya clumsily sidestepped as her staff was knocked from her hand. The woman's shoulder crashed into her. Panic flared at the fact she was weaponless. Freya grabbed the woman's weapon hand with her left and pushed her thumb into the delicate juncture where wrist met hand. Her attacker snarled again and tried to yank free, but Freya clung on. If she had to face this woman unarmed, she knew with certainty she would be killed. Her fingers ached with the force of holding on, locking the joints and digging in. Yet fear of what would happen if she let go made her cling even more tightly. The woman lurched forward. Her teeth sank into Freya's shoulder and Freya nearly let go. But the need to survive was too strong and she clung on through the surprisingly sharp pain.

Using the pain to fire her anger, Freya twisted the woman's wrist while using the same movement to ram her shoulder into the woman's nose. The woman grunted and her fingers spasmed open.

The weapon fell from her grasp, but her free hand came scything around, fingers curled into a claw. Filthy, elongated nails would have found Freya's eye were it not for a lucky jerk of the head. Instead, four lines of warm pain raked down her cheek.

The woman's face was close enough that Freya could see the lack of any tether to sanity. She realised she would be ripped apart by the teeth and nails of this savage woman and there was nothing she could do to prevent it. But the woman's snarling was competing with another sound – the woman's lifesong. Freya tried to focus on stilling it, but her opponent's struggles were too violent, requiring her to concentrate on keeping her grip on the woman's wrist. Without contact, she couldn't use her ability to save herself.

The woman drew back her free hand to make another pass at Freya's face, and Freya took the opening. She aimed a punch at the woman's stomach. Astrom had only taught her a little about punching, proclaiming her so weak that she'd do more damage to her own hand than an opponent. But Freya was a trained healer. She knew where to hit to drive the breath from someone. And she was fighting for her life. That desperation put extra weight behind her fist as it connected with the woman's sternum, right where the top of her stomach sat. It winded her attacker for just long enough. Freya pushed her attention to the woman's lifesong and clamped down on it with every part of willpower and desperation she had. The woman dropped like a weighted bag, dangling by the wrist that Freya still clutched.

Freya looked around. Stillness had returned to the street. Astrom, blade in hand, was standing over the slumped form of one of their attackers. The third of their assailants had been neutralised by the other Resistance member. Freya looked down at the limp form at her feet, expecting horror at the second life she had taken to form a shroud over her. But instead she only felt grim satisfaction that she was still alive. Besides, there were other matters requiring her attention. She let her attacker's wrist fall with a dull thud and went over to kneel by the Resistance member who had been cut down. Astrom crouched at Freya's side. She looked warily around the rest of the street as she spoke. "Is he all right?"

The depth of his wound sang an awful melody under Freya's fingers. But the blade hadn't pierced anything vital. She nodded, her focus on bringing him out of danger but keeping him unconscious. She took a bandage from the healer's bag and quickly wrapped it over the now-shallower wound. "He'll need to come to the Centre, though." She accepted the staff Astrom had retrieved for her.

"They were Dark Gods' Followers, weren't they?" Freya looked at the prostrate forms of their attackers. Their appearances spoke of a hard life; frayed clothes that had been patched countless times, skin marked by sunburn and scars. Freya wondered what purpose drove them to fight like deranged animals, to sow destruction and chaos.

Astrom walked over to the limp body of the woman Freya had fought. She nudged it with her foot. "I assume she's not getting up." She didn't bother to wait for Freya's response but knelt by the other two, checking to see if they were still alive.

One apparently was, because Astrom efficiently ripped part of his clothes up and used the strips to tie his wrists and ankles together.

"Should we...take him with us?" Freya asked.

Astrom shook her head. "Can't."

"So we just leave him here?"

Astrom shrugged. "Not ideal, obviously. We'll try to pick him up on the way back."

Freya wasn't certain that she was comfortable with the idea of leaving someone bound and helpless on the street, but she couldn't argue with Astrom's logic. In honesty, she had expected Astrom to execute the unconscious man. Leaving him tied up was a mercy of sorts.

She got to her feet. Her head swam for a moment and she swayed on the spot.

Astrom came to her side. "You're hurt."

The words seemed to bring to life the pain of her injuries. Sharp pain ran up and down the gouges in her cheek and her shoulder throbbed from the bite. She put a hand to her face. Her fingers came away smeared with blood. The woman's fingernails had been long and sharp. Freya closed her eyes and turned her focus inward to her own lifesong. The Follower's teeth hadn't drawn blood on her shoulder, but the force of the bite had inflamed the area. She remedied the injury from the bite entirely but could only lessen the severity of the gouges down her face; the other Resistance member had seen them. The pain retreated, although it still lingered in her cheek.

She opened her eyes. "I'll be fine."

Astrom ran a hand across her tight braid of brown hair. "Are you sure?"

Freya took a moment to assess herself, to collect her scattered concentration. It took all of her self-discipline to push aside the fatigue which clung to her bones, and the order the disarray to her thoughts caused by the use of her ability. But she did it. She nodded. "I'm sure."

"All right, come on. The Centre's not far off." Astrom groaned as she and the other Resistance member picked up their injured comrade. Between them, they began to half drag, half carry him along. Freya offered to help but was rebuffed. She was glad – the two nights without sleep were exacting their toll on her and the fight with the Follower had exhausted her. Her legs were rendered unsteady as nervous energy fled her but she had no intention of sharing that with Astrom. She forced herself to feel steady, to walk evenly, even though she wanted to sink to the ground and sob for a couple of minutes before they continued on.

Terror threatened to break free of the flimsy constraints she placed around it as they walked. Her head swivelled, searching every alley, every doorway, every shadow for a fresh assault. She wasn't sure that the three of them would be able to hold their own in another fight, not with the added burden of caring for a wounded comrade. And especially if they were attacked by more Followers. At least the Guardians seemed to fight along some rule set rather than the violent formless savagery Freya had only barely survived.

Perhaps the Goddess was smiling on them. They didn't encounter a single person the rest of the way and, after what seemed like an eternity but was probably only a few minutes, they reached the Healing Centre.

As they staggered up the steps and into the atrium, two figures stepped in between the archway at the top of the stairs, blades drawn. When they saw who was approaching, they sheathed their weapons and allowed them to pass. The alertness and the readiness to defend the Centre restored some of Freya's frayed sense of comfort.

Curious eyes followed them as they passed through the foyer toward one of the empty healing wards. Freya was conscious of the blood smeared across her cheek and the questions she knew people were asking about how she had been injured. With the last of her willpower, she pulled herself up to walk with a straight back and calm step.

Mish arrived, offering to help carry the wounded Resistance member, but she was waved away. Freya suspected that Astrom and their other escort had carried him this far and wanted to finish the job themselves.

"How's everything been?" Freya asked.

Mish shrugged. "As good as we could have hoped. People are starting to get a bit restless – to be expected, really. They've been here for two days with little to do. The bigger problem is that the food reserves are getting low."

Having placed the injured Resistance member on a bed, Astrom straightened up, frowning. "We knew this would be an issue. It'll be the same in all the major buildings we're holding. Unfortunately we didn't foresee that we'd be fighting on two fronts."

Freya took up a set of abandoned healer's tools and began to tend to the injured man. The familiarity of bathing the wound, stitching, dressing it, was comforting, and she felt the terror that had sought to possess her after the fight with the Followers slinking further and further away.

"Wait, two fronts?" Mish asked.

"The Dark Gods' Followers are in the city, That's who we ran into," Astrom replied.

"Oh dear," Mish said so quietly it was more a noise than discernible words.

"Don't worry, our people are working to corral them into the one spot where we can ambush them," Astrom said.

She sounded so confident that Freya couldn't find it within herself to entertain any doubt that Astrom's plan would work.

Mish evidently felt so, too. "How long will it take?"

Astrom made a slight noise of protest as Freya turned from the man she had finished tending and began to look over her. She subtly poked Astrom's side as a reminder that she was supposed to still be recovering from an injury. Obediently, Astrom let out a very convincing "ouch" and immediately shifted so that the leg that had been broken was now being favoured.

She had sustained a scrape in the fight and Freya cleaned it quickly before moving on to the final member of their party. She had received a cut to her upper arm that required stitches.

"My orders should be being enacted right now," Astrom said to Mish as Freya worked. "It was just our bad luck that we ran into a small group of those lunatics. I would expect that by nightfall, this part of the city should be safe."

"Is the Centre safe now?" Mish asked.

"Nobody's come near it?" Astrom asked.

Mish shook her head.

"Then yes, it's safe," Astrom confirmed.

Freya finished the stitches and surveyed her work with quick satisfaction. "Mish, would you mind getting Astrom something to eat? She won't if she doesn't now."

Mish obliged, taking the other Resistance member with her.

"You should tend your own injury," Astrom said, her voice quiet.

Freya pursed her lips, then nodded. Her ability would stop the wound from becoming serious, but she needed to at least clean off the blood which had spread across her face. She started to clean the blood off by feel.

"Stop, you're making a mess of yourself," Astrom said. "Tell me what to do and I'll do it."

Freya complied, directing her to sponge off the dried blood and clean the wound with the fresh water she had drawn. The stoneworker's hands were unexpectedly gentle. "Are you all right?" Astrom's question contained worry, and not just for Freya's physical state.

"There was a moment where I thought she was going to kill me," Freya admitted.

"I caught a glimpse of you fighting her. You did well."

It had been a long time since she had sought the praise of a teacher, but Freya found now that it soothed a ragged part of her that she hadn't even realised was roughed. "I don't know about that," she mumbled.

"You didn't get yourself killed, you didn't panic. That's basically all you need to do when you're in a fight." Gentle humour eased into Astrom's voice as her fingers caught the water pooling along Freya's jawline. "What now?"

"The balm." Freya pointed. "It should be rubbed onto the scratches."

Astrom dipped her fingers in the tub and traced the sore lines across Freya's cheek with the cool ointment. There was something very nice about being tended to by someone else. Freya hadn't been ministered to like this for as long as she could remember. It was her job to fix people, not theirs to heal her.

Astrom finished applying the balm and stood back. "I'm sure you'll help it on its way," she noted.

Freya nodded. "But gradually, over a few days."

"Good." Astrom squeezed Freya's shoulder. "Hang on. We're nearly at the end now."

"Except then comes the real challenge," Freya repeated Astrom's words from the previous evening.

Her friend smiled. "Yes. But different."

Mish returned with a plate of preserved meats and fruits.

"Eat. Healer's orders," Freya said.

The other woman laughed but complied.

"So what should we do about the people in here?" Freya asked while Astrom ate.

"Tell them that if they really want to leave, they can," came the calm reply.

Freya felt the bottom of her stomach swoop out all over again. "Are you sure?"

"We have to trust them, Freya. If they don't want us to lead them, we can't do much," Astrom replied.

EIGHTEEN

Astrom left, taking two Resistance members with her. One of the people guarding the Centre took the place of the injured fighter. Astrom had protested that one person accompanying her was sufficient, but Freya wouldn't hear it, and neither would any of the other Resistance members.

Freya remained alone in the ward, sitting beside the sleeping Resistance member for a short while, allowing her thoughts to settle. She considered the second death she had caused. Unlike the Guardian, who she had taken by surprise and killed almost out of instinct, she had made a decision to end the life of the Follower. Granted, it was a certainty that the Follower would have killed her, but Freya's entire adult life – and much of her childhood – had resonated with the message that it was her responsibility to save lives and never take them. Yet the people who had impressed upon her this responsibility had never offered the possibility that she may find herself in a position where it was a question of her life or another's. She tried to dredge up some remorse, but instead she only discovered she was glad to be alive and would act in exactly the same way again if it was required.

She turned her thoughts to contemplate how best to tell the people who she had effectively kept captive in the Centre that she trusted them enough to let them go. The night she had spent among them replayed over and over in her mind. How many of them would harbour resentment toward the Resistance, and by extension, the Pious, for the uprising? A great many voices had taken part in the whispered arguments under the safety of darkness. Granted, anonymity encouraged a bravery that was otherwise rarely seen, however the comments expressing anger and disdain toward the Pious served as a reminder that not everybody would easily accept a change of rule across the Third Country.

Finally she stood, her thoughts having resolved themselves into something useful. She left the ward, ordering Mish, who was waiting outside, to move the Resistance member into a ward with other patients. She walked to the foyer. The building was one of the older ones in Oranis, and the gentle pink of the stone from which it was built caught and held the morning light. She had walked this route at this time of day countless times, yet she had never properly admired the beauty of the building. Her steps slowed so she could better enjoy the experience. That she could still appreciate such simple beauty gave her comfort.

She entered the foyer and felt the eyes of the crowd turn to her. She felt such a distance between herself and them, even those she knew. The people with whom she had worked looked at her as they would a stranger, or a leader, not their equal. She supposed, though, that she had never been their equal, even if she may have briefly thought she was. The realisation didn't bother her as much as it might once have.

When she spoke her voice was strong, filling every part of the space. "We don't wish to keep you here against your will any longer. We have never sought to compel anybody through fear. If you wish to go back to your homes then nobody will prevent you from leaving.

"If you don't feel safe outside, then there will always be a place for anybody who asks within these walls."

As she spoke, she looked for signs of dissent or anger, but she saw no evidence of either. The only things she saw were fatigue and resignation.

As the echo of her words faded, she joined Mish in the outside corridor. They listened to the rumble of many people getting to their feet, speaking to each other, shuffling around the building. She held her breath without even realising it, waiting for the sound of a fight, for some kind of attempt to wrest control of the Centre back into the hands of Kade authority. Yet despite her fears, nothing of the sort transpired. The multitudinous footsteps had a quality to them which sounded almost docile. Once the noise had petered to nothing, Freya asked Mish to see how many people had left. Her second-in-command briefly left, returning to report many had chosen to remain.

Fatigue was slipping into the corners of her mind, dulling her thoughts. Certain that the Centre was devoid of any threat, she headed back to her rooms. Mish stayed by her side, a shadow simply observing Freya's actions with an inscrutable silence. For that, Freya was grateful. She didn't want to have someone constantly asking her questions, to whom she had to explain herself. Mish's unquestioning faith in Freya's judgment was an asset that Freya appreciated increasingly as the uprising dragged on.

As they reached her rooms, she turned to Mish. "I need to sleep." It was an admission she didn't want to make but she knew better than to push herself to the point of collapsing in front of others.

Mish nodded.

"We should do something about the people who have chosen to remain. They shouldn't stay in the foyer," she said. The prospect of sleep was seductive, pulling her thoughts away from anything else.

"I'll handle it," Mish said.

"Don't let me sleep for more than a few hours," she instructed as she went inside. Her rooms were as she had left them before the uprising began, despite bearing witness to the change in control of the Centre, despite bearing witness to the hours Freya had spent speaking with each worker from the Centre. It was eerie, and she had to look back to Mish to make sure she hadn't somehow dreamed the uprising.

She closed the door and pulled the pins out of her hair, allowing the dark brown locks to tumble to her shoulders. Then she lay down on the pallet set up for when she stayed late. It was so strange that her rooms looked exactly the same, and yet the Centre, like the city outside, was changing so completely. As soon as she closed her eyes, she fell deeply asleep.

She was awoken by knocking at her door. She sat up, struggling to clear her mind of the sleep to which it stubbornly clung. "One moment," she called, trying to force herself awake.

Resentfully, she levered herself up from the pallet. It wasn't particularly comfortable, but at that moment she thought it the finest bed in which she'd ever slept. She crossed the room and opened the door. Mish stood on the other side, waiting patiently.

"Come in. I won't be long." Freya turned and led the way back into the room, casting a glance at the shadow cast by the sun as it hit the timepiece on the wall. Exactly four hours after she had lain down. She went to a piece of polished metal on the wall and began to pin up her hair. Mish wordlessly followed her in.

"What's happened while I've been asleep?" Freya asked as she teased her tangled locks back into some semblance of order.

"Many people have come seeking safety here," Mish told her.

Freya paused in surprise and glanced over her shoulder. "Really?"

"Apparently word of your offer spread quickly. How, given the city's in complete disarray, I'll never know. People feel safe here...under your protection." As ever, her face gave nothing of her thoughts away. Something of her demeanour reminded Freya of Symon. She wondered if Symon had sought refuge in the Centre. It was unlikely

"Me specifically?" Freya asked sceptically.

Mish nodded.

Freya finished pinning her hair back and sat behind her desk, the motion one more of habit than any use the desk may offer. She pursed her lips in thought. "How many?" she asked finally.

"Oh, a couple of hundred. Not as many as we initially had in here with us. People keep showing up, though, so that may change."

A part of Freya regretted she hadn't had someone like Mish working in the Centre with her before the uprising.

"Do they want food?" Freya's thoughts went to their dwindling supplies. That many people hoping to be fed as well as protected would soon find themselves very much disappointed. In turn, that could lead to some very unpleasant scenes.

"Some have brought food and belongings, some have shown up empty handed. They genuinely believe that their homes may not be standing when this is all over." A trace of emotion made its way into Mish's voice, but it was so faint that Freya couldn't discern what it was.

"How do they seem?"

"What do you mean? Do they seem upset? Yes. At us? I don't really know."

Freya sighed ever so slightly. A loyal and efficient second-in-command, Mish was, without question. Someone who could read and understand the nuances of human emotion, she definitely was not.

"I think I should talk with them," Freya said.

Mish's eyebrows shot up and her eyes widened. "Are you sure about that? We have no idea who they are. Some could be here hoping to get to you."

Freya restrained her impulse to snap back. Mish did have a point. "I'm certain. I'll go now." She took a moment to compose herself before standing up and leaving the little pocket of her own space. Mish followed.

"Where are they?" Freya asked as they walked along the corridors. The middle of the day had come and gone. The afternoon sun had an orange quality to it, and where it slid across the walls, it made them look almost aflame.

"Most are still in the foyer. We haven't decided what to do with them. Those who have been here since the start I moved to the western ward. There aren't enough beds for all of them, but we have enough for the older people to sleep on them if they need."

"Good thinking," Freya said absentmindedly, her thoughts on the issue of the new arrivals. "We shouldn't keep the newcomers in the foyer either. Not if they're scared."

Mish said nothing.

The foyer held several hundred people, all who looked anxiously to Freya when she entered. Recognition flared in many faces and she paused, not expecting that she would be viewed so publicly or with such complex emotions. She looked at the people gathered before her, trying to tell if any of them were a threat to her Centre. For the most part, Mish seemed to be correct; they looked scared and a little angry, and they looked at her with shy hope. Some clustered together, others stood by themselves. Everybody shared the same posture of uncertainty. It was a terrible thing to fear that everything you had worked your whole life to achieve may be destroyed by an event entirely out of your control. Freya could remember the same feeling sweeping through her during the Kade's uprising. This time, she was fortunate enough to have been able to prepare herself. Most people in Oranis had not enjoyed that luxury.

Freya's eye was caught by an old woman who stood unsteadily; a younger woman held her arm to keep her stable. She went over to them and took the woman's hand, pressing her thumb into the woman's palm in the Pious greeting. It was an act that had been forbidden for the past seven years. Freya hadn't even thought to look to see if the woman was Pious, although she returned the gesture.

"Do you need to sit down?" Freya asked, casting around for a seat.

The shake of the woman's head was definite. "I'd like to stand, thank you, Healer Kuch." Despite her advanced years, her voice was without any tremor.

"Do you need food?" Freya asked, using her ability to discern the woman's physical vitality despite her age.

The woman's smile crinkled her face into a network of lines. "No, thank you. Please don't worry about me."

"Is this your daughter?" Freya looked to the woman holding the old woman's arm.

"No, my daughter...she is gone. This is a friend. Nikka."

Freya released the old woman's arm to take Nikka's hand, also offering her the Pious greeting.

"Is there anything I can do to make either of you more comfortable?"

Nikka smiled and shook her head. "Thank you for taking us in. It's a great comfort to be somewhere like this." Her hand remained on the old woman's arm as she spoke, steadying her.

"Of course." Freya smiled at the two women. Even if they weren't related, it was obvious that there was a strong connection between them. There was something lovely about it.

"Damesha, you should sit down," Nikka told the old woman with tenderness in her voice.

"I'm perfectly fine, Nikka. If nobody else is sitting, I don't need to," Damesha replied, tossing her head proudly. Freya hid her smile behind a hand.

"I'm relocating you to a ward with other people who have chosen to come here," Freya told the women. "Everybody should be more comfortable there."

She raised her voice so everybody could hear her. "I'm sorry that you've been kept waiting here. We just wanted to make sure we would be able to make you comfortable. Please follow me."

Trush and Mish, looking wary, walked beside her as she led the crowd out of the foyer but they reached the ward without any incident. Despite her confidence in her capacity to defend herself,

Freya breathed a sigh of relief as the group compliantly filed into the ward. Yet alongside her relief was a deeper running worry: Was this what her life was to be like, now? For how long would she be looking over her shoulder, waiting for someone to exact revenge on her for her treachery?

"I'm afraid I will have to ask you all to stay here," Freya told the group as Trush melted away, evidently satisfied that the Resistance members standing unobtrusively by the door would be sufficient protection. "As things currently stand, we can't afford to have anybody wandering around the Centre. That being said, if you need anything, please just ask."

Nods and agreeable murmurs greeted her words. As Freya went to leave, Damesha grasped her wrist. Freya gasped in surprise. At her side, Mish flinched, a hand suddenly on her dagger's hilt.

The old woman didn't appear to notice. Fortunately, nor did anybody else in the room.

"Do you have anywhere to be?" Damesha asked.

Freya shook her head. She probably should have been making rounds of the Centre to ensure everything was as it should be, but she didn't really have the heart.

"Stay and talk with me, Healer Kuch," Damesha said.

Nikka excused herself politely and went off, ostensibly to request a blanket.

Freya glanced around the room. Most people were settling themselves onto beds or chairs or the floor, quietly conversing among themselves. A few were watching her curiously, waiting to see what she would do. Curious as to why Damesha had requested her company, Freya forced herself to relax and sat down next to the old woman.

A long moment of surprisingly companionable silence passed. When it appeared the old woman was not about to say anything, Freya asked Damesha where she lived. It was a safely neutral thing to ask.

The old woman didn't answer her question but, in the way Freya had often observed among the very old, took it as a cue to start talking of what was passing through her own mind. "You know, there was an attempted uprising when I was very young."

Freya hadn't known that, but she wasn't given a chance to speak before the woman continued. "Most people don't know about it because it was quelled so quickly. It was our people, you know – the Pious. Do you know why they wanted it to be forgotten?"

This time, it seemed Freya was expected to respond. "I don't know," she admitted.

"Because the Dual Accord didn't want there to be any ongoing acrimony between the Kade and the Pious."

"So how do you know?" Freya asked.

"My father's brother was involved. It was a great shame for my parents, to be related to someone who would bring such violence to our community. I always wondered if the Kade who overthrew the Dual Accord those years ago knew about it and sat with that resentment for years until they were finally able to exact their revenge. Maybe the desire for power is just a part of human nature, though." She spoke beautifully, the cadence and phrasing of her voice attesting to years of education. Freya wondered what she had done in her younger years.

"Do you think that I'm doing the right thing?" Freya's question tumbled from her lips despite her best effort to remain restrained. She wondered if the old woman had an ability of the faithful, subtly urging Freya to speak what was truly on her mind. It would certainly be a far more subtle ability that any of the ones she had encountered, but the Resistance had no idea what was and wasn't possible. The secrets of faith had been lost with the Goddess' Children seven years previously.

Damesha shrugged, exhaling heavily. "Who am I to say?"

"Were you happy to live under the rule of the Kade?" It was a question she had only ever asked herself, Symon, and other members of the Resistance.

"I wasn't unhappy for the most part."

"Why?"

Damesha shrugged again. "When you get to be as old as I am, then everything is bearable."

"What happened to your daughter?" Freya couldn't help herself from being so unforgivably interrogatory. It all but confirmed her suspicion that this old woman definitely had some kind of ability.

A frown appeared on her forehead. "Daughter? I don't have a daughter,"

"But you said—" Freya began.

Nikka hurried over. "She can become very confused," she explained as she took Damesha's hand.

Freya nodded. As a healer, she had seen elderly people with whom one could have a perfectly rational conversation suddenly become almost incoherent for no apparent reason. The mind was one thing Freya's ability could not fix.

"Did she have a daughter?" Freya asked Nikka, unable to shake the curiosity that had bloomed inside her.

"Not that I know of. I'm a neighbour. I started to look out for her a few years ago. I lost my own parents in the uprising, so she cared for me until..." Tears sprang into her eyes and she excused herself as she wiped them away. Freya said nothing, placing a hand on the other woman's shoulder. It was the most contact and connection she had experienced with someone who was just an ordinary citizen in the longest time that she could remember. Nikka put a hand over Freya's, squeezing appreciatively.

"My lady?" Mish called softly from the doorway.

Freya excused herself from Damesha and Nikka – although Damesha seemed too lost in the forest of her own mind to notice – and walked to where her second-in-command waited. A few stares followed her. She wondered how many had watched her exchange with Damesha and what they had made of it.

"Yes?" She kept her voice low, not wanting to disturb any of the people who had just settled in.

Try as she might have, she could not help but feel a flutter in her chest at Mish's next words.

"Ashtyn is here to see you."

NINETEEN

He stood by the window in her rooms. His back was almost fully to her as he looked out onto the garden in the courtyard below. His hands were in his pockets and he appeared to be totally immersed in the view. She stood in the doorway he had left open and looked at him. Not for a second did she believe he wasn't aware of her presence. He was as aware of her as she was of him – she could see it in the slight angle of his shoulders. She wondered for a brief moment whether he had come to her rooms deliberately, seeking a private moment with her. But her pondering was pushed aside by the overwhelming rush of relief she felt at seeing him safe and in one piece. Even from across the room, his lifesong sounded clearly in her mind. She didn't stop to contemplate how she could sense like this from such a distance but instead took comfort in the vibrancy of its sound. Warmth spread through her, and the icy core that she hadn't even realised had formed around her heart at the worry he may be harmed, melted.

He turned and smiled at her. For a moment, they stared at each other. Uncertainty hung between them, thickening the air, prolonging the moment. A part of Freya wanted to rush over to him, to embrace him and feel his arms fold around her, but she held that impulse in check. She had pushed him away for so long that the fledgling repair of things between them did not feel strong enough to withstand the thundering wave of emotion such a gesture would unleash.

"Nice of you to drop by," she said, her voice light, even playful.

His smile broadened into a grin. "Well, I was nearby…"

She stepped in and closed the door. "Have you eaten?"

"Do you remember I used to worry about whether you were eating enough?" He chuckled and ran a hand through his dishevelled hair.

She blushed at the memory of his concern and the intimacy that had accompanied it. She had liked that he had cared for her so much. Nobody else did.

His eyes went to her cheek and worry darkened the green of his eyes. "You're hurt."

She put a self-conscious hand to the scratches left by the Follower. "I'm all right. I couldn't fix it up because too many people had seen it."

His eyes were still clouded. There was a nakedness to the way he looked her over to ensure she truly was otherwise uninjured. It called forth memories of how he had seemed to care so deeply for her wellbeing, and how she had loved the way that made her feel.

"How is the city?" she asked, desperate to divert the conversation. She didn't want to drown in her memory or sentiments. She couldn't, not now.

He straightened. "We've all but gotten rid of the Dark Gods' Followers."

She raised her eyebrows. It was excellent news, but the ease with which the Followers had been removed as a threat bothered her. "It seems such a small force for them to have sent in," Freya murmured. "Surely this was their great opportunity."

"Unless they have something else planed. If we learned anything last year, it was that they have plans within plans." Ashtyn wisely did not mention Zarech. He didn't have to. She knew they were both thinking of Freya's strange relationship with the leader of the anarchic group. It was disquieting to contemplate that the Resistance may have to face further threats from the Followers of the Dark Gods. Weariness swept over her at the prospect of yet another fight for control, another fight against someone else's ideology. Would it ever end? She marshalled her thoughts. Now was not the time for this kind of contemplation.

"And the people – are they supporting us?" she asked.

"The gildsmiths' district was quite easy to keep subdued. The people with whom I spoke seemed mostly glad to hear we were taking control of the city, especially once I assured them we'd look after their interests and let them be heard."

"It's that simple?" Freya asked.

"It helps I'm one of them."

"And charming," she said before she could stop herself. His teeth were white against the sooty black of his hair as he grinned, obviously delighted by her inadvertent compliment.

"Fortunately, the Kade's behaviour in the past few cycles has done most of the work for us. People are willing to support anyone who promises them a life without repression or fear," he added.

He ambled over to Freya's desk, hands still in pockets. He leaned his hip against it casually. All the while his eyes never left hers. It felt as though he was drinking in the sight of her, as she was him.

"For how much longer can the Kade hold out?" Freya asked as she settled into a chair.

"Well, that's why I'm here, actually. I'm a messenger."

Her eyebrows shot up. "From overseeing a district to messenger?"

"Don't worry, I haven't been demoted." His grin turned into a smirk.

"I never said as much," Freya protested.

His expression was pure amusement. She broke eye contact and they shared a good-natured laugh.

"I did wonder," she admitted, her lips twitching to contain a bashful smile. Her eyes made their way back to find his, almost of their own volition.

"Well, it's a promotion of sorts. We've gotten most of the city in our grasp. Most of the Kade leadership are holed up in the governance halls.

"We're going in for a big offensive to try to break through. If we capture the Kade leadership hiding inside, it means we've all but taken the city. Hopefully, that will end it."

"Hopefully?" Freya didn't bother to hide her concern at the qualifier. The prospect of an indefinite continuation to the fighting, and how that would affect the city, was an unpleasant one. The Resistance had captured the merchant gate and with it, significant stores of goods. For at least some time, carts would continue to arrive to deliver their wares; word of the struggle for control of Oranis would not reach across the whole of the God-skissed Continent for at least a few cycles. In that time, the Resistance would continue to collect whatever goods came in to the city. But having the supplies was largely pointless if they couldn't be distributed across the rest of the city.

"We think we should be able to do it. Especially given the strategy Makkyd's come up with. It's quite brilliant."

"We?" The cold around her heart returned in a rush.

"Yes. I'm taking part." He tried to simply throw the fact away, as though he weren't risking his life.

"Do you have to?" She couldn't hide her fear from him. She didn't want to.

"We need every fighter we can muster. This is our chance. We'll only get one."

Freya couldn't understand how he seemed so calm at the idea of putting everything – including his life – so completely subordinate to his commitment to his cause. It was ultimately why she hadn't been able to rekindle her romance with him. She knew she would never be as important to him as the Resistance. It was that truth that had overlaid every word she had spoken to him with such bitterness for so many cycles. She took a deep breath, trying to let it go. Now was not the time to hold onto something like that.

"On the way to you I found you a present."

She was grateful for the change of subject. If Ashtyn lost his life, she didn't want the last moments between them to be steeped in anger.

"A present?" she asked.

"A prisoner." He laughed at her expression. "We captured him as we made our way here. He tried to kill me. Came very close to it, in fact. I figured he'd be better locked up in here than roaming the streets."

"Why didn't you just kill him?" Freya saw the surprise flit across his face at her question.

"Didn't have to." His look of surprise transformed briefly into an expression of unease.

She wondered where her ruthlessness had come from. It concerned her that she could shock people like Ashtyn with comments that she thought were just practical. Not for the first time, she wondered what dark purpose had invaded her heart along with the rebellion.

She made an embarrassed gesture. "Do they need me near the fighting – to heal people?" She wanted him to forget her comment. To forget that she could be like that.

He shook his head. "No. You're better use here. Stronghold and all that. I just came to let you know what's to happen. Even though Makkyd feels we should win, things could still go either way, and you should know what's going on and what might happen."

"I appreciate it. We haven't really been getting much in the way of information." She smiled ruefully.

"Well, you should be prepared. Especially if we aren't the ones who win."

Hearing the possibility voiced in such blunt words was a shock. The assurance of victory had propelled many people into the Resistance. A sombre silence fell between them for a fleeting moment.

"Do you really think we may not win?" she asked.

"I don't know." His voice was quiet. There was no fear or uncertainty in it, just a simple statement of fact. She didn't understand how he could be so comfortable with such a prospect.

"So why do it?"

"I mean, we *should* win," he clarified. "But you never know what can go wrong."

"Are you afraid?" she asked.

It was some time before he answered. "Of losing? Yes. We've worked so hard for this. And if we do lose, the consequences would be so dire it hardly bears thinking about. Of dying? I mean, I'd like to avoid it. But I'm not afraid of it." Something in his manner made her think there was something else that he wanted to add, but he didn't say anything more and she didn't feel he would yield more than he already had.

"I'd rather you didn't die," she told him, working hard to keep humour in her tone rather than the desperation she felt.

"You'd miss me?" There was a playful note to his tone.

"Don't flatter yourself." She couldn't help the smile from creeping across her face at the warm mischief in his eyes.

"I always flatter myself," he replied. For a moment the seriousness that overlaid everything melted away. That was his magic, that he could take her away from her worries and troubles, even if it was only for a moment. But the severity of that which surrounded them only allowed her a moment or levity.

"How long until you have to go?"

"We'll attack in the darkest hour. Use the cover of night so we can come at them from all sides. I should be at the square on the corner of the merchants' and governance districts by sundown to help with the preparations."

"So when will you leave me?"

She caught her own words and saw in his stillness that he had too.

"Soon." It was said softly, and in it was a more complex apology than words could adequately capture.

"Ashtyn, if anything happens to you—"

He cut her off. "You don't need to say it."

"But what if I want to?" She raised her chin in a gesture of hollow defiance.

"But you don't need to."

Abruptly, he pushed off from the desk and walked over to sink to his knees in front of her. With his head slightly bowed, it looked as though he was offering her worship. The gesture of supplication unnerved her. She wasn't a god to be worshipped. She put her hand underneath his chin, tilting his head up so he was looking directly at her. The conflict on his face surprised her. She wondered what exactly he was feeling and thinking that made him look so torn.

"You know, I really do wish we'd met under different circumstances," he told her. His eyes were sadder than she'd ever seen.

"I really don't think it matters in the end, Ashtyn. All I can say is that I'm glad I met you," she replied. It was true. Despite the heartbreak, the agony, and the anger, she was glad that she knew him and that he was in her life, one way or another. She wouldn't have it any other way.

They remained still, her thumb against his chin, her index finger resting on his jaw. The stubble which had crept onto his normally clean-shaven face was rough underneath her fingertips.

She broke the long silence. "Do you really think that things will be different if we win?"

The way he smiled up at her made it feel as though her heart was squeezing in her chest.

"Isn't it worth trying to find out?"

She leaned even closer to him. Her hand slipped down to curve around his neck as though she was about to pull him forward so his lips could meet hers. Their faces were so close. His breath broke gently against her mouth.

"I guess I think it is." She smiled. This was an argument in which they had been engaged from the start. It seemed funny that after all this time, she had ultimately agreed with his point of view.

He closed the minute distance between them, resting his forehead against hers. She closed her eyes, wishing that the moment could last forever, that he wasn't going away to a possible death, that things with him weren't so complicated. She wasn't certain she wanted to be with him, but she knew that she didn't want to be without him. Her feelings for him were an exquisite agony. He put a hand on her arm and his fingers rested on the laastram.

"It served me well," she whispered.

The muscles of his face gave away his smile, even though she couldn't see it. "I'm glad," he replied.

They lapsed back into silence, simply resting against each other, enjoying the sensation of the other's touch.

It was Freya who broke away first, standing and tugging him to his feet. "If you don't leave now, I may give in to temptation and render you unconscious so you can't fight." The statement was only half a jest.

"I'm not certain I trust you around an unconscious me." He put his hand over his heart, feigning a shocked innocence.

She couldn't help but laugh, even if the sound also held her sadness. "I'm sure I'd be able to restrain myself."

"You say that now."

She laughed even harder.

"Stop!" she ordered him, gasping for breath.

"All right, I'll leave you in peace." He raised his hands in mock surrender and walked to the door. Freya stayed where she was. The weight of all the things she couldn't say to him almost tore her down. Foolish, that the only thing really stopping her from telling him what she actually wanted to was some tattered remnant of pride which barred the way for her to find any of the words to express how she felt.

"Ashytn?" she called.

He turned, his hand on the door.

For a fraction of a second, she would have told him everything. But she couldn't. She didn't know how to put it into words. "Please be careful."

"You're not worried about me, are you?" he asked, that mischievous half smile that made her heart beat just a little faster creeping across his features. "Watch that prisoner, by the way. He's a sneaky one. I'd feel very guilty if he hurt you in any way. Interesting, though, he seemed to be a true fanatic from what I saw."

He didn't give her time to reply. He opened the door and walked away, hands in his pockets in the deceptively casual manner with which she was so familiar.

It was only after he was too far away for her to call out to him that she found the words for all of the things she wanted to say to him.

TWENTY

She remained in her rooms for several minutes following Ashtyn's departure. Try as she might, she couldn't shake the sense that she had lost something precious. The sentiment rendered her temporarily paralysed. Something in Ashtyn's demeanour had unsettled her, almost as though he were saying goodbye to her in a very final way. If asked, she couldn't have elaborated on what it was, but something in his manner had seemed entirely out of character, and she couldn't simply put it down to the fact that they were in the middle of an uprising. Grief for this loss threatened to overwhelm her, but she would not let it. She breathed deeply, falling back into the familiar, comforting count as she drew in and exhaled breath, using that calm to forbid the tears that filled her eyes to spill down her cheeks. This was not the time for her emotions to overwhelm her. They were so close to the end. Once the city was secure she could enjoy the full depths of all the feelings which fought to make themselves known to her. Of course, along with those feelings would be the need to face Symon, to fling herself into an even more public position and everything that accompanied it. And there were those feelings for Ashtyn she had chosen to push aside for so long. Astrom was certainly correct – the hardest part was indeed to come.

Once she had pushed away this terrible sense of loss, she realised that she couldn't stay in her rooms doing nothing. Inaction, as always, sat poorly with her. There was no point her simply standing around while people were preparing to fight for control of the city. Once she was certain of her composure, she decided to check on Ashtyn's prisoner. His comment had aroused her curiosity, and it would give her a welcome distraction from what was going on in the governance district.

Walking along the quarantine ward evoked her memories of the cycles she had spent tending to Zarech. That time seemed both a short while ago and an eon before, and the Centre in which she had healed the injuries inflicted by torture performed on a man far more complex than a mere killer seemed both identical and entirely different to the building through which she now walked. Unlike the desolate silence that had permeated the quarantine ward in the Central Healing Centre, the number of Kade supporters imprisoned in her Centre meant the ward was suffused with the muffled sounds of life. Not even the heavy doors and thick walls could stifle that hum.

Three Resistance members patrolled the corridor. After witnessing the idle boredom of the Guardians in the prison during Makkyd's rescue, Freya had given very specific instructions on how the guards could stay alert when on duty. If she had learned anything from that nightmarish evening, it had been that one or two lax guards could be disastrous. It was gratifying to see her instructions had been carried out so carefully, even this many hours after they had taken the Centre. Now was the time when boredom stole away the alert edge that fear gave. The more prisoners who filled the cells, the more routine guarding became, and the more likely someone was to take advantage of a careless moment.

As she approached, the three paused their pacing.

"Healer Kuch, is everything all right?" the nearest asked.

"Yes. You're all doing an excellent job. It's kept the Centre safe across the last days," Freya said, remembering Astrom's easy compliments to her people and the obvious manner in which it buoyed them. Sure enough, she was offered three smiles.

"We try," the man said. "Can we do anything for you?"

"A prisoner was recently brought in?"

He nodded, pointing to one of the doors.

"I'd like to speak with him," Freya said.

The Resistance member obligingly unbarred the door and held it open for her while she entered. It closed behind her with a loud echo that resonated alongside the memory of a similar room holding a very different type of prisoner within it.

The Kade man in the cell looked up at her. A long cut ran all the way down his face. That it hadn't been tended was the first thing she noticed. The second was the fire of resentment and un-adulterated hatred that shone in his eyes. Hair the colour of dirty sand fell across his face. He angrily tossed his head to move his hair aside so he could glare at her unimpeded. She judged him to be around her age, perhaps slightly younger. That his arms were tied behind his back gave her pause. Her instructions had specified that only those deemed a significant threat were to be tied up in their cells. Were it not for the expression on his face, he certainly would have looked innocuous. Given what Ashtyn had told her, she had expected someone burlier, perhaps a bit older, too. Not this slender boy.

Rather than sitting on the bed, he was on the floor in the corner farthest from the door.

"What do you want?" he snarled before she had an oppor-tunity to say anything.

There was a time when Freya would probably have been in-timidated by someone who so obviously wished her harm. Then again, there was also a time when she thought that killing some-one was an act she could never have committed. She had changed a great deal. Rather than flinching away from the fore of the hate and anger he exuded, she remained where she was and looked at him in almost detached appraisal.

"Do you really care?" she asked, her voice cold.

For half a moment, he looked surprised. But he quickly re-gained his initial compose of seething hatred. "Not really. You're a Pious. You're all the same. Scum."

"Why?" She crossed her arms and tilted her head as though the slight variation of angle would offer some different perspective, allow her to see something about him and his fervour that she had initially missed. Her curiosity was piqued. Something about his certainty, his absolute hatred of her because of her identity as a Pious, was as fascinating as it was illogical.

"You're all ungrateful. You worship an inferior god, your ways are pointless. You can't appreciate what we were generous enough to give you."

"What exactly did you give us?" Indignation waited within her to arise, knowing whatever answer he gave would be some vitriol-tainted nonsense. She was not disappointed.

"Your lives. We allowed you to live." He followed with a string of expletives.

Freya raised an eyebrow, impressed by the range of his vocabulary. "Who exactly told you this?" Such complete contempt for the Pious was rare to find.

He spat at her. His spittle landed on the floor between them, the frothy white edges somehow obscene against the flat, polished stone. "Your cause will fail," he told her. His certainty was so absolute that for a moment she almost believed him.

"Why?"

"Because you are weak and pathetic." It came out more as snarls around which words were wrapped than actual speech.

Freya did not tremble as once she might have. He was all talk. She wasn't quite certain why she remained in the room with him, but this rabid zealotry was something she had never encountered outside of her fight with the Follower. Every other person who had been willing to go to extremes for their cause had acted in accordance with some logic. Zarech, the Chief Healer, even Makkyd. They were all fanatics for their causes in their own ways but they held to a form of reason, and eschewed senseless violence.

She could see that the man across the room from her didn't have the intelligence to be nuanced in his zeal. All he had was blind hatred for the Pious that he had nursed quietly until it had become a core part of him and the way he saw the world. It surpassed even the Kade governance's teachings about the Pious, seeming as though it was something he *had* to believe in order to justify his perception of his own supremacy. And then he had been given the opportunity to give it legitimacy; this group of people that he had hated, considered lesser due to their difference, was suddenly daring to challenge the legitimacy of his own people who in his view had rightly seized power seven years earlier. This was the excuse for which he had been waiting to unshackle his blind hatred.

"Well, I have news for you," she told him, unable to quite suppress the surge of vindictiveness that had blossomed at his hatred of her people. "We *are* going to take the city, and we *will* win. And there's absolutely nothing you can do about it."

She had to fight to stay where she was rather than take the step back the hatred distorting his features made her want to take.

"Do you really doubt for one second that I won't be waiting for my chance? Even if you take control of Oranis and the Third Country, if I'm given even a small opportunity to kill just one of you, I'll take it. And there are more like me. We'll take you down, one at a time." He spat again for emphasis.

Freya stared at the man. Contempt and anger for his small-minded hatred burned in her. For too long she had lived in fear of this kind of prejudice directed toward her on the basis of something she couldn't help. She hated that the limited prejudice of people like him had cowed her for so long. Yet the anger remained separate from her appraisal of the risk he presented to the Pious. He was certainly enough of a fanatic to have the abilities of the faithful. However, his hatred of the Pious meant she couldn't help but feel that his fanaticism was directed to the Kade rather than their gods. Something about him left her feeling as though he didn't really care about matters of divine beings. That fact alone diminished him in her eyes, made him seem less than human. Not a son or brother or friend. Not someone who made those he loved happy with the mere fact of his existence. Not someone who felt pain or happiness or sorrow or anger. Just a petty being. She crossed the room to stand in front of him, then crouched so she could look into his eyes.

"Are you quite sure that there's nothing I can do about that?"

His reaction was everything she expected: initial wariness wiped away quickly by dull and long-burning hate.

Killing him was easy. Some dark purpose overtook her and she was content for it to do so. There was no way he would not be a threat to the Pious or the governance that they hoped to create across the Third Country. He would always seek to harm Pious, and for that she judged him, found him guilty, sentenced him, and exacted her sentence. She didn't even need to touch him. Perhaps using her ability over the past few days had expanded its strength significantly. Perhaps the rage burning within her at his impudence gave it an extra strength. Regardless, she was able to reach across the space between them to feel the sound of his lifesong strongly resonating in her mind. She breathed in, pressed upon the vibrant sound with her will, breathed out, and it was done. The divide between life and death was so flimsy and she pushed him across it with ease, feeling a mastery over that thin difference between the mortal and divine realms. Whatever the reason, it seemed that the capabilities of her power were more immense than she had even imagined. It thrilled her even as it terrified her.

The slumped form on the floor in front of her lacked any menace. It was hard to believe that only a few moments previously, the sack of flesh that would soon begin to reek as it decomposed had been a person full of unadulterated hatred and malicious, violent intent.

She stared at the body. It didn't even surprise her that she felt nothing other than satisfaction that once more, she had survived when her opponent had not.

She left the room, saying nothing about the corpse in the cell to any of the Resistance members in the corridor. It would be far simpler for it to be found long after she had left. Certainly, some questions may be raised, but Freya gambled on the fact that her ability had left no mark on him. The death of one angry Kade man would be lost amid the chaos and bloodshed of the uprising. The few who did know of her ability would never hear of what she had done, and even if they did, most would agree with her assessment of the risk he had posed to innocent people and the action she had taken to protect them.

Late afternoon sunlight warmed the corridors through which Freya made her way to the wards, as though defiant of night's imminent arrival. The air outside looked so still, so calm, that it seemed absurd parts of the city were under siege. Only the smudge of clouds tinted dark orange served as a reminder that buildings were burning and lives were being taken in the name of liberating the city.

She didn't feel at all bad about the man she had just executed. She couldn't. It just didn't feel as though she had done something wrong. Killing was something to which she was becoming accustomed as she understood that taking a life to save others was a different way of fulfilling the healer's obligations to protect others. Her fear of taking that step had been born of the concern she would become a monster if she took a life, but she didn't feel like a monster at all.

In fact, she felt more herself than ever as she resolved to check on the refugees, perhaps talk with Damesha again, and do her rounds of the sick and injured. She had no desire to return to her rooms and await news on whether or not the final push to capture the Kade leadership had been successful.

Mish was outside the first ward, quietly conversing with one of the Resistance guards. She looked up at Freya's approach and surprise seized her features. "You decided to stay?"

Freya frowned in confusion. "What do you mean?"

"You decided to stay here instead of go and tend the wounded?"

"What are you talking about?" Freya wondered if Mish was finally cracking under the strain of so many days of the uprising. It wouldn't have surprised her to learn that Mish hadn't slept at all. She felt a twinge of shame at the realisation she hadn't bothered to find it out – she'd just assumed Mish would take care of herself as she had taken care of so much else over the past three days.

"What you were requested to do?" Mish asked the question in a manner just shy of a suggestion that Freya was herself touched in the head.

Catching herself before she snapped back a reply, Freya took a breath. "Mish, start from the beginning."

"I was talking with one of the people who came with Ashtyn – she said that they'd come to ask whether you would be willing to heal during the final attack."

Freya worked exceptionally hard to keep her face neutral. She had very specifically asked Ashtyn if she was needed. He had been very clear when he had replied with a categorical no. She stood in the corridor, feeling like an idiot as she sought to understand how Mish had heard something so different to what Ashtyn had told her. Only slowly did it dawn on her that he might have lied to her.

She didn't spare the time to wonder why he lied. All she could think of was that she needed urgently to be near the front line – that healing was something that she could do and it was something that may actually help the Resistance to capture the city, as well as save the lives of countless wounded. What was more, perhaps it was selfish, but for her own sake she needed to be present at the end, to take a direct part in finishing what had been started seven long years ago.

"Mish, I need you to take command of the Centre," she said with a calm that belied the raging thoughts churning through her head. She didn't wait to hear the response because she was all but running out of the Centre to take her place in the final fight.

TWENTY ONE

Freya remembered very little of how she got to the square Ashtyn had named. Perhaps it had been reckless of her to leave the Healing Centre without at least one guard. Yet the knowledge of what she had done to the man in the cell had uncovered a different kind of truth: she possessed the capacity to protect herself, the ability to take life with a mere thought. She hadn't even brought a weapon; her own ability would be of more use than a weapon she could only wield clumsily. Some part of her recoiled in horror at what she had done to the prisoner. She had acted in a way that aligned all too closely with the tyranny she abhorred. And that tyrannous impulse which sat within her was given scope by the godlike capacity she possessed. Yet a part of her roared victorious at what she had discovered she could do.

The square was one of those built by the Kade to force everybody to worship their gods – the fledgling trees which lined the square always gave away the fact that another building had been unceremoniously torn down following the days of the takeover to force their gods onto everybody else. Ashtyn had told her the Resistance would be launching their assault from here, but a festive atmosphere hung over the space. Perhaps it was the unusually large gathering of people in the one place – a rarity of late, especially thanks to the Kade's escalating restriction on people's freedoms. Something about it was vaguely reminiscent of the festivals of dance that were part of Pious religious worship before they, like every other Pious practice, had been banned. The distinctive shriek of weapons being sharpened was definitely not congruous with her memory of the festivals. But something smelled like stew was cooking over the fire which burned in the middle of the square, and the low hum of genial chatter circled around the space. And amid the diminishing light, they were just similar enough to what she remembered that a glance created the illusion of a beloved part of her past miraculously restored.

Freya was amazed at the number of people there. She had never dreamed that the Resistance could have so many supporters. She suspected numbers had swelled as the uprising gained momentum in their favour, but it was still a victory in itself that so many people wanted them to win. This many people gathered to fight against the Kade made her genuinely believe the Resistance would be victorious.

Makkyd appeared seemingly out of nowhere. She greeted Freya in the Pious way, her thumb pressing into Freya's palm.

"Glad you decided to join us," Makkyd said with a smile. Freya was surprised by the warmth of the gesture from a woman who was normally so unreachable.

Freya chose not to explain Ashtyn's lie. She simply returned Makkyd's smile. "How could you think that I wouldn't? Just wanted to clear a few things up at the Centre before I left."

The older woman clapped her on the shoulder and led her through the assortment of people readying themselves for battle. They gathered stares as they walked.

"I've arranged for the healers to be in this building." Makkyd gestured toward a building on the edge of the square. A sign painted on the building's side indicated it was a tailor's. Guilt squeezed at her as she wondered where Symon was. She pushed the sentiment aside. It would do her no good here.

"Why that building?"

"Large area in the front and one we could quickly clear. It was the best we could find in the area. Given how quickly we had to pull things together for the uprising, we might have tried to find somewhere with slightly more room, but it should do. We've cleared the bottom floor – what beds we have, we've lined up, and there are supplies there," Makkyd replied.

Freya nodded in satisfaction. She wondered where Makkyd had stored the supplies – presumably they were the very ones she had secreted away for so many cycles at Makkyd's direction. It seemed this had all been foreseen by Makkyd.

"Here's also a bit back from where we anticipate the fighting will be, so I think you should be safe here," Makkyd added.

"How will the wounded be brought here?"

"Those who can will walk, the rest will be carried by others," Makkyd replied.

"Not ideal," Freya noted.

She glanced at Makkyd in time to see her leader's lips thin in what looked to be unwilling acknowledgment. "Unfortunately it's that or they don't get any care. I'm not risking your safety." Finality lingered in her tone but Freya ignored it.

"What's the point if we could be closer?"

Makkyd stopped walking, forcing Freya to stop and swing around to face her. In the twilight, the nuances of Makkyd's expression were difficult to discern but the way she was exerting her command radiated from her. She spoke quietly enough that only Freya could hear but her voice was iron. "The point is you, Freyanna Kuch. The woman who defied the Kade's brutality to join the Resistance. You will be seen healing the brave wounded at this decisive moment. It makes your role in what's to come unquestionable."

Freya swallowed. She reminded herself of the balance she knew she had accepted; the number of lives saved in the long run was what she stood for. That required standing firm in the face of difficult decisions such as this one.

Freya nodded. Her gaze flicked around at the square. She wondered where Ashtyn was and what he would say to this. But she couldn't see him anywhere.

They entered the tailor's. The windows were shuttered and the gas flames were lit. The storefront had been cleared. People were setting out beds and supplies. As they noticed Freya, they stopped and looked expectantly at her and Makkyd.

A smattering of spontaneous applause crescendoed into cheers and whoops. The feeling of so many people buoyed by her mere presence was powerful. The truth behind Makkyd's claim about the importance of her simply being seen – the power she held as a symbol – was here before her.

"I'll leave you to it. We have a little time before dark falls fully; that's when we'll begin," Makkyd told Freya.

"Where's Ashtyn?" Freya asked before Makkyd could leave.

Makkyd raised her eyebrows. "Surely you two said what needed to be said to each other. I assumed that's why he volunteered to ask you to come here."

Freya kept her surprise from seizing her expression, but only just. That Ashtyn might have asked to deliver the message had never crossed her mind. "I just wondered..." she mumbled.

Makkyd didn't seem to care. "Good luck," she said before she strode off.

Freya hesitated after Makkyd's departure, wondering if she should give a speech. Certainly, the others looked at her expectantly. She had never been one to speak in front of people, but as it had in the Centre, the situation required it. She swept her gaze across the room. Twelve people stood before her. Two were healers from her own Centre. She hadn't known that they were Resistance members. Typical of Makkyd to not convey such information to her. Twelve to tend perhaps dozens of injured. If Makkyd's earlier comment about the tailor's being the best they could find on short notice, it seemed that the small number of people here was likely also a result of that. Certainly it was a challenge. She felt a little like throwing up.

"Thank you all for being here," she began. One or two people offered her smiles but the others maintained intense stares. "This won't be easy, and we may not be able to save everyone. But I know you're all here because you're fighting – in your own way – for a better world, and that makes all the difference." She wasn't sure of the words. They sounded like hollow platitudes to her own ears, but in response she observed the manner in which the anxious faces relaxed.

She directed one of the healers from her Centre to explain how they had set up the area. She could not stop satisfaction from spreading through her at the man's efficient explanation and the obvious use of techniques she had developed. She offered a few suggestions, directed them to change one or two things. As she shaped the room to her preference, she spoke with the others. She teased out that three were healers from across the city and the other three were simply volunteers, people who clearly were not capable of fighting due to their age or physical frailty. She ensured the people before her were as ready as they could be to face the onslaught of wounded, then told them to take a few minutes for themselves. Until the battle was concluded, there would be no time for rest or reprieve, and she had no way of knowing how long the fight would endure. For all she knew, it might drag on for days.

She returned to the square. Darkness had just fallen. She told herself she simply wanted to wander through the mass of people and enjoy the atmosphere of joviality and anticipation one last time before everything changed completely. Deep down, though, she knew she was looking for Ashtyn.

"Good to see our healers relaxing," Astrom called as she made her way across the square to Freya. "Obviously we shouldn't worry about whether or not you're ready."

Freya smiled, glad to see her friend in good health and good spirits. "We're as ready as we'll ever be," she replied as Astrom reached her.

They embraced warmly.

"How's your cheek?" Astrom asked.

Freya reflexively ran her finger along the scabbed lines down her face. "A little sore," she admitted. "But a lot of people are going to sustain far worse soon."

Astrom's face sobered, but she obviously pushed the sentiment away. "What's the point if one doesn't have a good battle scar to punctuate a story," she said with a joviality Freya almost believed.

"Are you ready?" Freya asked.

Astrom shrugged. "I'd like a bit more sleep before I go into battle." She smiled ruefully. "But then again, if the Goddess gave us all we asked for, we'd never be satisfied when things truly did go our way."

"You're going to be in the thick of it?" Freya asked, surprised.

"I'd never ask anybody to do something that I wouldn't do myself," Astrom replied.

Once again, Freya was reminded of why she liked this woman so much. Of why she would have charged into battle with Astrom if she had been asked.

"Be careful. I've already patched you up once," she ordered. "I don't want all my good work to go to waste."

"Don't worry, Freya. I'm sure I'll be all right," Astrom said.

They chatted for a few more minutes, joking as easily as they had over their many training sessions. Astrom must have been nervous – it would be foolish not to be – but she displayed no worry. She seemed the same relaxed, confident self she had always been, intermittently calling out greetings to people, answering comments of encouragement with those of her own. Everyone seemed to have a little more strength in their step after talking with her, even briefly.

"How are you feeling?" Astrom asked her in an undertone.

Freya bit her lip. "Nervous," she admitted.

Astrom laughed, running a hand over her tightly braided hair. "We'd be fools to feel any other way. Take heart." She embraced Freya once more then departed. Freya watched for a moment as her friend walked away, exchanging easy words with many of the people she passed. Worry snuck up on her, but she didn't allow it to claim her. Worry would only stop her from being able to save lives.

She resumed her own wandering, passing groups of people who were covering their anticipation with jovial conversation, triple checking their gear was in order, or taking a quiet moment to gather themselves. She accepted a bowl that was offered to her, not really looking at what the food was.

Surprise overtook her as she saw the unmistakable hairy figure of Olek talking with someone. Uncertainly, she walked up to him as she ate. In greeting, he gave her a lascivious look.

"I didn't think you would be here," she said.

"I heard you weren't coming." His coarse voice carried with it a hint of the uncertainty that he had shown when he had first met her. She wondered if it would always be like this – people silently wondering where her allegiance truly lay.

"Sorry I'm late, then." Pretending she hadn't noticed his look, she stared at him for a moment.

"What? Like what you see?" He all but smacked his lips. It was amazing that even with battle about to commence, he could still manage to be crass.

"Yes Olek, that's exactly it. I can barely contain myself, even at this very moment."

He roared with laughter. "You've got fire, I'll grant you that, Kuch," he told her. "Well, if I make it through this, I'll be sure to pay you a visit. Show you my many talents."

"I can't wait," Freya mumbled, uncertain what else she could say to that, while privately thinking that there was nothing that she would like less.

Olek appeared to have finished with her, turning back to the person with whom he had been speaking. She wandered to a quiet spot and finished her food in silence.

Total darkness crept over the city. Normally, Oranis's buildings were lit by this hour, illumination spilling from the buildings
into the streets and creating a cosy glow to see by. Tonight, as had
been the case for the past few evenings, even the gas streetlamps
went unlit; only the light of the stars shone down on the streets.
The day's warmth bled unobtrusively away along with the light
until Freya realised she was shivering. Soon it would be time for
the attack to begin, but she lingered on the street, savouring the
last few minutes of nervous peace, hoping for a glimpse of Ashtyn.
She didn't even want answers, just to see him one more time. Despite the darkness the street was still full of an atmosphere of en-
ervated camaraderie. The sound of so many people in the one
place, talking quietly, moving things about, readying themselves,
reminded her of the Oranis she loved. Not the city it had become
under the Kade's rule, but the one she remembered from her
childhood, full of warmth and shared humanity. This was the city
for which she was fighting.

Abruptly, the atmosphere changed. People quietened down,
tension filled the air like ripples across water. She didn't need to
be told it was time to return to the tailor's. The people – her people
– were waiting. As she walked into the cleared storefront, she
looked at them. Their expressions ranged from nauseous to ex-
cited. She entertained the idea of offering a few words of encouragement, but found nothing that seemed to fit what she wanted to
say, so instead she gave them a curt not and sat down to wait for
the arrival of the injured.

A great roar sounded outside followed by the noise of many
feet running through the streets. Once the footsteps had passed,
silence reigned. Freya strained her ears and thought she heard the
sound of distant fighting, but it could have been simply been a
trick of her imagination.

She hadn't considered there would be a delay between the beginning of the assault and the arrival of wounded, but she now

realised her error. Tension mounted in the building until it became an extra person in the room. Nobody spoke.

Wooden mannequins that had been cleared from the space stood pushed up against a wall. From the corner of the eye, they looked like fighters. She suppressed a shiver at the contrast: figures of fighting in a place of healing.

Long minutes passed, then a commotion sounded at the door. Immediately, everybody sprang to attention, ready to act. It was almost a relief.

Six fighters entered supporting two people between them. One of the injured was an older woman with a long gash across her face. Blood ran into her eyes. The other was a boy, barely eighteen, clutching a mangled arm. Freya fought the impulse to use her ability to heal the boy herself. She needed to be able to direct the people around her first and foremost. That was where her skills could do the most help despite what her instincts screamed at her. She called out instructions as she helped the woman sit down. Two of the other healers helped the boy to a bed. His whimpers and the efficient communication between the healers filled the silence that had oppressively weighed down the room only moments previously. The uninjured fighters departed immediately to throw themselves back into the fray. Freya wondered if they would be coming back to her as patients.

From then on, the injured came in a steady stream. Some were easily healed and most of them promptly returned to the fight, even if it was against Freya's advice. However, some were wounded so badly that they simply had to be tended to. While the battle raged in the halls of governance, a different kind of battle raged in the healers' room. The small group of people often won, but they also lost. Some had injuries that were too great. Some were simply not seen to in time. Even if Freya had been healing constantly with her ability, there was no guarantee that she could have saved that many more people. There was simply too much to do.

Reports trickled in from the injured and those who brought them – dribs and drabs of information that some part of Freya's mind processed as she continuously issued calm instructions. The Resistance had breached the governance building, battling through a barrage of deadly projectiles as they made their first charge. The doors had finally been beaten down and entry gained. Every step forward was costly. The Kade leadership surrounded themselves with the best. Armed with better weapons, relentlessly trained, and familiar with their surroundings, they certainly had the upper hand. Superior numbers were overwhelming them, but the constant influx of wounded was a testament to the fact that the elite Kade guards would take as many as possible with them.

Freya's voice became hoarse from giving unceasing directions. The muscles around her eyes began to register the strain of concentration as she gazed intently at each new patient to asses them as quickly as possible to move to the next person. Her teeth ached from the way she clenched her jaw. Fatigue, not from a lack of sleep – although that too – weighed upon her from the unending number of wounded. The distinctive smell of blood filled the room, mingled with the less clear-cut smells of fear, sweat and gore. Freya called for the shutters to be opened to allow the cool night air and provide some relief from the stifling miasma, but it offered little improvement. Bodies of those who had not survived were carried into a room in the rear where the bolts of cloth were stored.

Still, the wounded came, a flood of bleeding, broken bodies. Those who nursed injuries that weren't life threatening were directed to wait in the street outside, forming a line to wait for an escort back to Freya's Healing Centre if their injuries were not severe, or attention from one of the healers inside the tailor's if they couldn't move any further. The line grew longer with each passing minute.

Freya was proud of the people who followed her instructions with professional detachment. Stress and fatigue showed in their eyes but did not affect their demeanours.

Then a commotion sounded outside. Freya's body locked for an instant with fear that the worst had come to pass and fighting was taking place outside. But she realised those were not the sounds of battle, but panic. Urgent yells preceded the entrance of several people bearing an unconscious form, making it clear that someone important to the Resistance was being borne in. At her order, a bed was cleared. Moments later, eight people came in bearing Astrom's prostrate form and laid her upon the bed.

"No, let me," Freya yelled at one of the healers who rushed to attend. She stepped forward, a sliver of panic fighting to make its way through her wall of professional calm.

A blade had opened Astrom from above her breasts to below her navel. Freya didn't care who saw what. She held her hand above the injury and felt for the hum of Astrom's body. But no lifesong sprang into her mind. Frowning, she refocused, placing her hand on Astrom's skin. She assumed her exertion of focus had sapped her concentration, so she took a breath to calm herself, to collect herself, and once more felt out for her friend' lifesong.

The realisation was slow to make its way through to her. It took the form of a chill that enveloped her completely.

"No no no no no." A headache pulsed in the base of her head as she pushed her awareness into Astrom's very essence to try and hear even the faintest trace of a hum or melody. But this was simply a body before her. It seemed preposterous. Her ability could take life so easily. How was it that it could not restore it? She searched again. She would not accept that she could not save Astrom.

It was only when someone called her name that she looked up. More people were coming in. She was needed elsewhere. Tears threatened to obscure her vision as she looked down at Astrom's face. They could not fall. It was not the time.

Someone made to move Astrom from the bed. "No!" Freya barked. "Leave her there." Her eyes stung and her throat felt as though a rock were lodged in it. Her order was foolish, the bed was needed for others. She forced the words out, even though each felt like it cut her mouth to speak them. "My pardon. Take her to the back." It seemed an unfitting treatment for this woman, but there were other lives to save.

She wrestled her thoughts away from grief, locking it away so she could focus on those who would live.

Time took on a thickened quality, seeming to stop and speed by all at once. Grief and fatigue spread across her like a salve that numbed her to any awareness of how much time had passed. All she knew was the bodies that came in, the sweep of appraisal, the quick lift of her eyes from battered flesh to survey the room and determine what space there was, the near-instant decision on how to act. She helped where she could, affixing bandages, helping to clean wounds, taking a needle and efficiently stitching together flesh.

Then suddenly after hours, maybe days, maybe only minutes, her concentration was shattered as cheers and the unmistakable sound of celebration swirled into the room. The disordered foot-steps of chaotically joyful running passed the open windows, and borne back on the night breeze was the chant "it's over".

Freya looked up and found her jagged disbelief mirrored on the faces of everybody else, but she drew the focus of the healers back with a call. "It may be over for them, but not for us."

Her people didn't falter. Expressions of resolve flowed into each of their expressions, and they returned to their work. Freya sank back into that near-meditative space, her hands mending bodies unthinkingly as she gave instructions, called orders. With the knowledge that the Kade leadership had been captured, she could send those who were able to be moved to her Healing Centre, leaving only the worst cases here.

Light began to play about the sky when she straightened and realised there were no more people who needed her help. Almost as though in a dream, she made her way onto the street. The sound of distant revels travelled seemed to float through the air to caress her ears, but the cool predawn air was strangely peaceful. It seemed as though Oranis itself knew life would be returning to normal and had let out a breath. The menace that had held sway over the city had evaporated, leaving only the beautiful stone buildings staring unseeingly down on her. Her guilt and fatigue and grief receded as Freya breathed deeply, listening to the peace. There would still be parts of Oranis to secure, and the real work was to begin now. But she took the moment to savour the knowledge of what they had just accomplished. The city was theirs.

COMING LATE 2019

DARK HEART

The brutal Kade dictatorship has been overthrown, but the fight is only just beginning in the Third Country where tensions between the Pious and Kade religious community remain high.

In the fight to bring freedom to her country, Freyanna Kuch had to contravene everything her training as a healer taught her and learn how to kill. But living with the person she became in service of rebellion is no easy task.

Yet another threat prowls the streets of Oranis and Freya is uniquely able to protect the city she loves from further bloodshed. However, to do so she must face the very real possibility that there is no going back to who she was – and those she loves.

DARK HEART – PREVIEW
ONE

At a glance, the woman in the cell didn't look as though she had been someone important. Certainly, she didn't look as though she was dangerous. Her robes held the dirt of a garment worn unceasingly, only betraying glimpses of their original pristine white. Snatches of colour peeked through at the hems - purple, blue, crimson - but the hems were where the most grime had gathered, making the threads almost indistinguishable from dirt. The woman's pallor was wan, the sickly hue of someone who has not seen the sun in quite a stretch of time.

Her dirty state and the unhealthiness to her complexion made her seem quite unthreatening.

She reposed on the room's solitary bench, her eyes closed, as though her time imprisoned had imprinted her with a bone-weary fatigue.

But a second glance suggested this was not a woman to be trifled with. The way she held herself somehow apart from the filth of her dingy surrounds filled anyone who looked at her for more than a moment with the immediate understanding that one needed to be careful around her. Indeed, the line of her posture was not that of exhaustion but of anticipation.

It was for this reason that Councilwoman Freyanna Kuch stepped into the cell with extreme trepidation. It was for this reason too that the door was closed behind her with a rapidity that made her very aware that she was to all intents and purposes, on her own.

At her entry, the eyes of the Chief Healer - former Chief Healer, to be precise - snapped open, and the battle between the two women began.

ACKNOWLEDGEMENTS

Sitting down to write this once more only serves to remind me of how many people to whom I am indebted for their support, encouragement, excitement, and love.

As always, the first thank you goes to my parents, and immediate family. I can only imagine what they thought when I declared that I was going to pursue writing and through self-publishing, no less. I probably cushioned the blow somewhat by threatening to be an author from a young age, but kids do make some pretty interesting claims, so for me to follow up on that must have been a bit startling. Thank you to my mother who has gone into bookstores and sneakily bought copies of my books stocked there, photographed my books and sent them to me, and subtly spruiked me to a whole bunch of people. Thank you to my father for doing all of the behind the scenes tech and formatting work, and generally on really short notice and with vague instructions. You guys rock.

In terms of the team, I must extend again my thanks to Jason whose editing is just the best (and also scarily fast). Additionally, Sarena and Jess are the best writers group girls I could ask for. They have made this book a better one with their comments, feedback, and encouragement. Marcus has again taken my vague mumblings about 'something cool and strong' and made it into a great cover – from the other side of the world, no less! Thank you to all of you guys. You rock.

And then there is everybody else.

My bookstagrammers – you guys are so supportive and lovely. Thank you to the stars and back, because that's what you guys are; stars. Jayse, Blue, Jess, Jess (all the Jesses, really), Mel, Nat, Madi (who also made the launch products and whose store

Spark+Sparrow produces amazing stuff), Jem, Tay, Nil, Sam, Kat, Angie, Abi, Julie...I know I'm missing people, and I'm so sorry to those who I have forgotten.

All my wonderful real life friends who buy and read my books – I love you all so much for reading and liking and telling me you like it, and telling other people that you like it. I don't deserve such fabulous people as you.

And finally, thank you to Mitch. With every day that passes I come to appreciate that really, there are no words.

ABOUT THE AUTHOR

Alice Jane Boér-Endacott was born and raised in Melbourne, Australia.

She started writing at the age of six, although her work from that era which includes *The Wish Flower* is still too radical for the world.

In the intervening twenty years since she began writing, she has acquired degrees in the very practical fields of Anthropology and Executive Management, eaten a significant quantity of chocolate, been stung by a jellyfish in Malaysia (and still has the scars to prove it), and bitten by a redback spider in Melbourne.

She hopes to spend her next years writing, eating more chocolate, using esoteric concepts from her degrees to confuse other people, and avoiding all wildlife.

You can find her on Instagram @alicejaneboere.

And on twitter @ajendacott

Alternatively, her website is www.abendacott.com

READ OTHER STORIES FROM THE LEGENDS OF THE GODSKISSED CONTINENT

QUEENDOM OF THE SEVEN LAKES

Having grown up amongst the Family of Assassins, Elen-ai knows well the prices people are willing to pay to see their enemies fall quickly, quietly, and discreetly. When she is asked to preserve life rather than take it, she is surprised. Upon hearing that her charge is the Queen's only child Gidyon, who is secretly being groomed to succeed his mother, she is horrified. To ensure political stability, no man has ever sat on the throne of the Queendom of the Seven Lakes. Yet one does not easily refuse a Queen, and so reluctantly, Elen-ai accepts the contract.

Her fears only deepen upon meeting the sixteen-year-old Prince Gidyon, who treats her as no better than a petty murderer. However, following an attack on his life, Elen-ai is forced to admit that the danger of leaving this boy-prince alone may be even worse than leaving him to his own devices. Elen-ai reluctantly accompanies Gidyon across the country to identify those within the seven most powerful families who are responsible for the attempt on the Prince's life.

Somewhere in their travels from the calm waters of Lake Tak to the looming cliffs above Lake Bertak, the two form an unlikely yet profound friendship, and Elen-ai begins to see that Gidyon has the makings of a great ruler within him. As they meet with the families of power, it becomes increasingly clear that secrets and power games run far deeper throughout the Queendom of the Seven Lakes than either of them ever suspected.

THE RUTHLESS LAND

"Lying is not simply about telling a plausible story, it's about being able to tell what someone will want to believe"

To outsiders, the Fourth Country is an unforgiving place. Under the leadership of ruthless women, powerful families regularly wage brutal campaigns against one another to increase their land and wealth, and men live in a state of complete subjugation.

Lexana, heiress to the Farwan family, is sent to the Academy, an elite institution where the daughters of powerful families learn and refine techniques to maintain and gain power. There, she finds herself attracted to Jaxen, one of the teachers who defies convention and goes about unveiled. His apparent disregard for what is expected of him leaves her both uneasy and fascinated.

Then the impossible comes to pass, and disaster befalls the Farwan family. Lexa must leave the Academy to find her mother and help restore her family to power. Jaxen insists upon accompanying her, arguing that she cannot survive without his help. Lexa can't be certain that she can trust Jaxen, but he is right; she needs his help if she is to succeed.